THE TRAP

EVIE HUNTER

First published in Great Britain in 2022 by Boldwood Books Ltd.

Cover Design and Photography by Colin Thomas Photography Ltd

A CIP catalogue record for this book is available from the British Library.

Paperback ISBN 978-1-80280-252-8

Large Print ISBN 978-1-80280-253-5

Hardback ISBN 978-1-80280-251-1

Ebook ISBN 978-1-80280-254-2

Kindle ISBN 978-1-80280-255-9

Audio CD ISBN 978-1-80280-246-7

MP3 CD ISBN 978-1-80280-247-4

Digital audio download ISBN 978-1-80280-248-1

Boldwood Books Ltd
23 Bowerdean Street
London SW6 3TN
www.boldwoodbooks.com

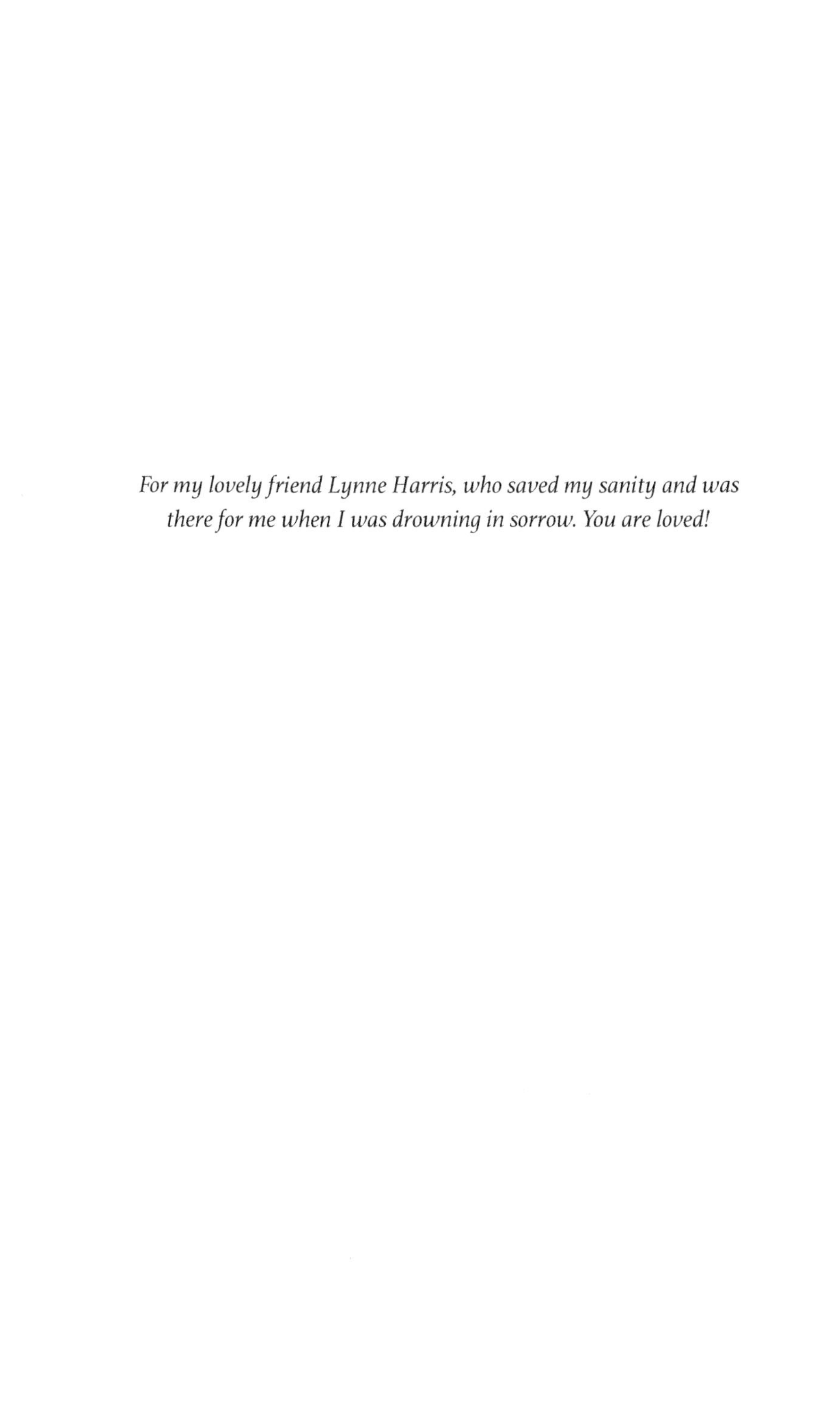

For my lovely friend Lynne Harris, who saved my sanity and was there for me when I was drowning in sorrow. You are loved!

PROLOGUE

As the wedding planner of the moment, all the big days blurred into one for Callie Devereaux. With the notable exception of the Blakely wedding, which was when her life changed forever.

It was the day she met and fell heavily for Mike.

Of course, that wasn't his real name; she knew that now and it probably explained why she'd had troubling equating the exotic and sophisticated man she'd fallen for with such a pedestrian name. But then, hindsight can be bloody irritating.

Callie closed her eyes, recalling the impressive figure he'd cut as he strode into the pre-wedding reception in his Savile Row suit as though he owned the hotel it was being staged in. Fashionably late. Callie suspected, when she thought about it later, that his timing had been deliberate. Mike liked to make an entrance, to say nothing of an impression.

Callie watched the other women at the wedding reception drinking in the sight of him like they'd never seen a handsome man in the last decade. She idly wondered who the lucky lady would be, instinctively knowing that he would score before the bride and groom took to the floor for the first dance.

It hadn't occurred to her that she would be his choice.

1

'No, not there!'

In a strident tone worthy of a sergeant major, the bride's mother's voice cut effectively through the activity of preparation. Callie, whose patience had already been worn gossamer-thin by the impossible woman's equally impossible demands, winced. She closed her eyes and took a deep, calming breath, counted to ten and reminded herself that she needed – really needed – this commission.

'The pedestal has to be there, Marion,' Callie said into the ensuing crystalline silence, as she moved the floral display back into its assigned position, 'or it will block the cinematographer's view when the couple exchange their vows.'

'A moment that must definitely be preserved,' Jason, Callie's assistant, added with a saccharine smile.

Marion Blakely sniffed and looked set to argue the point, just as she had argued over every minor detail with Callie throughout the interminable planning for a wedding that was costing a ridiculous amount of money. Callie breathed a sigh of relief when

Jason's charm appeared to work its magic and another battle of wills was averted.

'Oh, of course you're right, Jason,' she said, turning her attention to the menus and tutting. 'No, no, this won't do at all. I specifically said that I wanted Scottish wild salmon, not some cheap substitute that's probably farmed and...'

She bustled off with menu in hand, presumably to berate some hapless chef.

Callie drew in another deep breath, reminded herself just how much she would benefit financially if everything went off without a hitch – which it would, if only Marion would stop interfering – and turned her attention to the next item on her to-do list.

'Why does she bother to employ us if she wants to manage everything herself?' Jason asked, *sotto voce*.

'Brides get a bad press,' Callie replied. 'But trust me, they aren't the ones who make our lives difficult.'

She glanced at Marion's ramrod-straight back and was convinced she could sense the antagonism radiating from the woman. Even by mother-of-the-bride standards, this one was especially difficult, giving Callie instructions and then undermining them at every turn. The bride and her soon-to-be husband looked petrified of her, barely opened their mouths and would likely have preferred to run off to the nearest registry office.

'Tomorrow will be the happiest day of her daughter's life,' Jason, who enjoyed nothing more than a good gossip, remarked, 'but not because she's marrying that gorgeous hunk of manhood,' he added, going all gooey-eyed. 'Anyway, little Maddy would likely marry the Hunchback of Notre Dame if it got her out from under *her* thumb.'

Callie stifled a smile as she consulted the endless to-do list on her tablet. 'I dare say little Maddy has a healthy trust fund so could be independent now if she wanted to be.'

'I shall be hearing that strident voice in my nightmares for the rest of my days and will likely need therapy to get past it,' Jason said, shuddering.

'Make yourself useful and check that the table plan is being adhered to before she finds fault with it.'

Jason sashayed off in his skinny white jeans – one of the few people of either sex who could pull the unforgiving look off – and fluttered his fingers at the handsome barman polishing glasses. Callie stood back to examine the bower decorated with trailing flowers, beneath which the couple would stand in this sumptuous ballroom to pledge themselves to one another for the rest of their lives.

Or until one of them strayed, Callie thought cynically.

There was a problem with the caterers, whose van had broken down on the motorway. The florist hadn't received Marion's email changing the design of the bridesmaids' bouquets at the eleventh hour and that created another almighty argument that Callie was required to arbitrate.

'You should apply to the United Nations,' Jason said in her ear as he floated past, trailing ribbons destined for the top table, which Callie knew his talented fingers would weave into a glorious festoon with consummate ease. His artistic flair was one of the reasons why she had employed him. That and his wicked sense of humour and unswerving loyalty in a profession that was known for its bitchiness and underhand tactics. 'With you mediating, the Middle East would be at peace within weeks.'

Callie barely had time to smile before her mobile buzzed and she was immersed in yet more conciliatory negotiations with the beautician. The woman had had it up to the neck with Marion Blakely's unreasonable demands and felt inclined to withdraw her services on the grounds that she did not, as she bluntly pointed out to Callie, need all this crap. Who did, Callie wondered, as she calmed the girl down, reminding her just how well she was being paid to endure the crap in question. A mantra that Callie was obliged to repeat to herself at regular intervals in her line of work.

'Ah, this must be the mysterious daddy,' Jason said, as a tall, elegant man in his fifties with a sweep of thick, greying hair and a sophisticated air strode into the room. The trophy wife on his arm couldn't have been older than the bride but was a good twenty years younger than his former wife, which explained a lot, Callie decided.

'Well, well,' Jason muttered. 'If looks could kill then Daddy dearest would be six feet under by now. He just pulled up in a Lamborghini, by the way. Nothing like being ostentatious. But still, who am I to argue? If you've got it, flaunt it, that's what I always say.'

'I almost feel sorry for Marion,' Callie said, sensing the animosity coming off her in waves. 'It can't be easy for someone so aware of her appearance to be replaced by a much younger model.'

'If you want to feel sorry for anyone, spare a thought for our mousy little bride. It's supposed to be her big day, but Mummy and Daddy are in danger of turning it into World War Three.'

'Mummy is. Daddy appears oblivious to Marion, which must infuriate her. No wonder she's spending so lavishly on this shindig. Her ex is footing the bill.'

'Hit him where it hurts.'

'Are we going to get this started?' Marion demanded imperiously.

Robert Blakeley made a show out of kissing his young wife,

escorted her to a prominent chair in the front row, and then offered his daughter his arm.

'Shall we show them how to make an entrance, darling?' he asked.

'You know I'm not good at that sort of thing, Daddy.'

'Don't worry about it, buttercup. I am.'

The bride gave an uncertain smile and fell into line, just as she had likely been doing for her entire life.

'How did he make all that luscious loot for his ex to fritter away?' Jason asked, as he and Callie stood to the side, watching proceedings.

'Property, I think. Exclusive pads for the rich and deserving,' Callie replied, smiling.

'Hmm.' Jason had been brought up in care, never knew either of his parents, and had gone through some tough times. Precocious and fun for the most part, he understandably had a massive chip on his shoulder when it came to those who made money out of other people's misery.

* * *

'Gin,' Callie told Jason emphatically when the rehearsal came to an end, with the bride's mother mercifully concentrating the majority of her venom on her ex-husband. 'I need a hot bath, scented candles and gin, not necessarily in that order.'

'Sorry, darling, no can do. I have plans.'

'Well, then, go and have fun and I'll make do with Jinx for company. At least he never disagrees with me.'

'He's a cat, darling, so don't assume that he likes you. He simply tolerates you because you feed him.'

'I'll see you bright and early tomorrow for the fun and games.'

'Wouldn't miss it.' Jason grabbed his bag, blew Callie an exaggerated air kiss and headed for the door. 'Toodles.'

Shaking her head at her irrepressible assistant's style, Callie gathered up her belongings and headed for her ageing Beetle, tucked in the corner of the car park, well away from the showy red Lamborghini that had been parked directly in front of the entrance to the hotel, blocking the steps.

She drove home to her isolated cottage, buried deep in the countryside near Chichester. It had belonged to her grandmother and represented a safe haven from Callie's otherwise disjointed childhood. Small and in need of renovation it might be, but Callie loved it just the way it was and sometimes thought she could still sense her grandmother's calming presence in the miniscule rooms.

Jinx, her ginger cat – he of questionable loyalty – wound his way round her legs and miaowed pitifully the moment Callie walked through the door.

'I haven't been gone for that long,' she protested, scratching the cat behind his ears. 'Anyone would think you haven't eaten for a week.'

Callie opened a can of cat food and decanted the contents into Jinx's bowl. He bent his head, gave the food a sniff and deigned to delicately set about it.

'Don't you dare prove Jason right!' she demanded, smiling in spite of herself as she turned her mind to her own supper. She opened the fridge and was confronted with almost nothing other than out-of-date ham and half a mouldy lettuce. 'Ah, well, beans on toast again,' she said resignedly.

Callie wasn't hungry anyway. She had been inundated with tempting morsels from the hotel's kitchen and it would have been impolite to decline. Such organisations weren't beyond a little subtle bribery, aware that Callie could bring more business to their doors if they made a good impression. She really ought to say no to the offerings that came her way. She had gained weight and struggled to fit into any of the three outfits she kept to wear on wedding days. After this wedding, she would definitely exercise more self-control.

Probably.

She made her snack, consumed it without tasting it, and then stripped off in preparation of the bath she had promised herself.

On the basis that gin didn't count on the calorie front, she emerged from the bath wrapped in a towelling robe and poured herself a healthy measure. Then she curled up with her glass and a bridal magazine. It was essential in her line of work to keep up with the latest trends, and evenings at home were the only times she found to do her research.

She hadn't turned two pages before she heard the back door open. Jinx, who had condescended to curl up beside Callie and actually purr, lifted his head and sniffed the air.

'It's only Maisie,' Callie scolded, 'not an axe murderer. You're not an axe murderer, are you?' she asked when her friend put her head round the door. 'Jinx wants to know.'

'Not yet, but I very easily could be,' Maisie replied cheerfully. 'Is there any ice?' she asked, taking a glass from the cabinet.

'Are there seven days in the week?'

'Sorry, silly question. Just a mo, I'll get myself some sustenance and then tell you my latest woes. Do you need a top-up?' Maisie chuckled when Callie thrust her glass in her direction like a prize fighter going in for the kill. 'Another silly question.'

With strong drinks in hands, the girls settled down for a good natter. Maisie and Callie had grown up together and knew one another's darkest secrets. When she looked back on her fractured childhood, Callie firmly believed that Maisie's indefatigable good nature had been the catalyst that saw her through the worst of her mother's neglect and her mostly absent father's squalid ways. Callie's grandmother and Masie between them had been her salvation.

Maisie and Callie had gone different ways once school was behind them and lost touch for a while. Maisie went off to university and, from the reports that found their way to Callie's ears, had partied her way through her course. Even so, only Maisie was surprised when she came away with a first in economics without, as she freely admitted, putting in much work.

Callie, on the other hand, was required to take paid employment. More by luck than judgement, a vacancy came up in a wedding boutique and she fell into her present occupation when asked to assist the owner with the arrangements for a last-minute wedding. Callie reckoned even then that she could have made the affair far more spectacular, even on a limited budget, and set about proving it when the next opportunity came along.

Ironically, with no qualifications other than a will to succeed, Callie had established herself and was well on the way, as Maisie put it, to becoming an entrepreneur. Maisie, with her sharp intellect and shiny degree, married a guy she'd met at uni and produced her first child six months after the ceremony. Now the mother of two boisterous children, she worked from home as a bookkeeper for local businesses, as well as keeping her lazy husband in the style to which he aspired to become accustomed.

Dan hadn't held down any sort of job for more than five minutes in all the time the couple had been married. He had no sense of responsibility and needed, as far as Callie was concerned, a boot up the backside. Callie had to bite her tongue to prevent herself from telling Maisie that he was a waste of space. He was fabulously good-looking; she was convinced that he had affairs and that Maisie must know it. Close as they were, it wasn't a conversation that Callie felt she could instigate.

'What's he done this time?' Callie asked, aware from Maisie's expression that she had come round to grouse about Dan's lack of ambition. And to have a respite from her demanding kids.

'Only got fired from the bookies,' Maisie replied with an exaggerated sigh. 'I mean, how is that even possible?'

In Dan's case, Callie thought but did not say, very easy.

'How hard can it be to take bets? God alone knows, he's been placing them all his life. He ought to be a natural.'

'Why did they let him go?'

Maisie took a big slug of gin and shrugged. 'I didn't even bother to ask. He reckons it was too menial and that he's capable of more.'

'Perhaps he should decide what it is that he actually wants to do and focus on getting there,' Callie suggested mildly, knowing better than to criticise Dan. Maisie could, and frequently did so, but anyone else who voiced a word against Maisie's Adonis had better watch their backs. It was the only subject upon which Callie and Maisie had ever disagreed.

'Do you need help?' she asked, hoping Maisie would say no. Lending money to friends was the fastest way for the friendship in question to fracture, she knew, but she owed Maisie so much that she would make an exception in her case. She sighed, seeing her nest egg and future plans being blown in the bookies from whose employ Dan had just been summarily ejected.

'Thanks, but no. We'll manage. At least with him at home, he can look after the kids and I can concentrate on the backlog of work that's piling up.'

Except, Callie knew, his idea of caring for the kids was at best spasmodic. There always seemed to be good reasons why he couldn't have them when Maisie most needed him to. And when he did take charge, he let them get away with murder, never saying no to anything they wanted, which made him the favourite parent. He handed them back to Maisie when they were full of E numbers and bouncing off the ceiling, leaving it to her to instil discipline and be despised because 'Daddy let them do it'.

And yet, Maisie stuck by him.

If that was love, then Callie was glad that all her attempts at romance had failed. She was far better off on her own. She thought back to the grand romance she had entered into at the age of eighteen, naïve and with stars in her eyes. She only found out that he was a serial cheat when he gave her an STD. Talk about coming back down to earth with a bump. Was it any wonder that she was so cynical when it came to abiding love? It all seemed pretty one-sided to her, which made her choice of profession that much harder to fathom. Then again, perhaps being hard-hearted when it came to love and romance was a necessary qualification for her line of work.

'How are the little monsters?' Callie asked.

'Noisy. Josh wants to start judo and Saffron is banging on about riding lessons. Why can't my kids have cheap hobbies?'

'Are there such things?'

'Swimming, camping, tennis lessons down the local leisure centre. Falling out of trees, playing in the park.' She ticked the possibilities off on her fingers. 'Or make their own fun, like we used to. We were never ferried anywhere or needed every second of our holidays micro-managed. Just as well, in my case.'

'True.' It was Callie's turn to take a large slug of gin. It went down the wrong way, causing her to splutter. Maisie thumped her on the back until the coughing subsided.

'Any new men on your horizon?' Maisie asked.

Callie shook her head. 'Only Jason.'

'God, he's a dream! Such a tragedy that he's not straight.'

'He wouldn't be nearly as good at his job if he was. He can

handle my latest bride's-mother-from-hell far better than me. She's putty in his hands.'

'Well, anyway, you should spread your net, join a singles club or something. You're not getting any younger and...'

'If you say my body clock's ticking then I swear I'll throw my drink at you.'

Maisie chuckled. 'No, you won't. It would be a terrible waste of gin. Seriously though, Cal, you want children of your own, don't you?'

Did she? 'Not at any price,' she said evasively. 'It would mean getting married, or at least being in a serious relationship, and you know how I feel about that sort of thing.'

'Just 'cause you got burned once, babe...'

'More than once,' Callie replied absently, thinking of her other failed attempts at happily-ever-after, all of which had ended in disaster, usually because the guy cheated on her. There must be something about her that signposted her gullibility, she'd always thought. Anyway, it had put her off men. There was no such thing as a happy marriage.

She should know.

They had another drink while Callie told her friend all about the wedding she was currently working on. Unlike Callie, Maisie was a born romantic and sighed when Callie described the bride's dress.

'Sounds divine,' she said enviously.

'So it should. It's a Vera Wang.'

'My one regret is not wafting down the aisle in white. Ours, as you know, was a quick registry office job which isn't the same thing at all.'

'Half my brides who spend so lavishly on their big day finish up divorced within five years. It's an established fact.'

'That is *so* depressing. I hate dealing in reality, which is why I never watch the news. I don't need much of an excuse to turn to the gin at the best of times...'

'Marion Blakely is getting her own back on her ex by having such an expensive bash but the gesture's lost on him. He can afford it and it probably salves his conscience to give his daughter all the works. I gather he walked out when she was ten and barely sees her now. I reckon she's probably older than his trophy wife.'

'Men can do that and no one bats an eye. I mean, there's no such thing as an ugly rich man. But if the tables are turned and a wealthy older woman takes up with a toy boy, the world struggles to cope with the drama.'

Callie yawned and put her empty glass aside. Maisie took the hint and scrambled to her feet. 'I guess I've given him enough time to bathe the monsters. Not that he actually has to bathe them, but you know what I mean. He knows I'm pissed off because he lost his job so he's being ultra-helpful. I'm taking advantage whilst it lasts. As for you, get yourself off to bed. You need an early night so you look your best for the wedding tomorrow.' Maisie leaned over to kiss Callie. 'Who knows, a guest might prove to be the man of your dreams.'

Callie laughed as she waved her friend off. 'I would have to dream about men for that to be possible,' she replied.

2

Jack Carlisle felt his muscles protest when he swung the pickaxe and met with solid resistance that vibrated up his arms.

'Fuck!' he muttered, dropping the axe in disgust. 'This was supposed to be a simple job.'

'It is,' Frank replied, laughing. 'You're getting soft, is all. All that suit wearing and sucking up to investors has taken its toll.'

Odin, Jack's large, shaggy mongrel, lifted his nose from the interesting smell that had caught his attention and woofed his agreement, making both men smile. Jack shrugged, unwilling to admit that he privately agreed with his foreman.

'You're mistaking me for Logan. He's the clothes horse.'

'There's no mistaking you two. Stand back and watch, son. You might learn something.' Frank swung the pickaxe with similarly discouraging results.

'Remind me which of us is going soft?'

'Yeah, well, you need to bawl Logan out for committing us to this shit without checking out the feasibility.' Frank leaned on the pickaxe's handle, looking hot and uncomfortable. 'Who owns this site, anyway? I can't see us getting permission to build on it. We're wasting our time.'

'That's more Logan's department than mine. He's the brains, I'm the brawn in our partnership, as well you know. We both play to our strengths and, let's face it, Logan could sell ice to Inuits.'

'Just because he has a fancy degree in something obscure, it doesn't make him the better man.'

'Come on, Frank, we've been together, the three of us, through thick and thin. Logan has his faults, just like the rest of us, but he's 100 per cent committed to expanding our business opportunities. He's hungry and ambitious, which can't be a bad thing.'

'That's as may be, but I was happy with the way we were. I guess I'm just not cut out to be an entrepreneur. Even so, I won't apologise because I like to sleep at night without worrying about my investments.'

'I understand why you didn't want to become a partner and I respect you for that. I'm just glad that you agreed to stay with us. It wouldn't be the same without you.'

'Don't go getting all soppy on me. You'll be wanting a group hug or some shit next.'

Jack laughed as he dropped a hand to absently tug at one of Odin's ears. 'You're safe from my dubious advances.'

'Well, anyway, we won't get away with surveying this site with a pickaxe. We'll need to get the earth-moving equipment in on Monday.'

'Just like you predicted.'

'Yeah, but I remain to be convinced that it's worth it.'

'There's no telling unless we go through the preliminaries.' Jack slapped Frank's shoulder. 'Come on, it's hot already and it's Saturday. We'll knock off and I'll buy you a beer.'

'That'll work.'

The two old friends moved towards Jack's truck but before

they could climb aboard, a Porsche 911 screeched to a halt in front of it.

'What's up, guys?' Logan asked, getting out of his car but leaving the engine running. 'Finished already?'

'What's with the whistle?' Frank asked, eyeing Logan's silver-grey suit, crisp white shirt and flamboyantly patterned crimson tie. 'Bit over the top for a site visit, ain't it?'

'Robert Blakely's daughter's getting married today. Need to keep him onside.'

'Our potential investor?' Jack asked, seeking clarification. Logan could be surprisingly close-lipped about such things, perhaps because Jack seldom bothered to ask. He trusted Logan and wasn't interested in the details.

'He owns this crappy piece of land that we are going to turn into a goldmine,' Logan replied, absolute certainty underlying his words. That was one of the reasons why Jack and Logan got along so well, Jack had always thought. Logan saw the bigger picture and wasn't afraid to chase the dream. He was much better at brown-nosing it with the high-flyers than Jack, who was more at home with a pint of local ale than a flute of vintage champagne. 'What can I tell him about your findings?'

'Will he want to talk business at his daughter's wedding?' Frank asked, sounding surprised.

'Robert is always willing to talk business. He never wastes an opportunity; that's what I like about him. And why I'm bothering to go. He will be in a celebratory mood and off his guard. A great time to push his buttons.'

'Yes, well, today might not be the day to tell him that we'll have to bring a digger in,' Jack said. 'The ground is solid and we can't dig down deep enough by hand.'

A look of annoyance filtered across Logan's features. 'Damn, are you sure? I promised him some feedback today.'

Frank squared up to Logan. 'Feel free to have a go yourself, if you remember how. We'll be happy to hold your coat.'

'Use the minimum amount of machinery and try to keep it low profile,' Logan said. 'Robert doesn't want word getting out that he's thinking of developing. It will bring all the environmental nutters out from the woodwork and he can do without that sort of hassle. It might put him off the entire idea and that will be a disaster.'

'You'd best get going,' Frank said. 'You don't want to miss the nuptials. Or the opportunity to brown-nose,' he added in an undertone that was deliberately audible.

Jack sighed, worried that something would have to give between Frank and Logan before the antagonism impacted upon the bottom line. Locking them in a room and leaving them to slug it out sprang to mind. This business needed them both and they couldn't carry on at one another's throats indefinitely. Logan pretended not to notice Frank's growing aggression – he was good at ignoring anything he didn't want to confront – but even so...

'Catch you later,' Logan said, climbing back into his car and tearing off with a squeal of tyres, leaving a plume of exhaust fumes in his wake.

Frank and Jack got into Jack's truck. With Odin taking up the entire back seat with his rangy body sprawled across it, he drove them the short distance to their local in silence.

'Why do you let him do it?' Frank asked, once they had pints in front of them and occupied bar stools where they could keep one eye on the football match being shown on the big TV screen that every pub seemed to find essential nowadays.

'Do what?' Jack asked, taking a healthy swig of beer and placing his glass in the centre of a drip mat.

'Logan talks down to you, to us both, but never gets his own hands dirty. As the kids would say, he's disrespecting you.'

'Nah. Logan and I go way back, as well you know. Like I say, we play to our strengths.'

'But you're equal partners in the business. You don't take orders from him.'

'Logan has his demons, just like the rest of us, but he's basically good people. I wouldn't know how to start looking for backers, whereas Logan can smell them at twenty paces with the wind in the wrong direction.'

'I hear you, but there's something not right about this latest fiasco.' Frank put his glass down and scratched his ear. 'Bullshit is something I can smell, very distinctly, and right now Logan's dealing it out to us like we were prize chumps. It's something to do with this latest site, I can sense it. Wish I knew what it was.'

Jack smiled at the barmaid when she came to check they had everything they needed for the third time, then placed a bowl of water on the floor for Odin.

'You're in there, mate,' Frank said, chuckling when the girl walked away, swaying her hips provocatively. 'Don't know what there is to like about an ugly bastard like you but from what I've seen, you can take your pick. It don't seem right.'

Jack laughed. 'You can have too much of a good thing.'

'Wouldn't know, myself. My missus would knock me into the middle of next week if I even thought about straying.'

'Logan can be brash, I'll grant you,' Jack said, returning to their earlier conversation, 'but that's because he was brought up in a different world to ours.'

Frank sniffed, unimpressed. 'His family have a few bob and live in a mansion. So what? His shit still stinks, just like the rest of us.'

'I saw it all, remember.'

'Because your mother cleaned for his family and you got to

play with the son and heir.' Frank's expression made it clear what he thought of the demarcation lines.

'Logan's pa ain't quite so wealthy now. The family estate, Logan's inheritance, is long gone and he has grown up with a driving ambition to turn things around. To impress his old man, if you like.'

'An old man who's gaga and shut away in a home.' Frank supped his ale and screwed up his features. 'Welcome to the real world, Logan. Well, real by his standards. The first thing he did when his old man lost all his investments was to marry an heiress. That's not exactly making his own way, is it?'

'It's a matter of degree. Logan's privileged world fell apart but he's pulled himself up by his bootlaces—'

'More like his Senna Wingtips,' Frank said in a sneering tone.

'He'll tell you that you have to look the part if you want to be taken seriously.'

'Well, he'd know more about that than I do, and I'll be the first to accept that he does bring in the business.' Frank scratched his chin. 'It's just that I worry that he's getting over-ambitious, to say nothing of secretive.'

'Is that why you decided against investing as a partner?'

'I guess. Well, partly. My missus was dead set against it. She reckons we need our savings to help the kids and can't afford to risk losing the lot. She's right an' all.'

'You've never really taken to Logan. I've never understood why.'

Frank gave a wry smile over the rim of his glass. 'You wanna know why? Okay, I'll tell you.' But he paused to take a long sup of ale before doing so. 'I really liked Sally Faulkner and in our senior year she agreed to go out with me. I was well made up, I don't mind telling you. Then you introduced Logan into our circle and he took her from me, simply because he could. He walked on water as far as all the girls were concerned, you both did. Us lesser mortals had to fight over your leftovers. That's why Sally agreeing to go out with me meant so much. Anyway, Logan had his way with her and then dumped her, at which point she came crawling back to me, wanting to lick her wounds and expecting me to welcome her with open arms.'

'I didn't know,' Jack said. 'I'm sorry. Logan's my best mate but I'm not blind to his faults and I can well believe he'd do something that spiteful.'

'Yeah, well, it's water under the bridge now. I met Yvonne the following year, kept her well away from Logan and have never regretted marrying her.'

Jack nodded. He had never taken the matrimonial plunge himself but sometimes envied Frank his chaotic yet harmonious family life. Odin's company was all well and good but sometimes it wasn't enough for him. But the fact of the matter was that Jack, although he'd dated more than his share of attractive women, simply hadn't met anyone he'd be willing to spend the rest of his life with.

'You beat him hands down eventually,' Jack said. 'You have a wife you love, some well-adjusted kids, and a happy home life. Logan lives in a show house, not a home. He doesn't love his wife, still screws anything with a pulse and barely knows his kids' names.'

Frank cocked a brow. 'That's normal behaviour, is it?'

'Define normal. My point is, material wealth doesn't bring happiness.'

'But it sure as hell helps.'

Both men laughed as they drained their glasses and stood to leave.

As he drove home with Odin riding shotgun, Jack reflected upon Frank's rant against Logan, mentally springing to his friend's defence, just like always, even though recently an element of unease had trickled into his mind with regard to Logan's behaviour. Was there a grain of truth in what Frank had said about Logan being over-ambitious or did he still bear a grudge following Logan's unreasonable behaviour all those years before?

'What do you reckon, Odin?' he asked. 'Should I be reining Logan in? No point asking you, I suppose, because the two of you have never got along. Logan's scared of you, even if you are a big softie.'

Odin woofed, making Jack smile and increasing his conviction that Odin understood every word he said.

'Come on then, mate,' he said, pulling into the driveway of his modest semi and cutting the engine. 'Let's find you something to eat.'

Callie was up with the dawn but struggled to pull the zip up on her favourite wedding outfit – the one that ordinarily forgave the odd added pound or two. It seemed that there was a limit to its tolerant nature.

'Damn it,' she muttered, breathing in and holding her breath until the zip reluctantly slipped into place. 'I am definitely on a diet from Monday.'

She arrived at the hotel with Jason, bleary-eyed, hot on her heels.

'How was the date?' she asked.

'Phenomenal,' he replied, closing his eyes for an expressive moment. 'I think I am in lust.'

Callie smiled, glad that one of them was getting laid. 'Again?'

'Hey, we're not all as selective as you are.'

'Okay, let's quickly gloss over my lack of a life and get this show on the road.' She consulted her agenda, divided up the tasks that remained and they beavered away in efficient harmony for over an hour.

'It's so much easier without Marion getting in the way,' Jason said, standing back and admiring the floral displays. 'It's going like clockwork.'

'Don't jinx it,' Callie said, but she smiled, equally pleased with the way that the ballroom looked. 'Not even Marion will be able to find fault.'

Jason shuddered. 'Now who's jinxing it?'

Callie offered up a wry grin. 'Good point. Now, let's do one final check.'

The registrar arrived shortly after that and before Callie could draw breath, the first of the guests filtered in. They were directed to their allocated seats by the ushers whom Marion had insisted upon. All the trimmings of a church wedding in a hotel ballroom, as was so often the case nowadays. Callie and Jason stood unobtrusively at the back of the room, close to the point where the French doors were thrown open to a terrace and the manicured grounds beyond. The sun had even emerged from behind a bank of cloud. Well, of course it had!

'The elements wouldn't dare to rain on Marion's parade,' Jason muttered, echoing Callie's thoughts. They both knew this was not the bride's day.

Both slightly on edge, Callie and Jason waited, ready to swoop on the dozen or more disasters that could and inevitably did strike at the eleventh hour.

'It's getting close to showtime,' Jason muttered, tapping the fingers of one hand edgily against his thigh.

Callie blinked when one of the most handsome men she had

ever seen strode across the lawns and swept into the room as though he owned it.

'The damned car park was full,' he told Callie, as though she deserved an explanation. 'Had to hoof it from across the road.'

'Bad luck,' Jason said, batting his outrageously long lashes at the man.

'Making an entrance as usual, I see,' one of the ushers said in a loud voice, pumping the man's hand and conducting him to a seat close to the front. Callie noticed the appreciative glances that he gathered carelessly in his wake as he strolled down the makeshift aisle, nodding to acquaintances as he went.

'Will you look at that!' Jason was practically panting. 'Who is he?'

'I thought you were spoken for.' She paused. 'Again.'

'Darling, I'm too young to tie myself down to one man.'

Callie rolled her eyes. 'A business connection of the bride's father, I think.'

Callie watched the commotion caused by the man's arrival as he took his time settling in his seat, almost as though he wanted to be sure that he'd been noticed. She fought the urge to assure him that he had nothing to concern himself about in that respect. Not a single person of either sex had missed his entry. He was an outrageously handsome man, comfortable with who he was, Callie reckoned, and one who was accustomed to creating a stir wherever he went, enjoying the accolades.

At six foot or there abouts, he wore a sophisticated air with the ease of a man born into a privileged position. His dirty blond hair was clipped short at the sides and his perfectly aligned features were almost too... well, perfect. They were enhanced by piercing blue eyes and a lazy smile that made its recipient feel as though she was the chosen one. Callie knew because he'd given her a long look when he walked into the room and now glanced over his shoulder at her, almost as though he sensed her intense interest in him.

Annoyed to have been caught gawping in such an unprofessional manner, Callie's cheeks burned as she hastily returned her attention to her lists. Marion swept in, wearing an apricot creation that floated around her slim figure like a shroud. The handsome hunk glanced at her, dipped his head as she passed his position and then again glanced over his shoulder at Callie, a hint of amusement in his expression, as though sensing Callie's impatience with the woman's pretentions.

'Get a grip,' she muttered. Pretty faces of either sex did not influence her as a general rule, especially men she met during the course of her working life. She accepted that she had lousy taste when it came to the opposite sex and had decided they were not worth the effort. Callie had a plan, was determined to succeed and that plan left no room for distractions, emotional or otherwise. Besides, she had a dismal track record with men, had wrapped her heart in a protective cocoon of ambition and would never allow it to be dented ever again.

The bride entered to a fanfare of Wagner and gasps of appreciation for the guests when they caught sight of Maddy's tastefully restrained gown. Callie often wondered at the wisdom of brides who insisted upon a strapless gown and then spent the rest of their special day worrying about it staying up. She noticed the chief bridesmaid, a remarkably pretty girl, glance at the hunk in the silver-grey suit. She almost collided with Maddy because she was so slow to look away again and hadn't realised that the bride had reached the flowered bower that acted as a modern-day altar.

Callie breathed a little more easily as the ceremony went off without a hitch.

'Let the fun begin,' Jason murmured as the guests mingled, taking champagne from the trays of the waiting staff who circulated whilst an endless stream of photographs were taken and videos filmed.

Callie slipped away and entered the kitchens, which were in a state of organised chaos. Two more hours and her duty would be done. Her feet ached in her four-inch heels and she thought longingly of her squishy sofa, her PJs and a large, well-earned glass of wine.

* * *

Logan stifled a yawn as he greeted acquaintances and distributed charm and light banter with an even hand. He didn't consider himself to be a vain man particularly but enjoyed being admired and creating a stir. He was careful in situations such as this one not to flirt with the wives, almost all of whom came onto him with decreasing degrees of restraint as the wine flowed. The chief bridesmaid was a case in point. She was recently married herself, so he'd been told, to one of the ushers – a man built like a rugby full-back – but it hadn't prevented her from giving him *the look* throughout the entire ceremony.

A yawn threatened to escape when he thought how easy it all was nowadays. There was no thrill of the chase any more; success a foregone conclusion. Not that he was on the prowl for an easy conquest today, he reminded himself. He and Blakely were on the point of going into business together, as he had pointed out to Jack earlier, and it was down to Logan, as always, to make it happen.

A couple of female guests had attached themselves to him and he listened to their chatter with half an ear, all the while glancing around the room, looking for opportunities. Blakely wasn't the only influential man in attendance, and this was a perfect chance to make a good impression. Investors were thin on the ground in this day and age, more cautious than they had once been but still subconsciously willing to be won over.

'That's Callie Devereaux,' one of the female guests told him when his glance fell upon the slightly overweight woman he'd noticed when he made his entrance. Dressed in cream and turquoise that fell just below her knee and left a tantalising expanse of shapely leg on display, it also glanced over a stomach that wasn't flat but showcased impressive curves. 'She's obviously a little too fond of the canapes,' the woman added bitchily when Logan's gaze lingered upon Callie.

Logan smiled, refraining from pointing out that he preferred a little meat on his women's bones.

'She's making quite a name for herself in the wedding planning business,' the other woman said. 'She started out as an assistant in a wedding boutique and built her own business from there. She's in great demand nowadays. Well, she must be good, otherwise Marion wouldn't have given her the time of day.'

'Is that her partner?' Logan asked, nodding towards the man he'd seen her standing with earlier.

'Her business partner,' one of the women informed him. 'Word is, she lives to work and has no time for relationships. Perhaps that's why she's let herself go. I mean, if she doesn't care what people think of her...'

Logan tuned the catty remarks out. His decision not to tell his wife Portia about the wedding invitation had been vindicated, he decided, as he looked at Callie with renewed interest. A businesswoman, driven to succeed, equated to a woman after his own heart. Not that he would have brought Portia with him, even if she'd known about the invitation. Someone had to ferry the kids to their weekend activities. This was work and he couldn't forge connections when he had to worry about entertaining his wife, who was high maintenance and had to be watched to ensure that she didn't drink too much and then run her mouth.

Portia was a little too fond of recreational drugs too and didn't know when enough was enough. Logan blamed her father for that and so much else about the nervous, self-deprecating daughter he'd bribed Logan into marrying. A wealthy man, he had indulged his little princess for her entire life and she now expected everything on her own terms.

Logan bitterly regretted a marriage that he had entered into only because Portia's father's support had paved the way for his successful career. He wondered now if he would still have taken that route had he known just how controlling his father-in-law could be. Portia ran to him with exaggerated tales of neglect every time Logan sneezed, or so it felt, and his three children were equally demanding. He wondered if there was something wrong with him because he didn't take any paternal pride in his offspring. Not to put too fine a point on it, he found them irritating, but he pretended otherwise, if only to ensure that they were Portia's first priority.

It became increasingly obvious that Callie was blanking him as the day wore on and he failed to catch her eye, which only increased Logan's interest in her. He knew she had noticed him when he made his entrance and that she had liked what she saw. What was not to like? Well, Logan's competitive nature had been roused from its lethargy. Even so, he understood the value of patience. He would get through this meal, network with the money men, and then turn his attention to curvy Callie.

As good as his word, Logan didn't glance at Callie for the next two hours but was conscious of her unobtrusively moving about the room, checking on the arrangements in a subtle manner, always alert. He liked that about her. She wasn't willing to relax and didn't trust anyone else with the finer details, not even her assistant. He understood her drive because he was the same way himself.

Finally, the speeches were over with, the cake had been cut, and everyone got up to mingle. Logan gravitated towards the bar, where he found Blakely and his high-powered friends knocking back Louis XIII Magnum cognac. Invited to partake, Logan didn't hesitate, despite the fact that he was driving. The trophy wives had been temporarily abandoned as the men talked telephone-number business deals. Logan so desperately wanted to be able to play at the big boys' table that he almost salivated, simply because they had accepted him into their conversation.

This is what I want. What I was born to be.

It was his due, he decided, which is why he'd married Portia. But her father hadn't proved to be as generous as he'd given Logan reason to suppose would be the case when he'd taken his mentally unstable daughter off his hands. He had, however, proven to be controlling and openly critical of some of Logan's business decisions, which infuriated Logan. Yes, he'd made the odd mistake but it wasn't possible to make an omelette without cracking a few eggs, or so he had tried to make Ed Farquhar understand. But the older man looked upon any setback as failure and made sure that Logan knew it.

It was humiliating and yet also spurred Logan on. He would prove him wrong or die in the attempt.

Dancing had started and the trophies reappeared to drag their men into the fray. Blakely laughed, kissed the top of his child-bride's head and sent Logan a *what-can-you-do* look. The trophy, Logan was pleased to notice, fixed him with a speculative look and was slow to glance away again. Not that Logan would have even thought about playing with her. It was her husband's backing that he craved and he wasn't about to burn that particular bridge for the sake of a quick fuck.

'Call me next week,' Blakely said to Logan, 'and we'll finalise the arrangements once you get the results of that survey.'

'Will do,' Logan said easily, knocking back the rest of his drink and enjoying the slow burn created by the ruinously expensive brandy as it trickled seductively down the back of his throat.

Satisfied with his day's work, Logan decided that he'd earned the right to play and sauntered slowly into the reception in Blakely's wake.

3

Callie stood back and watched the dancers becoming progressively more raucous as the alcohol flowed in one direction and inhibitions went the opposite way. Even Marion jiggled about with a surprising lack of coordination for such an ordinarily controlled individual. She watched as the man in the silver suit twirled her round. She bumped into the person behind her and almost toppled over, giggling like a schoolgirl when the man grasped her forearm to prevent her from hitting the floor.

Callie had found that her gaze was frequently drawn to the handsome stranger. She was fascinated by his sophisticated manner and refined tone of voice. Her momentary fixation concerned her. She wasn't as shallow as the rest of the women here, was she? They all appeared to be drawn to a pretty face like moths to a flame. She reminded herself that she had given up on men. Even so, there was no harm in a little window shopping. If she had been looking for a relationship, she knew her own limitations. A man who could take his pick wouldn't settle for the hired help. Hired help who could do with dropping ten pounds or more. Hired help who had no time for a personal life and an underlying mistrust of all men.

With a sigh, she wandered into the kitchen to talk to the chef. She had just received another enquiry about a wedding that she hoped to persuade the bride's parents to stage at this hotel, using today's success as an incentive, since she knew there would be a big write-up in the local rag.

Her reputation was only as good as her last triumph; a fact she would be well advised to keep in mind. Things were going right for her at last. She was establishing herself as the go-to wedding planner for those who required the very best of everything and her bank balance was steadily rising along with her reputation. The days of her hand-to-mouth childhood were long behind her, thanks to her own efforts, but the scars ran deep and it would be a long time, if ever, before she felt completely secure.

'Thank you, Marcel,' she said, shaking the temperamental chef's hand. 'You excelled yourself, as always.'

'That Mrs Blakely is a tyrant,' he said, shaking his fist. 'She dared to suggest that my salmon tartare had too much lime. Ha!' He threw up his hands. 'The only bitter taste around my kitchen is the one left in my mouth when she interferes.'

'Complaining makes her feel important, Marcel. Don't let it trouble you. I have heard nothing but praise about your cuisine from everyone else.'

'Which is how it should be.' Marcel folded his arms defensively but appeared mollified.

With Marcel in as good a frame of mind as he was ever likely to be, Callie told him about the next wedding she hoped to stage at the hotel and the culinary requirements necessary to make it successful.

'The bride's family can't afford anything this lavish but at least they are easy to handle.' Callie grinned. 'Well, as easy as one can hope for in a bride's mother.' Callie paused, sensing Marcel's disinterest. 'She did ask to stage the wedding here solely because she ate here once and hasn't stopped raving about your food ever since,' Callie added persuasively, stretching the truth by playing to Marcel's vanity.

'Well, provided she doesn't interfere and gives me free rein, I suppose...'

Callie smiled, once she had secured Marcel's promise to prepare a suggested menu in accordance with a budget that had made him twitch his nose disdainfully. A budget that was more than adequate. 'How am I supposed to shine with such restrictions placed upon me?' he asked, muttering to himself as he walked away.

But Callie knew that he would rise to the challenge and that his mind would already be buzzing with ideas. She turned away and walked straight into a wall.

'Steady!' A pair of strong hands grasped her shoulders to steady her.

'What are you doing here?' she asked ungraciously, taken aback when she looked up into the stranger's face and felt disadvantaged by his obvious self-confidence. 'I mean, guests aren't permitted in the kitchens.'

'Truth to tell, I was looking to escape.'

'Never heard of gardens?' Callie asked, turning towards the cacophony of noise coming from the ballroom.

'I had to make a quick escape.'

'From what?'

'The Macarena.' He shuddered. 'Have a little compassion. There are limits.'

Callie smiled. 'Extenuating circumstances indeed,' she agreed. 'I don't suppose the gardens would have guaranteed your safety from that particular form of torture.'

'It astonishes me that sophisticated adults can be reduced to... well, whatever it is that damned song reduces them to.'

'You get used to it in my line of work.'

'You're the wedding planner, I take it.' He hesitated. 'Mike Logan.' He held out a hand and Callie slipped her own into it. 'It's a pleasure.'

'Callie Devereaux,' she said, reacting all the way to her toes to the feel of his fingers closing around hers. Annoyed with herself for being so predictable, she snatched her hand back but she could tell from the smug nature of his expression that he knew precisely what he had just done to her. What was less obvious to Callie was why he would feel the need to bother.

'You deserve to be congratulated. Marion Blakely can't be easy to handle.'

'I've known worse,' Callie replied diplomatically, unsure how friendly he actually was with the bride's mother but knowing better than to speak out of turn. Innocent comments tended to be twisted out of shape with each retelling. Callie's career was too important to her to take the risk, even though Mike seemed trustworthy. 'It stands to reason that all mothers want their daughters' big day to be special and it's my job to weave the necessary magic.' She cocked her head to one side. 'I think it's over – the Macarena, that is. It's safe for you to go back now.'

'I'm in no particular rush. I like it here.'

Callie sent him a curious look. 'In the corridor to the kitchens?'

He smiled. 'I was referring to the company.'

Callie was annoyed when she felt herself blushing. 'You didn't seem to lack for company in there.'

'Watching me, were you?' He cocked a brow in a way that ought to have come across as arrogant but somehow didn't.

'It's my job to watch everything.'

'Ah, right, that would explain it.'

Callie felt awkward, standing in the narrow passageway with a total stranger. Besides, it was unprofessional. She headed for the back door, which she knew led to the gardens. He followed along. 'You're only as in demand in this business as your last success, if that makes any sense,' she said, feeling a need to explain herself. 'Ninety-nine per cent of the wedding might go off without a hitch but it's the one per cent that gets talked about and can ruin a career.'

'Not in your case. I don't take much interest in weddings, but I've heard your name mentioned in connection with them in the most glowing of terms.'

'Have you really?' She snapped her head round and met his piercing gaze. 'Good to know. Anyway, I'd best get back to work.'

'Surely your day is done and I can buy you a drink.'

She laughed. 'Thanks, but my day is never done, not until the last guest leaves.' She walked away from him, then turned back. 'Oh, and it's a free bar.'

'I didn't mean here,' he said, extending his long legs and easily catching up with her. 'I noticed a nice little bar around the corner, where I'm pretty sure they don't play the Macarena.'

Callie was sorely tempted, but she also smelled a rat. 'Why?' she asked, annoyed with herself for being drawn in by him. She was serious about steering clear of romantic entanglements that were both distracting and usually ended up with her heart taking a battering. She was far too trusting and believed whatever line she was spun because she wanted it to be true – a sure recipe for disaster, but she never seemed to learn from her mistakes. She glanced at Mike and decided not to take the risk.

'Why what?' He looked genuinely confused.

'You can take your pick from the women in there. Why me?'

'You intrigue me,' he replied. 'You've made something of yourself through your own efforts. I admire that.'

She frowned. 'How do you know that about me?'

'Okay, I can see that you're going to make this hard for me so I'll fess up.' He gave a self-deprecating shrug. 'I asked your assistant.'

'You did what?'

'Hey, I'm sorry. Don't get mad.' He warded her off by pushing his hands towards her, palms first. 'Do you always jump down a guy's throat when he invites you for a drink?'

Callie didn't want to admit that she couldn't remember the last time that anyone who interested her had made a play for her. 'I work a lot,' she said lamely. 'Speaking of which, I really do have to get back. It was nice to meet you, Mike. Perhaps some other time.'

Logan watched her walk away, barely able to believe his eyes. She really wasn't interested and his own mild interest in her grew exponentially as a consequence. He wondered why he hadn't given her his real name. She could find it out easily enough if she asked around, but that was a risk he'd been willing to take. She'd only have to Google his name to find out about Portia and the kids. Some women didn't care if a guy was married and had responsibilities. Callie, he sensed, would have a conscience about that sort of thing and he fully intended to have some fun with her. Toying with nervous little mice who didn't really know how attractive they actually were was a temptation he simply couldn't resist.

'Well, well,' he muttered. 'It seems the chase is on.'

He sauntered back into the ballroom, keeping well clear of flying elbows and wayward feet as he skirted the dancefloor, watching Callie with renewed interest as she went from group to group, answering questions and soothing feathers that inevitably became ruffled as the booze took hold. He *had* heard her name mentioned deferentially by a group of Portia's friends, that much was true, and now that he had met her in the flesh there was something about her efficient self-containment that appealed to him. That was why he'd asked her assistant about her. He wouldn't waste his time if she had a significant other but, according to the loquacious Jason, she was cynical about the entire happily-ever-after scenario and seldom dated.

Music to Logan's ears.

She was just his type of woman, in all respects.

Up close, he liked what he saw. He had enjoyed their lively exchange and looked forward to going back to her place, where he would have happily given her what she so obviously needed. She was way too uptight and Logan recognised sexual frustration when confronted by it. He *knew* that she was attracted to him. It had shown in the way that she glanced at him so often during the course of the day. Logan was used to attracting the attention of women of all ages and this one, he had sensed, would be an easy conquest.

Except that wasn't proving to be the case.

Perhaps she had succeeded in business because she took nothing at face value. Just how successful she actually was, Logan fully intended to find out. He worked too damned hard himself, keeping Jack, Frank and their crew in gainful employment. Everyone deserves a little recreation.

* * *

Two days after the Blakely wedding, at six in the evening, Callie had sent Jason home. She remained in what she liked to think of as her tasteful business premises, making calls to try to satisfy a bride who, for some obscure reason, wanted to exchange vows in a hot air balloon. At least it would be good publicity for Callie's business, *if* the arrangements went off without a hitch, and she would ensure that they did.

Annoyed by the distraction when someone tapped at the door, she opened her mouth to say they were closed but snapped it shut again without speaking when she saw Mike Logan, tall, elegant and sophisticated, standing outside in the drizzling rain, holding a single red rose up for her inspection. She had thought about him a lot – far too much – since the Blakely wedding. His engaging smile turned her insides to mulch and there wasn't the slightest possibility of her sending him away.

'What are you doing here?' she asked, unlocking the door and letting him in.

'You asked me the same thing the last time we met.' He presented the rose to her with a flourishing bow.

'Thanks, I think, but the question is worth repeating.'

'I was in the area and thought I'd press you to go for that drink.' He held up a hand to prevent her from turning him down, as had been her intention. 'And don't ask why? Just go with the flow. I'll even buy you supper.'

'I'm on a diet.'

'That's a shame.'

'What, that I won't have supper with you or that I'm on a diet?'

'Both, but especially the latter. You don't need to diet.'

She rolled her eyes. 'Now I know you want something.'

'Seriously, Callie. I would have called but I knew you'd turn me down, so I decided to chance my luck in person.'

'I'm not sure that I believe you.' And she didn't. His behaviour made her highly suspicious.

'Take a chance. I promise that I'm not a pervert.'

Callie capitulated, closed her computer down and picked up her bag. 'Okay, you win. Where are we going?'

'I saw a little wine bar around the corner with quite an extensive menu.'

And so, over a decent bottle of red and more nibbles than she ought to have consumed, Callie found herself relaxing in ways she had forgotten were possible. Mike encouraged her to talk about her work and actually listened to her responses, seeming genuinely interested. Better yet, he ignored the admiring glances sent his way by all the women and some of the men in the bar and concentrated his attention exclusively upon her. Slowly, her doubts about his motives fell away. Perhaps he really was a decent guy in need of company who could see through her not especially attractive exterior and admired her entrepreneurial qualities.

Stranger things had been known to happen.

She figured that conversation with bimbos must be pretty limiting.

He told her about his own struggles to make something of himself and she listened in fascination, worried about just how drawn to him she actually felt.

'I had it all as a kid,' he admitted. 'Posh home, private education, all the bells and whistles. Everything other than love and encouragement. It was simply assumed that I would be successful. Anything else was out of the question.'

'I certainly know how it feels to be neglected,' she agreed, playing with the edge of her napkin.

'I'm not comparing my own situation with yours, which sounds horrendous,' he replied, covering her hand with his own. Callie was conscious of warmth seeping through her and knew she couldn't blame the wine. 'At least I had all the creature comforts.'

'So did I. I had my grandmother, whom I adored and still miss to this very day. I sense her presence in every room of the cottage that I inherited from her. Everything I strive to achieve is only possible because she encouraged me to believe that I had the ability to become whatever I wanted to be, despite a poor education, and ought not to be held back by my humble origins.'

'She sounds like a wise woman. I wish I could have known her.'

'I think you would have liked her.' Callie leaned her elbow on the table and cupped her chin in her hand. 'You were telling me about your own struggles. I still don't know what it is that you do.'

'I build luxury houses. Well, not personally, but I have a partner who does the heavy lifting. It's my job to find the sites and interest investors.'

'Something that comes naturally to you, I suspect. We must all play to our strengths. I saw the way that Blakely took to you.' And his young wife, but Callie decided not to mention her obvious interest in Mike Logan. She wondered if Blakely had noticed and if so, whether it would affect his decision to invest in Mike's latest project, the details of which he insisted were confidential.

The time sped by and Callie was surprised to look around and discover they were the only people left in the wine bar. It was gone eleven and the staff clearly wanted to pack up. Callie offered to pay her way but Mike seemed offended by the suggestion.

'I'm old-fashioned about that sort of thing,' he said, dropping a credit card on the waiter's tray. 'Besides, it was my invitation. Now, can I drive you home?'

She told him no, since she had her own car and hadn't drunk enough to prevent her from driving. She wondered if perhaps he had but decided he was a big boy, certainly old enough to make his own decisions.

In the event, his Ford was parked opposite her yellow Beetle. He kissed her on the cheek, said he'd enjoyed himself and asked for her mobile number.

* * *

And that was how it started. After their third evening out, she invited him back to her cottage and they finished up in bed. It was disappointing, over quickly, and she hadn't come. If Mike noticed, then he made no mention of it and seemed smugly satisfied with himself. It didn't matter, Callie told herself, it was just a bit of fun.

He didn't stay the night, claiming an early start in the morning, but she saw him again later that week and this time she cooked for him. She liked to cook but seldom bothered for herself. Now she found herself seeking out new recipes and shopping for unusual ingredients in the hope of impressing him.

Everyone close to her noticed the changes almost immediately.

'It's that guy from the wedding!' Jason clapped his hands. 'I just knew it! The man has taste, I'll say that much for him.' Jason settled in for a good natter. 'Now come on, girl, dish the dirt. I want all, and I mean *all*, the gory details.'

Maisie was equally keen for the lowdown when she saw how happy Callie was; how she was gradually lowering the barricades and letting Mike in.

'I told you so!' Maisie said smugly one night when Callie sang Mike's praises for a good ten minutes, barely pausing to draw breath. 'You're in love, girl. You've got it bad, and not before time.'

'I'm not sure about love, but we do get along well.'

'Have you been to his pad? Where does he live?'

'Southampton way somewhere, I think. He's not there much. He travels a lot, looking for investors. Besides, I need to be here seven days a week, so cosy overnighters aren't feasible,' she said, wondering why she sounded so defensive.

'Where's his latest building project?'

'How should I know?' Callie grinned. 'We don't waste time talking about work.'

'When do I get to meet this Adonis, then? Do you have any pictures of him? Any selfies of the two of you making gooey eyes at one another?'

Callie didn't like to mention that they'd almost had their first row when she'd tried to snap a picture of him with her phone without telling him first. He apologised for overreacting, she said she understood, that she didn't like having her picture taken either, and they hadn't referred to the incident again.

'I hope he's coming for the weekend, then you will – meet him, that is. I'll cook for the four of us if you can get a sitter. Anyway, I'll let you know if he can come. He said he'd try but he's at the beck and call of his investors.'

Maisie frowned. 'At the weekend?'

Callie shrugged. 'What can I say? He's driven.' The fact that he was the polar opposite of Dan, Maisie's husband, who was again out of work, went unsaid.

As it transpired, Mike was unable to stay that weekend, or the one after. Maisie made the odd comment about it being strange but Callie understood Mike's fierce desire to succeed; it was the same desire that gave her a reason to get out of bed in the mornings and so she never pushed him for a commitment. They saw one another when their respective workloads permitted and that was enough for Callie. Despite her growing feelings for Mike, she still didn't believe in happily-ever-after. She could count on the fingers of one hand the number of weddings she had organised that had stood the test of the first five years.

Cynical, perhaps, but she would settle for happy-for-now.

And she was happy, she realised, albeit unfulfilled in the bedroom. She couldn't think of a way to tell Mike that he didn't satisfy her without piercing his manly ego. The fault had to be hers, anyway, not his, so she pretended in the way that women had since the beginning of time and Mike remained none the wiser.

It was a perfectly ordinary morning when the letter that changed her life came from the bank, stating that her mortgage payments were overdue. She sighed. She had a manic week ahead of her and no time to waste on the phone sorting out the mistake.

And it had to be a mistake because she didn't have a mortgage.

4

Jack sighed when his mobile went off in the middle of a site meeting. He glanced at the display and let out a second sigh when he saw Portia's name light up. He was fond of Logan's wife but she was a bit of a flake, high maintenance, emotional and nervous. And not his responsibility. She only ever called him when she wanted something. Usually it was because she thought Jack could resolve her marital problems for her. It didn't seem to occur to her that even a seasoned marriage counsellor wouldn't be able to fix that particular car crash.

He excused himself from the men he'd been discussing drainage with and stepped away to take her call.

'Hiya, Portia. What can I do for you?'

'Have you seen him?' Her words were slightly slurred and it was still only eleven in the morning. She was high on something; either booze or the pills she got from somewhere to calm her nerves. 'I can't raise him on his phone.'

'He's up in Manchester talking to investors. He said he'd been gone most of the week. I expect he's switched his phone off if he's in meetings. Is it urgent?'

'He hasn't left me enough money and I...'

He could hear the hysteria building in Portia's voice and wished for the thousandth time that Logan would give her access to a credit card. It was ridiculous in this day and age for anyone to try to survive on cash. Jack had helped her out before and not seen the money back. He was damned if he'd go down that route again.

'I'm sorry, love. Keep trying Logan, or else ask your dad. I can't get away right now. How are the kids?' he added as an afterthought.

'They're good.' He could hear her voice trembling but hardened his heart. Portia really wasn't his problem. 'If you hear from him, be sure and get him to call me.'

'I will. Take care now.'

'Will you drop by and eat with us this evening? The kids would love to see you.'

Jack knew that it wasn't the kids who craved his company. Portia wasn't good without Logan there to lean on and had tried to substitute him with Jack on more than one occasion.

'Don't count on it. I have meetings coming out of my ears. I might not be able to get away.'

Jack pocketed his phone, wondering when he would learn to say *no*. Wondering where the hell Logan had taken himself off to this time. He was tired of covering for him when he was having one of his frequent dalliances and astonished that Portia didn't seem to suspect a thing. Well, perhaps not so astonished, given how trusting she was. Even so, he didn't approve of Logan's behaviour, especially as it impacted upon him, as it appeared to do with increasingly regularity. He had told Logan not to marry Portia; that he would live to regret it since he was marrying for all the wrong reasons.

But for Logan, chasing money was his only motivation and he

was convinced that the rewards dished out by Farquhar would be far-reaching.

As it transpired, he'd got that wrong too and the master manipulator had been played by the hand of an even greater expert.

Logan had been out of touch for two days now, which was unusual enough to worry Jack. He always took Jack's calls or returned them promptly if he was otherwise engaged. He ought to be here now, reassuring their new investors, which was an aspect of the business he never trusted to anyone else. And with good reason. Jack wasn't the right man to gloss over the cracks in their building projects – quite literally. He preferred to be upfront and thought investors deserved to understand the risks. Logan disagreed and nursed their egos with kid gloves. Another aspect of their working relationship that threatened their friendship, Jack realised as he sighed, plastered a smile on his face and returned to the fray.

Callie sat on the floor, surrounded by paperwork, sobbing her heart out against Maisie's shoulder.

'If you dare to say you told me so,' she gulped, stroking Jinx's back so violently that he mewled in protect and jumped from her knee, 'I swear I won't be responsible for my actions.'

'Hey, it's okay. I'm as much to blame as you are. I should have found the courage to voice my concerns but you seemed so happy that I didn't want to burst your bubble. Besides, I was the one who encouraged you to find someone and have some fun. I just never dreamed...' She swept her arm in an arc to encompass the mess on the floor and allowed her words to trail off.

'Everything I've worked for, every sodding thing. How could

he? More to the point, how did I let this happen? Why didn't I see it coming? I thought I was a grown-up in full control and that I was dating a driven businessman who shared my values.'

In the two days since Callie had discovered that the bogus mortgage wasn't bogus, she had also discovered that a credit card she hadn't applied for had been maxed out, too.

'How the hell did he get hold of my pin number?' She shook her head. 'He never stayed the night and never once asked me about my finances. He must have somehow got access to my files, I suppose.'

Callie lifted a tear-stained face to meet her friend's concerned look. 'You think he copied my house key and I never suspected a thing.'

'The best conmen are entirely believable. That's how they get away with it.'

'It all makes a weird sort of sense, I suppose. His never being available when I wanted to show him off to you. His hissy fit when I tried to take a selfie of us. But he was so plausible, Maisie. I was cautious at first but also completely taken in by him. He never let me pay when we went for a drink and seemed to be flush with cash.' She grunted. 'Other people's cash, most likely. Not that we did very often; go for a drink, I mean. We fell into the habit of meeting here and I cooked for him. He said he enjoyed the cosy home life. Said he was brought up in a mausoleum of a house with no affection and looked after by servants. I felt sorry for him, but I was probably supposed to. I expect that was a lie too and that the upper-class accent was bogus; just like all the rest of him.'

'What will you do?'

Callie spread her hands. 'I feel like such a fool. I thought I was so clever, knew it all and would never get scammed.'

'Well, the way I see it, you can either sit here feeling sorry for yourself or you can get off your arse and think of a way to get even.' Maisie gave Callie's shoulders a gentle shake. 'None of this is your fault. You were taken in by a master manipulator. You now have to decide whether you intend to let him get away with it.'

'How often have I said that when something seems too good to be true it almost always is?' Callie mopped her eyes and gave her nose a hefty blow. 'I smelt a rat when he came on to me at the Blakely wedding. I mean, there were a ton of better-looking females there who'd made their availability plainly apparent. So why settle for third best?'

'Oh, Callie!' Maisie shook her head. 'Sometimes I could shake you.'

'He'd obviously decided that I'd be so grateful that I'd be an easy mark, and how right was he?' Jinx returned to her lap and she stroked his sleek back more cautiously.

'Stop it!' Maisie's strident tone caused Callie's head to snap back. 'Stop blaming yourself and put your energy into thinking about how to put things right. You've put a stop on your credit cards, including the bogus one, right?'

Callie nodded and pulled a face. 'Much good it will do me.'

'You need to involve the police?'

'Much good that will do me as well. I doubt whether Mike Logan is his real name and even if it is, I can't prove he's the culprit. Like I say, he's been ultra-careful not to leave a trail.'

Maisie gave a considering nod. 'This cottage is pretty isolated but he can't have known that when he picked you up. When he saw it, I guess he thought it was his lucky day and just couldn't help himself. Where are the nosy neighbours when you need them?'

'Anyway, if I go to the police, I can't guarantee that word won't get out and what will that do for my business? If I can't manage my own affairs, why would people trust me to manage the most important day of their daughters' lives? Think of the huge budgets I'm entrusted with. If there's a question mark over my ability to manage my own finances, potential clients will think twice before trusting me with theirs.'

'That's the least of your worries. You've made a name for yourself and you need to exploit that fact whilst you're at the top of your game.'

Callie threw a handful of pages in the air and watched them flutter back down to the rug. 'Ha!'

'What about the mortgage company? How much did he take them for?'

'A hundred grand.'

Maisie let out a low whistle. 'Wouldn't they have wanted to survey the property before lending that much dosh?'

'That's where he was clever. He asked for less than thirty per cent of the value. Well, he asked for it in my name. The money went into my account and then straight out again before I even knew it was there.'

'He must have done this quite recently, then, because he couldn't risk you seeing that transaction.' Callie nodded. 'Why are they demanding payment so soon then?'

'They weren't. It was just confirmation of the due date.'

'Why didn't they email it?'

'Well, he wouldn't have given them my real email address, would he? Sorry,' she added sheepishly when she realised that she was shouting. 'I don't know why they used snail mail. If they hadn't, I wouldn't have found out so soon, so I'm glad that they did.'

'Well, if they believe you didn't make the application then presumably they will take steps to get their money back.'

'But they won't look into Mike,' she screeched, 'because I can't prove a connection to him and so they have no reason to. As far as they're concerned, the problem is mine.' She sighed. 'I'll have to place it in the hands of my solicitors, which will take forever and cost me even more money that I no longer have.'

'Then we shall just have to track him down and ask him not so nicely to let us have your money back, with interest to make up for the stress, naturally.'

Callie threw back her head, closed her eyes and sighed. 'You make it all sound so easy.'

'It doesn't have to be difficult. People don't just disappear. Unless he's done this to a hell of a lot of other people, one hundred grand won't keep him in designer jeans for long. We could perhaps start an online campaign, asking anyone who knows him to come forward. I bet we'd get a ton of responses,' Maisie said enthusiastically, warming to her theme.

'And send him scuttling deeper under cover.'

'Ah, I hadn't thought of that.' Maisie paused. 'What about his car? Do you know the reg number? I have a friend of a friend who can trace that sort of thing. Don't ask me how. Not sure if it's strictly legal. He's a computer whizz who knows his way round the dark web but hell, what does it matter? Your Mike hasn't played by the rules, so why should we?'

'It was just an ordinary grey Ford Sierra. I did wonder about that. It seemed a bit tame for such a flamboyant man who was anything other than grey.' She closed her eyes. 'I think I remember the number.'

She reeled it off, Maisie jotted it down, then picked up her mobile and spoke to someone. 'He's on it,' she said, cutting the call.

They talked round in circles for a few minutes. In actual fact, Callie did all the talking and Maisie made sympathetic noises at the right moments. Callie wanted to curl up, lick her wounds and drink herself into oblivion, but feeling sorry for herself would achieve nothing, she reasoned. When Maisie's friend called back to say that the car had been rented from Gatwick airport, instead of feeling even more defeated, something changed inside of her and a slow, burning anger chased away the pity party.

'I bet I am not his only victim,' she mused. 'You're right about that. And I wonder just how well Robert Blakely knows him. Blakely was supposedly investing in one of Mike's building projects. I told you that, right?'

'You did, and they must have been close associates, otherwise Mike wouldn't have been invited to the wedding,' Maisie replied, following Callie's line of thinking. 'He will have to be your first port of call.'

'I don't know.' Callie pensively nibbled the end of her index finger. 'It's humiliating. Besides, would he believe me?'

'True about the humiliating part, but if he's done this to you, what's to say that he hasn't done it to Blakely as well? Now he's powerful enough to get more answers than we ever will.'

Callie felt an enveloping sense of calm as she slowly nodded. 'Possibly, but I get the impression that Blakely's a self-made man, so he won't be so easy to dupe.' She glanced absently out the window as a summer squall sent rain pattering against the glass. 'Blakely's not nearly as gullible as me and he would have checked out Mike's credentials before even considering doing business with him.'

'Well then, give him a call, make up some excuse and ask him for Mike's contact details. What's the worst that can happen?'

Callie nodded, tipped an indignant Jinx from her lap and went to the files she kept in a cabinet in the corner of her tiny sitting room. An unlocked cabinet that contained all her bank documents. It hadn't even occurred to her to hide them away, so comprehensively had she trusted Mike. She glanced accusingly at her laptop, sitting innocently in the centre of her tiny desk, and wondered if Logan had managed to hack into it. It would explain how he'd come across her credit card pin number and probably couldn't believe his luck when he checked the balance on her bank account. She had the access details coded in an email file but if he could hack a laptop then cracking her amateur code would have been child's play.

Thank God she didn't keep anything to do with her business account at home, she thought, going hot and cold when she considered where that might have led. A spell in the nearest prison for fraud, she imagined, shuddering.

She found the file for the Blakely wedding and the contact details she had been given for the bride's parents. Fortunately, Robert Blakely had given her his mobile number, meaning that if she called it she would likely get straight onto him without having to get past layers of minions.

'Go on, then,' Maisie encouraged. 'What have you got to lose?'

'I don't suppose I can look like a bigger idiot than I already do,' Callie said, keying in the number.

'You don't have to tell him the truth. Make something up.'

'Blakely,' an irritated voice snapped at the end of the line.

Callie wasn't in the mood for playing games, so she got straight to the point. 'This is Callie Devereaux, Mr Blakely.'

'Who? How did you get this number?'

'Your daughter's wedding planner and you gave it to me.'

'Ah, right, sorry. It's been a fraught day.' Callie nodded, even though he couldn't see her, well able to empathise, thinking fraught didn't come close to cutting it in her case. 'How can I help? Not more unpaid bills, I hope. How much can one wedding cost?'

'Nothing like that. I'm trying to contact one of the guests. He left something behind at the hotel, no one has been able to contact him and so I got landed with the job.'

'And you think that I can?' She could hear the surprise in his voice.

'I gather he's a business associate of yours.'

'Does he have a name?' She heard him say something in an apologetic undertone to someone else, implying that he was not alone and that she was interrupting something important.

'Mike Logan.'

'Who?'

Callie shared a quizzical look with Maisie, who'd heard everything, since Callie had put her phone on speaker. 'The handsome gentleman in the silver suit. I saw you in the bar with him at one point.'

Blakely's voice turned glacial. 'Sorry, can't help you. We didn't go into business together and if you want my advice, you'll steer well clear of him.'

'How did you contact him, if you don't mind my asking?'

'Actually, I do. If the man has lost one of his possessions, then he only has himself to blame for his carelessness and if I were you, I wouldn't waste my time trying to reunite him with whatever it is. Now, you really must excuse me.'

And with that, the line went dead.

'Seems odd that Blakely didn't recognise Mike's name,' Maisie remarked, glancing out at the steadily falling rain and then at the clock. 'There's obviously been a falling out amongst thieves since he didn't sound like a fluffy bunny. Anyway, it's five o'clock somewhere,' she said cheerfully, retreating to the kitchen and grabbing a bottle of chilled Pinot from the fridge. 'Besides, this is an emergency, so the usual rules of engagement don't apply.'

She filled two glasses to the brim, handed one to Callie and clicked hers against it. 'To revenge, sister,' she said, taking a healthy sip. 'Now, what next?'

'What indeed...' Callie slumped back into her vacated seat,

drawing a howl of protest from Jinx when she encroached upon his space. 'So we're no further forward.'

'Don't be so defeatist. Now then, put your thinking cap on. It's obvious that he went to great lengths to conceal his identity from you. Mike may not be his real name since Blakely didn't recognise it. Blakely will know his real identity, but he clearly wasn't in the mood to share. Most good lies are based on a foundation of truth, you know, so I'm reckoning that he used his middle name or something close to it.'

'I didn't know that and can't help wondering how you do.'

'I read it somewhere, I expect.' Maisie waved a dismissive hand, in full Miss Marple mode. 'Anyway, it makes sense. It's easier to remember what you've told a person if it's founded in reality, so if he was attempting to do business with Blakely then he must be in the building game. That's what Blakely does, after all.'

'True.' Callie took a swig of her drink and felt it settle her gyrating nerves.

'So, it stands to reason that there must be a company in his name somewhere locally.'

'But we don't know his real name!' Callie cried.

'Even so, we have a motive to find it out. Think, there must be something he let slip that will lend us a clue.'

'He did mention a partner once, as a matter of fact, but I don't recall his name.' Callie pouted. 'I doubt he even exists and was just another figment of Mike's cruel imagination.'

'What did he say about him? Try and think, Callie,' Maisie urged when Callie shrugged.

'Just that they'd been friends forever. His mum was the cleaner in the grand house that Mike lived in. He and the kid were about the same age and played in the grounds together.

Mike reckoned he'd been lonely so welcomed the company and I actually felt sorry for him.'

'Bastard!' they said together, then burst out laughing.

It felt good to laugh, despite the circumstances, Callie decided, as she closed her eyes and struggled to recall the conversation in question. They had been in bed at the time and Callie has been distracted by Mike's wandering hands, wishing, hoping, that this time they might actually hit the spot, and so she hadn't paid a great deal of attention to his words.

'He said his friend was better at getting his hands dirty, whereas Mike was the man who brought in the investors.' She gave a disgruntled snort. 'I was actually impressed, if you can believe it.'

'I can,' Maisie said, squeezing Callie's arm. 'Men like him have to seem entirely genuine. It goes with the territory.'

'I suppose...'

Maisie grabbed her ever-present mobile and started scrolling.

'What are you looking for?'

'Local building firms with the name Logan in the title.'

'Ah, good thinking, always assuming Logan is part of his name. That should have occurred to me.' Maisie was sitting on the floor at Callie's feet and she peered over her shoulder. 'Any luck?'

'Nothing jumps out at me. He clearly didn't use anything as obvious as his real name, but then if he's a conman I suppose that shouldn't surprise me.'

'A conman.' Callie threw back her head and roared. 'We'd only been seeing one another on and off for a couple of months. To think that I let my guard down and believed every word he said to me in such a short space of time. Time that he didn't waste, it seems. Mortgages take a while to organise.'

'Except you weren't entirely taken in by him. You were still taking it slow.'

'Perhaps.' But Callie knew that if he'd suggested cohabiting, she would probably not have put up too many objections, despite her aversion to commitment. A part of her still hadn't been able to believe that a man who looked like Mike was the real deal but the rest of her wanted to believe it so desperately that she'd closed her eyes to the cracks in their fledgling relationship; most particularly to his inability to satisfy her in bed. His selfishness in putting his own needs first. His constant absences and her inability to reach him when she tried to ring. Who knew she was quite *that* needy? That admission would be one humiliation too far, though. 'How the mighty cynic has fallen,' she said derisively. 'Hoist with my own petard, whatever the hell that's supposed to mean.'

'Sounds all Shakespearean to me,' Maisie said, shuddering but not looking up from her phone. 'This is no good. There are too many building firms with the initial L in the name for us to be able to narrow them down. Never mind, help is at hand.'

Callie watched listlessly as Maisie phoned her hacker friend again and gave him crisp instructions.

'He's on it and will get back to us,' she said, ending the call.

'How much do you have to pay him?'

'Don't worry, he does it because he likes to show off. Our cause is better than him trying to prove a point by hacking into banks or whatever and getting himself arrested.' She rolled her eyes. 'I wouldn't put it past him. Anyway, he's taking a peek at Companies House as we speak.'

'Ah, I get it.' Callie nodded. 'Mike's name would have to be registered if he's a director.'

'Right.'

Maisie drained her glass. 'All this sleuthing is thirsty work,' she said, reaching for the bottle and topping off their glasses. 'To us, the invincible duo. Mike bloody Logan won't know what hit him and will regret the day he ever messed with us!'

Callie smiled, grateful to her friend for doing the thinking for them both but unable to see any light at the end of a bleak tunnel. The thought that she might well lose her grandmother's cottage filled her with despair. Granny had had faith in her and she had let her down in the worst possible way. She had been so damned stupid! It defied belief. Stupid, and pliable and so needy. God, she felt angry now. Ready to commit murder. It was all so blindingly obvious now and she had been too invested in Mike's admiration, his compliments and the way he appeared to open up his heart to her to see the wood for the trees.

They had almost finished the bottle and were contemplating the wisdom of a second when Maisie's phone rang.

'That took a while,' she said, answering the call. 'Companies House got the better of you, did they?' She laughed at whatever her friend said in response. 'Course I don't doubt your abilities. Why else would I call you? Well, other than the fact that you're cheap.' She laughed again. 'Yes, yes, and the best. Now give, before I die of old age.'

Maisie indicated that she needed a pen and paper. Callie obliged and watched as her friend scribbled down an address in writing that was barely legible.

'Yep, thanks, Gary,' she said. 'That sounds like the place.'

She cut the call and grinned at Callie. 'Your Mike isn't quite as clever as he thinks he is. Tra-la!' She turned her scribbles in Callie's direction, but they were still almost illegible. 'AW Construction. With directors Logan M. Armitage and one Jack Carlisle.'

'That's it!' Callie cried, optimism highlighted by a lightbulb explosion. 'Jack. That's the name of the cleaner's son.' She turned to Maisie, her eyes glistening with triumph. She could taste blissful revenge on her tongue. 'And presumably the M stands for Michael. He simply reversed his first two names. We have them!'

Logan drank brandy almost as decent as that supplied by Blakely at his daughter's wedding and savoured the rich burn as the fiery liquid trickled slowly down the back of his throat. His moment of triumph was briefly clouded when thoughts of Blakely intruded upon it. The fat cat who got away, he thought, sighing with regret. Blakely had withdrawn his support for Logan's ambitious new plans at the eleventh hour, obliging him to fall back on Plan B. It rankled but happened occasionally. You couldn't win 'em all.

Damn Jack and his determination not to cut corners. Of course they couldn't have broken ground on that damned site. Logan had known it all along, which is what made it so perfect. A bodged survey, impressive paperwork from his bent mate in the planning office to convince the average punter that permission had been applied for and would be looked favourably upon, a few hints about profitability for those who had the foresight to get in on the ground floor and Logan's long-term plans would have come to fruition.

This was to have been his swansong, but he'd underestimated Blakely, got sloppy when the invitation to his daughter's wedding fell on the doormat and he assumed he'd sold Blakely the dream. Greedy men were seldom cautious, but he admitted to himself now that he had misjudged the man.

Fortunately, he always had a failsafe. A rueful smile graced his lips when he thought of the failsafe in question. Callie, so suspicious of his motives at first and yet so easy to win over in the end. It was a shame that he'd had to scam her, but needs must...

She'd get her money back, or most of it, eventually, and would learn to be more cautious in the future.

It was funny but his eye really had been drawn to her at that wedding with nothing more serious than a roll in the hay in his thoughts. If she'd obliged then he would have walked away and been none the wiser about her nest egg. He had known the worth of that cottage the moment he had walked through the door and from that moment on, her goose had been comprehensively cooked. Her security, such as it was, had been a doddle to breach.

He'd come to like and respect her determination and drive, to say nothing of her modesty. It was no hardship hanging out with her. He looked forward to their time together – something that hadn't happened to him in a long time. He made excuses, altered his schedule so that he could be with her. He enjoyed the sound of her husky voice. Liked to watch her moving around her small kitchen with elegant economy as she cooked proper food for him, taking extra trouble to source ingredients that he'd mentioned were favourites of his.

When had anyone last cosseted him with no expectation of reward, other than to win his approval?

But that was done with and it was time to move on. He needed another week to tidy up a few loose ends and then he was away from England – from his wife and kids, from his father-in-law, from Jack... from the whole damned circus, where endless demands were placed upon his time and talent and no appreciation shown by his dependents for his efforts.

He signalled for another drink and the waiter in the glamorous London hotel attended him with alacrity. He wondered if it should bother him that his conscience – if it existed – didn't... well, bother him. But the fact of the matter was that it had only very briefly raised its head when he helped himself to Callie's worldly goods. Leaving his wife and kids barely warranted a second thought. They, Portia in particular, had brought it on themselves. Callie's only crime was to be too trusting.

Portia would be okay. She'd run to Daddy, who would take care of her and the kids. He had never really trusted them to Logan's care anyway, otherwise he would have signed the house he gave them as a wedding present over to Logan rather than leaving it in his own name. That still rankled. Logan was good enough to take his flaky daughter off his hands but not to be trusted with the family silver.

Was it any wonder that Logan had had to reinvent himself? Why would he have married someone like Portia if it wasn't in expectation of a generous reward? He blew air through his lips, irritated to be reminded that he'd been played by a master conniver when he ought to be enjoying his moment of glory and plotting his strategy.

He smiled when the waiter delivered his new drink and then stood to greet the gorgeous escort who drew every male eye in the place as she glided up to him on legs long enough to make a race-horse weep with envy. She introduced herself in a husky voice that went straight to Logan's groin. He turned on the charm, kissing the back of her hand in an old-fashioned gesture that would probably impress even a seasoned brass. He then downed his drink in one, took the woman's arm – he'd already forgotten her name – and steered her in the direction of the lifts. He had a room upstairs and champagne on ice. After all the work he'd put in, he deserved a reward.

The conscience he was unsure he possessed actually did trouble him a short time later when the woman expertly brought him to climax and he cried out Callie's name.

What the hell was that all about?

5

Callie hadn't been able to find any business premises for AW Construction, which increased her suspicions about Logan, as she must now think of him, and his supposed sidekick, the cleaning lady's son. During the course of a busy working day, hindered by the hangover from hell because she and Maisie *had* polished off the second bottle the night before, Callie was distracted and kept making mistakes, mixing up two weddings as she spoke to a bride's mother. Jason had to cover for her.

He remarked upon her *faux pas* several times, pointing out that she wasn't her usual sharp self and wanting to know what was wrong. Callie waved his concerns aside and put the blame on her hangover. She wasn't about to tell him, to admit to anyone, what a prize idiot she had been.

'How's the dreamboat?' Jason asked, standing back to critically examine a table design he'd just come up with for a demanding bride who insisted upon a nautical theme. 'All well in paradise?'

Callie's phone rang, providing her with an excuse to evade the question. She could not, however, avoid Jason's increasingly concerned glances as she stumbled from blunder to blunder.

'Get a grip,' she muttered aloud, when Jason was out of earshot. 'I will not let Logan destroy what I have left.'

Having pulled herself together after a fashion, she managed to get through the rest of the day without alienating another bride's mother, who had now changed her mind three times about the reception's theme and with whom Callie was rapidly losing patience.

'Who came up with the idea of themed weddings anyway?' Jason asked.

'Someone like me who saw a profit in it, I expect,' Callie replied absently, poring over her computer as she did some intense online digging into AW Construction. 'You can get off now, if you like. We're done here for the day.'

'It's still early and I'm not in any rush,' Jason replied, hitching his backside onto the edge of her desk. 'Anything I can help you with?'

Callie suppressed a smile. No one could ever accuse Jason of minding his own business. 'Nope. I'm about to get off myself. There's nothing more we can do today. Let's have an early one.'

'O... kay.' Jason grabbed his man bag but hesitated in the doorway, looking genuinely concerned for her. He was the one man she could depend upon. 'Call me if I can help, or when you decide you need to talk.'

'Will do. Bye.'

Left alone, Callie devoured the contents of AW Construction's glossy website, which was high on accolades and short on useful information. The contact details offered up one of those annoying online forms to fill in but didn't give an actual address. She tried the phone number listed and it went straight to an answering service. Her suspicions mounting by the minute, about to give up, a snippet at the bottom of the home page caught her eye.

'A new proposed development in west Chichester, details to follow. Hmm.' There was a miniscule map which Callie enlarged, taking note of the names of the streets surrounding a patch of brown and green. 'Ah ha!'

Mildly triumphant when she recognised the area, Callie decided to go and take a look. She jumped into Bessie, her faithful old VW, and smiled when the engine purred into life at the turn of the key. She might be old – the car, that is, although Cassie was feeling her age too – and not especially trendy, but she was well maintained, cheap to run and even the most desperate of thieves would think twice before targeting her.

'Much they know,' she said, giving the dashboard an affectionate pat.

Traffic was light and she reached the development area before she had decided how she would react if Logan was there. She crawled past a portacabin sat on the edge of a fenced off area, where there was little sign of life. A muddy pickup truck and an equally muddy 4x4 were the only vehicles present but it was knocking off time, so she wasn't especially surprised by the lack of bodies. What did surprise her was the fact that there was no sign of any building work having got under way and no glitzy billboards singing the praises of the homes to be erected.

She could see lights on in the portacabin, so someone was presumably toiling away. Unprepared to face whoever was there, even though she was convinced it couldn't be Logan – he wouldn't be seen dead in a pickup – Callie drove slowly away. She needed to think about her approach. Presumably, anyone in authority here would be in on Logan's scam and if she showed her hand, it would put her at an even greater disadvantage. It wasn't as if she could walk in there and ask the person to kindly have Logan return her money or else she would involve the police. If she had intended to call the police in, anyone with half a brain cell would have expected someone to come knocking long before now.

Callie circled the block and returned to the site. She pulled into a space across from it and simply watched for a while, unsure what she expected to see. A man stepped out of the portacabin and engaged in a brief, heated discussion on his mobile. He glanced in her direction and she resisted the urge to duck below the steering wheel. It wasn't her who ought to be hiding, she reminded herself, renewed anger burning through her oesophagus when she recalled what Logan had done to her and how easily he had managed it.

As if she could forget!

Even so, she started the engine and drove away, convinced that the man had to be watching her. She regretted now that Bessie was such a distinctive shade of yellow, hard to miss. She ought to go home and think things through, but some instinct prevented her from doing the sensible thing. As she passed the site for a third time, a sleek black car she hadn't seen before pulled away, with several men inside it. They must have parked on the other side of the portacabin, she assumed, causing her to wonder what they were hiding from.

The 4x4 had gone as well and only the pickup remained. Without considering the wisdom of her actions, she drove in and parked where in the spot that the Jeep had just vacated. She sensed someone watching her from inside the portacabin as she climbed out of Bessie and walked towards it. The door opened before she could knock and the same man she had seen on the phone earlier filled the aperture with his musculature.

'Something I can do for you?' he asked, subjecting her person to a slow perusal. She couldn't tell from his expression whether he liked what he saw and upbraided herself for caring. She was not here to win friends, or to make an impression. Even so, there was something about the man, about the fact that he clearly didn't mind getting his hands dirty and had the muscles to prove he was no stranger to hard, manual work that made her want to trust him. She almost laughed aloud at that absurd possibility, thinking of Logan and reminding herself that her judgement when it came to the male of the species was most definitely not to be trusted.

'Um, is Mike about?' she blurted out, when the man's steady gaze and his apparent comfort with awkward silences made her feel compelled to speak.

His expression darkened and she felt wary of him, sensing that he would be a dangerous man to cross. A sweep of thick black hair fell across his forehead – hair that would benefit from the attention of a brush – and cool green eyes regarded her with suspicion.

'Well, is he?'

'Why?'

'Why?' So he knew who she meant. He obviously did go by Mike. She planted her fisted hands on her hips, feeling disadvantaged. 'What do you mean why?'

'It's a simple enough question.'

'And none of your business,' she snapped.

Her fit of pique caused a slow, lazy smile to grace the man's rugged features, transforming him into every woman's vision of masculine perfection. He was the polar opposite to Logan in all respects. Logan with his clipped hair sculpted to his head and kept in place with a variety of products that must have cost him a small fortune. Logan with his style, charm, expensive suits and elegant sophistication.

She suspected that this man was the owner of the pickup and

that he wouldn't drive anything else even if he could afford to. You could tell a lot about a man from the car he drove, which is why she had always found Logan's humble Ford so hard to equate to the man she thought she knew. She understood now that the car had been part of an elaborate ploy to gain her trust and she still shuddered when she recalled just how easily that ploy had succeeded.

'Well, then, I guess we have nothing more to say to one another.' He turned away from her, revealing an expanse of strong shoulder that created an inappropriate distraction and caused Callie to momentarily forget her lines.

'Wait!' she cried, convinced that he actually would walk away if she didn't say something to prevent him. 'I met a man calling himself Mike in London recently and when I told him that I was house hunting he told me about a development of apartments here that he thought might interest me.' Her explanation sounded pathetic, even to her own ears, but she forged ahead regardless. 'I was in the area but couldn't reach him on the number he gave me, so I thought I'd drop by on the off chance.'

'Where and when did you meet this man?'

'What's with the interrogation? Is this how you treat all potential purchasers? If so, I'll take my money elsewhere.' *Or would if sodding Logan hadn't appropriated it.*

'Just need to know.'

He didn't elaborate but instead remained on the portacabin step, muscular arms folded over an impressive torso, demonstrating once again that he was perfectly at ease with silences. 'I saw him on Monday, in a London hotel. Not like that!' she added, blushing furiously when he raised one eyebrow.

'No, you didn't,' he said quietly. 'The man you know as Mike was in Manchester on Monday. I know because I spoke to him myself on a video call. I saw the clients he was there to meet. What is it that you really want?'

'Forget it! You're obviously up to your neck in his grubby little scheme.' Callie closed her eyes and blew air through her lips, struggling to contain her growing frustration. She had handled this all wrong but was too angry to temper her words. 'I never should have come here.' Callie turned on her heel and walked towards her car. 'Tell him I've involved the police,' she said, looking back over her shoulder.

She climbed back into Bessie and turned the key but her hands jerked and it took her three attempts to start the engine. She stalled when she tried to reverse out of the site, sensing all the while that the man was still standing there, watching her with that enigmatic smile on his face.

'Damn!' She thumped the dashboard this time. 'I've just made matters ten times worse.'

Aware that she was too emotionally distraught to drive anywhere, she noticed a pub further along the road and pulled into the carpark, leaving the car straddling two spaces and not bothering to lock it.

Jack scratched his head as he watched the woman drive jerkily away in her silly yellow car. He had seen her earlier that day. He'd glanced at the old VW Beetle as it drove past the site office three times in quick succession. It was a classic car in good condition and it stood out. He idly wondered why it was touring this back-water. Then the phone had rung. When didn't it, he thought, rolling his eyes. He'd taken the call, dealt with the latest crisis and put the car out of his mind. He had more pressing matters to hold his attention; like finding his missing partner before the shit really did hit the fan.

'What the hell was that all about?' he asked Odin, who simply flapped his tail.

He thought at first that she might have been Logan's latest conquest, but she wasn't his type. He liked them tall and thin and without much between the ears. Logan hoped that his visitor had more sense than to fall for Logan's slick lines. He liked the fire in her eyes and... well, quite a lot of other things about her too. He could tell that she was seriously upset and wished now that he'd handled her more sensitively, but she had caught him at a bad time. The potential investors were, he sensed, on the point of pulling out and he urgently needed Logan to smooth their ruffled feathers.

Where the fuck are you, Logan?

Logan had disappeared off the face of the earth and he sensed that the woman had probably seen him more recently than Jack had. But it was equally obvious that she had no idea where he was now, or what his real name was for that matter, which caused Jack to revise his earlier surmise that Logan hadn't hit on her. Jack knew it amused his mate to give his conquests false names. He justified it by saying it helped to prevent them from tracking him down when the affairs had run their course.

Jack scowled, thinking it was another part of his friend's behaviour that he didn't approve of, along with a steadily growing list.

'Face it,' Jack muttered, 'you've had your doubts about his activities for a while.'

Jack felt disloyal for even admitting to the doubts in question but they couldn't be shoved on the back burner indefinitely. There was a limit to the time that Jack could close his eyes to Logan's increasingly bizarre conduct and this woman's visit could well be the catalyst that forced him to address the issues in question.

Perhaps.

'Time to take the blinkers off,' he said, accustomed to conducting one-sided conversations with Odin. At least the dog never contradicted him in the way that a wife undoubtedly would. 'This is my business too.'

Sighing, he switched off his laptop, turned off the lights and whistled to Odin. He climbed into his truck and drove off, intent upon a hot bath and a cold beer, when a flash of yellow in the Oaks' car park caught his attention. It was badly parked across two spaces and the lights had been left on. Without stopping to question the wisdom of his actions, he pulled into the car park as well and left the truck next to her car.

'Let's go see what she thinks she's doing,' he said to Odin, who jumped happily from the cab, wagging as always. 'She'll be hit on every which way she turns in this dive.'

He found the woman sitting at a small corner table, being harassed by a man with more tattoos than braincells.

'Hiya, Jack,' the barmaid said, ignoring someone else waiting to be served. 'The usual?'

'Please.'

Jack paid for his beer and sauntered over to the woman, whose attempts to ignore the Lothario were being ignored.

'Sorry I'm late,' Jack said, putting his beer on the table and taking the vacant chair that tattoo man hovered over.

The woman sent him an alarmed look, then appeared to relax when she recognised him. 'No problem.'

Tattoo man swore and took himself off.

'What are you doing here?' the woman asked.

'We got off on the wrong foot,' Jack replied, noticing that she had a large glass of wine in front of her and that half of it had already disappeared. She was either more upset than he'd realised or had forgotten that she was driving.

'Did we?' She sounded disinterested. Defeated. 'I asked you a civil question and you blanked me. End of.'

'Shall we start again?' He smiled, surprised by the degree of his determination to banish the bleak expression from her eyes. 'Jack Carlisle.' He held out a hand. 'And you are?'

She looked at his hand for several seconds before reaching a decision and slipping hers into it. 'Callie Devereaux.'

'Nice to meet you, Callie.' Odin, who had squatted down beside the table, woofed once. 'Oh, and this is Odin. He can be demanding when ignored.'

Callie smiled and dropped a hand to pet the soft mutt. 'I have a cat who's equally full on.'

They each took a sip of their drinks, eyeing one another warily over the rims of their glasses. Odin's presence helped to ease the tension as Jack struggled to think of a diplomatic way to break the ice, fully aware that she only allowed him to sit down because he was a lesser evil than tattoo man.

'Why are you really looking for my partner?' he eventually asked.

'Why are you so reluctant to tell me where he is?' she countered.

'You aren't interested in buying an apartment, are you?' She drained her glass and stood up, clearly intent upon purchasing another. 'Steady,' he said. 'Don't forget you're driving.'

'What are you, my mother?'

Jack threw his head back and laughed. 'I've been accused of being many things, but a mother is definitely a first. Sit down. I'm buying.'

He took her empty glass from her hand and got her a refill. Odin remained with her, which surprised Jack. Ordinarily, he was

Jack's shadow. When he returned to the table with her replenished drink, he sensed that she would happily have poured her heart out to Odin, much as Jack himself often did, but getting her to confide in him would be a much tougher nut to crack. She had been hurt, and badly. Why did he find it so easy to believe that Logan had done the hurting?

'He told you his name was Mike?'

Callie nodded. 'Mike Logan.'

'Mike's his middle name. He hates it. Thinks it's too common.'

'Why does that not surprise me?'

'I've known Logan since we were kids,' he said, thinking that if he opened up to her then she might reciprocate. It was clear that she needed to talk to someone and equally clear that the booze had gone straight to her head. He could already see the effect that the wine, knocked back so quickly, was having on her. Her focus was no longer straight, and her words were slightly slurred.

'Your mother cleaned for his family.'

Jack shot her a surprised look. 'He told you that?'

'Is it true?'

'Yeah, pretty much.' She covered her mouth with her hand and hiccupped.

'You're a fair way to being drunk,' Jack said, watching her as she moved her hand from her mouth and drained her glass again. 'And in no condition to drive. Come on.'

He stood up, ignored her weak protests and marched her from the pub. He unlocked his truck and all but lifted her onto the passenger seat. Odin jumped in next to her and rested his big head on her shoulder. It seemed to comfort her, but also made her sob. Jack didn't know what to do about that. Every instinct he possessed screamed at him to pull her into his arms and comfort her. Whatever Logan had done to her, he'd hurt her big time and right then, Jack could have killed him with his bare hands.

He resisted the urge to offer comfort, sensing that any personal contact would be resented. Callie had only got into his truck because she was three sheets to the wind, but she still didn't trust him. He'd take her back to his place to sleep it off and wanted to be able to assure her that he had behaved himself when she came to.

Without saying a word, he started the engine and drove the short distance to his cottage, which was a work in progress. He never seemed to find the time to do all the jobs in his own place that their high-end clients expected as a matter of course. Even so, he kind of liked its rustic, half-finished charm, especially in winter when he had flames from massive log fires dancing up the chimney and thick curtains closed against the intrusive outside world. As far as he was concerned, their clients could keep all the chrome and glass and fancy gadgets that they found indispensable. He wouldn't swap what he had here for their modern easy living, not for any price.

Callie had fallen asleep, head lolling to one side. He pulled up on his driveway and cautiously opened the truck's door, catching her before she tumbled out. She mumbled something but didn't object when he swept her into his arms and carried her into the cottage. He laid her on a couch, removed her shoes and covered her with a throw. He then rummaged in her bag, found her car keys and told Odin to stay with her.

'Won't be long.'

He knew that if he left her car where it was, it would be either nicked or vandalised before morning. He stretched his long legs out and walked back to the pub, covering the distance in less than ten minutes. He reached the car, which appeared to be undamaged so far but was receiving speculative looks from a gang of kids across the street. He got behind the wheel and swore when he bashed his knees against it.

'No good deed goes unpunished,' he muttered, pushing the seat back as far as it would go and turning the key in the ignition.

He drove the car back to his, parked it beside his truck and let himself back in. Callie and Odin were both sound asleep.

'Great company you two are,' he said, retreating to the kitchen to rustle up something to eat.

6

Callie woke with a pounding headache and with no clear recollection of where she was. She opened her eyes cautiously but blind panic set in when she failed to recognise her surroundings. She sat up, pushed a throw from her body, took a deep breath and tried to focus. But focusing was challenging with a thumping head and a wet nose pressed against her arm.

A wet nose!

She screeched, snatched her arm free and looked down at the offending nose, which was attached to a shaggy dog who wagged his entire body in a non-threatening manner. Callie breathed a little more easily, groaning as her sluggish brain cranked into action. Closing her eyes again, she felt convinced that if she didn't die of alcohol poisoning then embarrassment would finish her off. Now would be a good time for the ground to open up and swallow her whole. It would be a merciful release. But death, she figured, wasn't that obliging. It wasn't like you could log onto the hereafter and book a delivery slot or anything.

Callie sensed she wasn't alone in the room, but when the recollections came crashing down in disjointed bursts, she couldn't bring herself to check. She had stormed from Logan's workplace, that much she did recall, and then hit the nearest pub. She would have thumped her forehead in punishment for her stupidity if she wasn't already in so much pain, both physical and mental. What had she been thinking? She'd drank too much the night before *and* she'd been driving.

Bessie! She jerked upright and groaned when the sudden movement set a jackhammer off inside her skull. What had happened to her beloved car, her pride and joy? She hadn't driven, had she? She was responsible to a fault in that respect, aware that if she lost her licence her business would go down the toilet. Surely she hadn't broken her golden rule and got behind the wheel when she was over the limit? She simply couldn't remember the important things, like where she was and how she'd got there, but did recall some Neanderthal hitting on her. She rubbed her forehead, willing this not to be his place. Struggling to suppress a panic attack.

'Hey, welcome back.'

Callie's head swivelled in the direction of a deep, throaty and somehow unthreatening male voice.

'You!'

She gasped when she recognised Logan's partner seated in front of a handsome brick fireplace with one foot casually crossed over his opposite, denim-clad thigh. A whole raft of conflicting emotions struggled for supremacy inside her head as she tried to decide if she felt more relieved or annoyed that her rescuer had also been Logan's partner in crime. Clearly, he had ulterior motives and wasn't to be trusted. She glanced down, relieved to see that she was still fully clothed, but for her shoes.

'Don't worry. I prefer my women to be sober.' Amusement fuelled his expression. 'And conscious.'

'What time is it? What day is it, come to that, and where am I?'

'It's still Thursday. It's seven at night and you're in my cottage. I didn't know where else to take you.'

Callie forced herself into a sitting position and swung her legs onto the floor, waiting until the room stopped spinning before deciding which of the dozen questions forming inside her brain she needed to ask first.

'Stay where you are.' He got up, disappeared and returned almost immediately with a tall glass of water and a couple of white pills. 'Aspirin, not Rohypnol,' he explained when she looked dubiously at the pills, then at him.

Callie was too dehydrated to argue. She grabbed the glass, swallowed down the pills and drank half the water in several unladylike swallows.

Jack had resumed his chair and his dog rested his big head on his master's thigh, looking up at him through adoring eyes. The man himself watched Callie with a stillness that unnerved her, compelling her to speak.

'I need to leave,' she said, staggering to her feet and falling straight back onto the couch when the floor swayed.

'Need me to call you a cab?'

So much for Jack wanting her to stay, she thought indignantly, wondering why she found his gallantry so disarming. 'I need to get my car.'

'It's outside.'

'Outside?' She frowned at him. 'You went through my bag and took my keys?'

'Well, I didn't jump start it.'

'What else did you take?' His expression darkened and she knew she had said the wrong thing. 'Sorry,' she said hastily.

'I would advise against driving for a least a few hours yet. You need to eat and sober up first, or else risk being arrested.'

'Why do you care?' More to the point, why did Callie feel a need to argue with him when he'd actually behaved well?

'You're welcome,' he said, sounding amused.

Callie dropped her head and sighed. 'You went and got my car. That was thoughtful,' she said.

'Not need to pour on the gratitude,' he said, chuckling. 'Stay put. I'll get you something to eat.'

'The thought of food makes me want to throw up.'

'I'm not *that* bad a cook.'

He levered himself to his feet with surprisingly lithe grace for such a muscular man and disappeared into what was presumably his kitchen, the dog at his heels. Callie welcomed the opportunity to get herself together and wondered how she could have been stupid enough to put herself at this man's mercy. He'd been kind and considerate, she'd give him that. He must have rummaged in her bag to find her car keys and she reached for it now, unwilling to accept that he hadn't touched any of her other possessions. Being conned by Logan had clearly made her ultra-suspicious.

Her overlarge bag was her life; it contained everything that mattered to her, and would have given away her identity in seconds flat. Of course he would have snooped, she reasoned, probably knew from Logan who she was anyway, and was being the good Samaritan for a reason.

She glanced around the room, noticing the unfinished walls and the mismatched yet comfortable furniture. She had never seen Logan's apartment but knew it would be the polar opposite – all glass and chrome and sleek modern lines. Somehow she preferred the shabby chic that reminded her of her own cottage, where there always seemed to be something in need of fixing and never enough time to get it fixed.

Except it was no longer *her* cottage, she reminded herself, reining in her meandering speculations. There was every possibility that it would be repossessed because of a mortgage that she had not taken out and in all probability the man in the kitchen was party to the fraud. In his own way, he was as disarmingly charming as Logan. As a team, they clearly played to their strengths – Logan had told the truth about that. It was the only honest insight he had let slip regarding his true purpose, probably unintentionally.

She stood up, pleased that she felt a little more stable on her feet and that her headache was slightly less severe, and wandered across the room to inspect the only picture decorating the walls. It was obviously an original likeness of Jack's dog, and quite well executed. She wondered if Jack was the budding artist but wasn't about to ask him and fall for his smarmy charm as easily as she had Logan's.

Once bitten...

She wandered into the kitchen and watched the muscles at work in Jack's bulging biceps as he moved economically about between a range and the work surface. He was stirring something in a pot and the enticing smells made her stomach give an embarrassing rumble.

'Not hungry, huh?' He turned to look over his shoulder, wooden spoon in one hand, and grinned.

'What are you making? Can I help?'

'No offence, but the state you're in, you'd be more of a hinderance. Sit down and take a load off. It won't be long.'

Feeling like she was back at school and in detention, she obediently took a seat at the scrubbed pine table dominating a room that was... well, ramshackle. The range looked like an ancient Aga, none of the cupboards matched and there were bare wires dangling above her head. She wondered if that was safe but didn't bother to ask. It seemed that builders didn't believe in busman's holidays.

Even so, the room was warm and inviting, its walls painted duck-egg blue, with old-fashioned gingham curtains framing the windows. There were rows of pans dangling from ceiling hooks, mismatched plates lining the shelves of a dresser and even pots of herbs growing on a windowsill. This man clearly enjoyed cooking, as Callie herself did. Logan had once told her that he appreciated her skills in the kitchen, being incapable of boiling an egg himself.

Logan and Jack were very different and unlikely bedfellows, but Callie had learned her lesson the hard way and wasn't about to be taken in by this display of domesticity. Men were most definitely not to be trusted!

'Here we go.'

Jack dished up eggs scrambled with smoked salmon, then reached into the oven and produced roasted new potatoes and a vine of baby tomatoes that he tossed in thick balsamic. He placed the loaded plate in front of her with a flourish, adding cutlery, condiments and fresh, crusty bread.

'Enjoy.'

From feeling ready to throw up at the thought of food, Callie was now famished. She had barely eaten since discovering Logan's treachery and so, mindful of the fact that hangovers required feeding, she dug in without restraint. The eggs were fluffy and creamy and she closed her eyes in appreciation as the first bite slid down her throat. Jack leaned his backside against a counter, folded his arms and watched her.

'You not eating?'

'Already did while you were sleeping it off.'

'Oh. Well, thanks for doing this,' she said, sounding ungracious. 'It's good.'

'Don't go overboard with the compliments.'

She cleared her plate and sat back with a sigh. 'Where did you learn to cook?' she asked.

He shrugged. 'Anyone can scramble a few eggs.'

'Logan can't.'

She wished the words back the moment they slipped past her lips. A shadow passed across Jack's features and the atmosphere grew tense.

'Coffee?' he asked, making no comment about her *faux pas*.

She nodded as she carried her plate back to the sink, watch by Odin, who was clearly disappointed that there were no leftovers.

'Go and sit down again before you fall down,' he said curtly. 'I'll be right there.'

Callie wanted to say that she was leaving but something held her back. This man had been good to her and she was no longer convinced that he had done so because he was in league with Logan. Too many things simply didn't add up, and the scale of the anomalies grew in her mind as her brain became less befuddled.

She moved back into his living room and resumed her place on the couch. True to his word, he followed her a short time later and handed her a mug of coffee. She helped herself to cream and shook her head when he passed across a sugar bowl.

'Now then,' he said, leaning back in his chair as he fixed her with an unwavering look, 'why don't you start from the beginning? Tell me why you were really looking for Logan. Perhaps we can help each other out.'

* * *

Jack affected a relaxed pose at variance with his turbulent thoughts. He had changed his mind a dozen times about this woman's connection to Logan and was no nearer to deciding upon what it could possibly be. She was clearly deeply upset. Going into strange pubs alone and drinking herself silly was not, he sensed, the way in which she normally conducted herself. He still shuddered when he thought what might have happened to her, had he not interceded. Despite the supposedly equality between the sexes, there were still places where a woman had to be a fool to venture alone.

That dive of a pub was a case in point. A man's local that Jack occasionally frequented because it was close to home, and because they served first-rate beer.

Jack pushed aside his fears for Callie's wellbeing and hardened his heart. Logan was on the missing list, he had Portia calling him a dozen times a day sounding increasingly frantic, and backers on the verge of pulling out because Jack was useless at calming their jitters. The tribulations of a stranger, albeit a very cute one, were not his burden to bear.

He waited without speaking, content to bide his time and make that silence work for him. Besides, it was no hardship looking at her, even though she wasn't at her best right then. Her hair was like a bird's nest where she'd slept so soundly for over an hour and her eye make-up had run, leaving her looking like a distressed panda.

Even so, there was something about her that held Jack's interest and made him want to protect her from... well, from whatever it was that had her chasing Logan's shadow. She wasn't the first hysterical female who'd tried to track his partner down but definitely wasn't out of the same mould as the others. This one had class and, he suspected, more than a few brain cells.

'Logan, or more to the point, the man I knew as Mike, and I are an item,' she said, lifting her chin. 'Or were.'

'An item?' Damn, Logan *had* strung her along. Jack felt disproportionately disappointed because she'd fallen for Logan's toxic form of charm, even if he'd yet to find a woman who could resist it when his partner turned it on. He schooled his expression into neutrality, though, keen to keep Callie talking. 'Logan doesn't do long-term.'

She rolled her eyes. 'Well, I know that now, obviously.'

It wasn't obvious to Jack. 'How often did you see him?'

'We've been together for two months now.'

'What!'

Jack jerked forward in his chair. She'd just said the first thing to surprise him. He had assumed that they would have met once or twice, Logan would have given her all sorts of crazy assurances to get her into bed and then moved on to his next conquest. Love 'em and leave 'em. That was the ways he always operated.

And yet... and yet, she'd known that his mother had cleaned for the Armitages. Jack's brain went into overdrive. That wasn't something that Logan would ordinarily tell his conquests. In fact, he never told them anything personal at all, given that he had a wife and three kids waiting patiently in the wings.

'There's no need to sound so surprised.' She rippled her shoulders indignantly. 'I'm not *that* unattractive. Besides, I assumed you knew. Why else would you have followed me to that pub?'

'You think I'm like him? That we're joined at the hip?' Jack shook his head, discomposed by that possibility. Jack loved Logan like the brother he'd never had but he didn't like him very much, disapproved of his conduct and constantly warned him against putting it about. It was asking for trouble. If his father-in-law got wind of it... well, Farquhar was a powerful man who adored his fragile daughter – a daughter who could do no wrong in his eyes.

'Well,' she replied, a combination of anger and hurt flashing through his eyes. 'Aren't you?'

'I didn't know your name until you showed up today and that's the God's honest truth.'

'But—'

Jack held up a hand to cut off her protest. 'If you aren't willing to take my word for it then there's nothing to stop you leaving. You ought to be all right to drive now.' Not that Jack cared much either way. He felt tired, all of a sudden, and was done with resolving Logan's problems for him.

'I'm sorry,' she said meekly into the crystalline silence that followed Jack's angry retort. 'I can sense you aren't like him. It's just that... well, I don't seem to be able to trust my instincts right now.'

A tear trickled down her face and it took all Jack's self-restraint not to pull her into his arms. 'What did he do to you?' he asked softly, sensing it was bad. Very bad.

She looked directly at Jack through huge, liquid eyes. 'He's taken me for almost every penny I have and I just don't know what to do about it.'

The single tear turned into a flood. Jack, astounded by what he had just heard, left her crying and went in search of a box of tissues. He was furious with Logan, couldn't understand why he'd do such a thing, and was now very worried. What the hell was he playing at? It was essential to get more information out of Callie before he could decide. He handed her the tissues, resumed his seat, and waited for her to compose herself.

'Sorry,' she said eventually, dabbing at puffy red eyes with the corner of a tissue. 'But I thought you and he were...'

'Were in the business of scamming trusting women out of their life's savings.' He growled with frustration. 'You have me confused with someone else.'

'I know that now, but you must see how it looked.'

Jack could see, all too well, and didn't much care for the view. 'How did you and he meet?'

'At a wedding. It's what I do. I'm a wedding planner.'

'Ah, I remember. Blakely.'

'Yes. You know him?'

'We've met once or twice. Logan was trying to rope him into an investment that I knew wouldn't take off but the man checked his facts, didn't take Logan at his word—'

'Logan makes a point of scamming his investors as well as his girlfriends, does he?'

'Not as far as I am aware. Everyone he's persuaded to come in with us has seen a decent return so far. But I knew there was something not right about the site he wanted Blakely to invest in,' he added, almost to himself.

'Yes, well, he took an interest in me at that wedding and I thought it was too good to be true. There were a ton of other women there who would have walked on water for him. Besides, I was there to work.' She shook her head. 'I should have gone with my instincts, but he was so convincing.'

'Conmen always are.' Had Jack just called his best friend a conman? He blinked when he realised that he had, and that he'd done so out loud. It was one thing harbouring doubts, but surely his first loyalty ought to be to the man whom he'd known most of his life rather than simply accepting the word of this stranger. She'd hardly lie about something that would be easy to disprove, though, and worse yet, a part of Jack wasn't surprised.

'You sound like Maisie.'

'Who's Maisie?'

'My friend. She got suspicious about Logan when he kept inventing excuses not to meet her.'

A sudden thought occurred to Jack. 'You were aware that he's married?' he said softly.

'Separated.' She threw up her hands. 'He told me he was separated from his wife, but I expect that's a lie as well.'

'I'm afraid so. He has a wife who lives not far from here and three kids at private school.'

'Children, too.' She let out a deep sigh and seemed to shrink in on herself, justifying Jack's belief in her. She *had* been taken in by Logan and wasn't a homewrecker. Her tortured and shocked expression when Jack mentioned the children left no room for doubt in that respect. 'Oh, dear God!'

'Tell me it all.'

'We should go and see his wife. She will know where he is,' Callie said, her voice manic as she jumped to her feet. 'Besides, she deserves to know just what a scumbag he is. And I want to assure her that I wouldn't have given him the time of day if I'd even suspected...'

'She's called me a dozen times over the past couple of days, looking for him,' Jack replied. 'She doesn't know where he is either, which is what's got me so worried. He missed an investors' meeting today and that's completely out of character.'

'But he wouldn't walk out on his wife and children, surely?'

Jack said nothing.

'Heaven knows why I'm defending the louse,' she muttered. 'I suppose I just don't want to think of him as being quite *that* bad.'

'Portia is very fragile. She will fall apart if he's done a runner, and if she finds out about his infidelities, for that matter.'

'If he hasn't scarpered, the credit card fraud people will want to talk to him. And her, I expect. We can't keep it from her indefinitely. No one's protecting my finer feelings.'

Slowly, in disjointed bursts at first and then with growing anger, Callie explained how she had been taken in by Logan and how he had royally screwed her, in all senses of the word. Jack felt for her but was also really worried about his own situation. Logan clearly did intend to pack it all in, confirming the doubts about Logan that Jack had been suppressing for too long. Well, no more. It was time to look out for number one, so the burning question now was: where did this mess leave Jack?

Jack knew that Logan had found it increasingly demeaning to have to grovel to Ed Farquhar when times were tough. His father-in-law enjoyed the power he wielded and extracted a high price for his help, manipulating Logan in all sorts of ways. If he had reached the end of his tether and was looking for an easy way out, Callie's situation would have been like manna from heaven.

Easy money extracted from a vulnerable victim. Not that Callie would see herself as vulnerable, Jack suspected. She would prefer to think of herself as a woman of the world, a business-woman in her own right, and that was true as far as it went. But Logan was a class act. Callie had taken a while to trust him, but Jack suspected that when she did trust, that trust was absolute and it wouldn't once have crossed her mind that she was being played.

'Why did he do this to me?' Callie was clearly almost as desperate for an explanation as she was for the return of her money. 'I thought you and he had a good business going. And he has children...' She looked lost and bewildered. 'How could any man walk out on his children?'

'What you need to understand about Logan is that he's always been driven to succeed. Born with the proverbial silver spoon, it was simply assumed that he was a cut above. He was also starved of parental affection.'

'Weren't we all,' Callie said stiffly.

'It's hard to feel sorry for a person in that position – I'll be the first to agree with you there. I grew up on the local council estate but I had a full set of parents and an abundance of love, even if there was never enough money for me to have what all the other kids had. I resented it at the time but can see now that I was way better off than Logan, despite all his latest gadgetry and fancy cars.'

Callie sniffed. 'He drove a Ford Sierra every time he came to see me.'

'He what?'

'I never thought it suited his personality.' Callie managed a wan smile. 'It was all part of the big con, I suppose, which shows just how much planning went into it. No one can accuse Logan of operating on the fly,' she added scathingly. 'Anyway, we traced the car back to a rental firm at Gatwick, Maisie and me, and that's when I knew beyond doubt that I'd been played.'

'Ordinarily he drives a Porsche 911. It's not at home. Portia told me.'

'Even so, it will be easier to find than a common Ford.'

'Clearly a lot of planning has gone into whatever it is he's doing, so my guess is that you won't find him unless he wants to be found.' Jack damned well would, though. 'My partner is a wily individual.'

'Going back to what you were saying just now.' Callie swung her legs onto the couch and tucked them beneath her bottom, in the way that women often did. It felt good to see her relaxing in his home, always supposing she would ever be able to relax properly ever again. 'I can see that you made a good partnership, bringing different skill sets to the table, but if you were doing so well, why has Logan done a bunk?' She paused, fixing Jack with a sad yet resigned look through liquid brown eyes.

'Well, there's the question.' And one that Jack was currently at a loss to properly answer. Even so, he fully intended to get to the bottom of things, for his own sake as much as Callie's. His reputation was now on the line. He'd worked damned hard to establish himself and would not be tarnished by his association with

Logan. 'Perhaps he'd had enough. His parents lost their money in quite a spectacular fashion when Lloyds collapsed. Logan then married Portia, who's the only daughter of a wealthy property investor. But, and here's the thing, Portia is mentally fragile. Logan knew it but thought he could handle her, mainly because the extent of her frailties was kept from him.'

'That was dishonest.'

'Right. Her father was generous and bought them a nice house as a wedding present, but he's a control freak too. I don't think he ever entirely trusted Logan and so he kept the deeds in his own name, preventing Logan from doing what he did to you.'

'Wise man,' she said with a wry smile.

'Right, and his generosity became optional once they were married. I guess he felt he'd done enough to support them and it was up to Logan from there on in. Once they started having babies, of course, the old man's attitude changed. His only son isn't married and shows no sign of tying the knot so—'

'So Logan saw an opportunity to sire an heir to his pa-in-law's empire,' she finished for him, rolling her eyes. 'I'm starting to get the picture.' She took a moment to reflect. 'Do you really think he's decided to run off and go it alone somewhere else, just because he's tired of playing happy families?'

'I don't know what to think. Frankly, I'm worried because he's on the missing list. Like I say, that's out of character, and why I came after you. I thought you might know something that I didn't.'

'Bet you regret it now.' Her sense of humour was starting to come through, despite her dire situation, and Jack liked to see her fighting spirit emerging.

'I'm just relieved that you don't think I'm in this with Logan.'

'I did wonder, at first. No offence.'

'None taken. In your situation, I'd have been highly suspicious too. What do you intend to do about the bogus mortgage?'

She let out a long breath. 'I shall have to put it in the hands of my solicitor, see what he can do about it. Either that or I shall have to come to an agreement with the mortgage people. Get them to let me pay it off in small chunks.' Her eyes blazed with a combination of anger and determination. 'One thing's for sure, I am not going to lose my grandmother's cottage because a smooth-talking bastard took advantage of me.'

'That's the spirit!'

'I still don't get why he'd walk out on a profitable business,' Callie said, shaking her head.

Nor did Jack, not yet. 'You'll get the money back on your credit cards, I assume, and can prove that you didn't take out the new one.'

She shrugged. 'I hope so.'

'Did he use them for anything that would point us in the right direction?'

'Us?' She blinked up at him.

'Sure. The way I see it, he's shafted us both. I don't know if he's taken any of the capital out of the business, but it wouldn't surprise me. I'm as trusting as you are and left that side of things to him and our accountants.'

'Shouldn't you look?' she asked incredulously.

'I should, but he keeps the books at home. I will have to call and see Portia and take them away with me. Obviously, I have access, but frankly never have the time or inclination to look at them, which makes me as trusting as you, albeit in a different way.'

'Take me with you. I'll pretend to be from your accountant's.'

7

Logan switched off his mobile, threw it across the hotel room and let rip with a string of violent curses. The person he'd paid over the odds to provide him with a fake passport had taken his money and scarpered. Logan couldn't track him down without putting himself at risk and the man knew it. That's what came of making arrangements on the fly. You couldn't trust anyone.

Fuck! It was just the sort of thing that Logan himself would have been tempted to do, but he failed to see the irony.

'What the fuck am I supposed to do now?' he asked his reflection, scowling at the sight of his bloodshot eyes and unkempt appearance.

There was nothing else for it. He would just have to risk going home and make up some excuse for being out of reach. Portia would believe anything. She was so fucking gullible. Anyway, he wouldn't have to see her for long. He couldn't afford to linger. Those who wanted an urgent word with him, and he wasn't referring to Jack or the fragrant Callie, would soon hear he was back. He had borrowed heavily from some pretty unsavoury types who now wanted their money back at an extortionate interest rate.

Logan suspected that they were watching his place, which made returning there that much more of a problem. But still, if he timed it right, he could nip in when Portia was taking the kids to school, grab his real passport and leg it, with no one being any the wiser. He hadn't wanted to travel under his own name. It wouldn't be long before he was on the official wanted list as well as that of the loan sharks, and it would make him that much easier to trace. But still, needs must. He'd do what he did best once he got to where he was going and reinvent himself.

Again.

Then, unencumbered by a clinging wife and demanding father-in-law, to say nothing of a partner who lacked vision and wasn't prepared to take the risks necessary to succeed, he'd show the world what he was really capable of. Not that he could shout about his achievements, he accepted – not without drawing the attention of unsavoury characters with long memories. But still, the satisfaction of becoming a self-made man to reckon with would be more than enough.

The effect of the expensive whore's ministrations had already worn off and Logan felt tense and edgy, as well as hungover. For some obscure reason, thoughts of Callie kept distracting him, which really bugged him and didn't help matters. Portia would have persuaded Jack and Daddy dearest to send out search parties by now, he reckoned. He picked up his phone and switched it back on, his ears assaulted by a constant ping of incoming messages. A dozen from Portia and two from Jack, as well as a ton of other even less welcome threats.

'Damn it!'

He thumped the wall, cracking both the plaster and his knuckles, attempting to keep the dreaded red mist blurring his vision at bay. He took a mini bottle of scotch from the room's bar. He knocked it down in one slug and reached for another. Then changed his mind. He needed to keep a clear head. He could still pull this thing off, if he didn't panic.

Logan reached for his wallet, extracted a sim card and replaced the one in his phone. The moment it came to life, a dozen frantic text messages from Callie appeared. This was the number he had given her and he should have been prepared for the deluge. Even so, the sound of her voice asking him to get in touch momentarily stirred a conscience that had chosen a damned inconvenient time to trouble him. There was just something about her that created lingering regrets, which in itself was astounding. Logan didn't form attachments to his women, emotional or otherwise.

Not that he was to blame for the way things had turned out, he reminded himself, hardening his heart. Callie was too trusting and he had just taught her a valuable lesson. It wasn't as if he'd left her potless. He had a good idea how profitable her business was, and he knew that her services were in great demand. It wouldn't take her long to recover, and in some respects he'd done her a favour. She would be more careful about who she let get close to her in future.

Only a couple of other people had this number and the messages left by one in particular turned Logan's blood to ice. Damn it, he thought he'd have more time! He switched the sims backs, packed his things and checked out, trying not to wince at the astronomical charges. After all, Callie had paid.

He got into his beloved Porsche, resigned to abandoning it to a used car dealer who would do him over because Logan wasn't in a position to bargain. Not that it mattered. The sacrifice would be worth it, he reminded himself, thinking of the broader picture and what he stood to ultimately gain.

He fired up the engine, enjoying the sound of the throaty roar, and pointed the car in the direction of his home.

* * *

Jack shook his head. 'Best let me do this alone,' he said, thinking that Callie, in her highly emotional state, might well let something slip to Portia, tipping her over the edge.

'Not a chance!' Callie crossed her arms over her torso in a gesture of defiance. 'Either you take me with you, or I'll call on Logan's wife alone. She deserves to know the truth.'

Jack cocked a brow. 'You don't know where she lives.'

'I found you, didn't I?'

She had a point. 'Portia will find out soon enough, *if* Logan's done a runner. What good will come out of telling her that her husband hasn't only abandoned her and his children, but that he's also been playing away?'

'I'm not the woman scorned, out to hurt others in my quest for revenge, if that's what you're thinking. Well, not against Logan's wife, but all bets are off when it comes to Logan himself when we find him, which we will, no matter how long it takes. I will *not* be his victim!' Callie's eyes glistened with determination. 'Nor am I spiteful enough to tell Portia the truth about him. None of this is her fault, but I will admit that I am curious about her. Besides, she might let something she isn't aware she knows slip if I chat to her that could point us in Logan's direction. Women have a tendency to exchange confidences.'

'I can understand why you might feel that way. What you need to bear in mind though is that Logan's a user. I've always known it but didn't realise until now quite how unscrupulous he actually is. I should have taken more interest in his side of the business. I guess I kinda knew he often cut corners but turned a blind eye because... well, because Logan did things his way and didn't take kindly to interference.' Jack ran a hand distractedly though his hair, hoping to persuade Callie to see the matter from his perspective. The last thing he needed was for her to run around independently of him, stirring up trouble. Until he had a better handle on what Logan had done and more to the point why, Callie needed to keep a low profile. 'Perhaps now I understand why. You and I meet new people and pass the time of day with them. If Logan meets the same people, he sees them as opportunities.'

'To exploit them?'

Jack shrugged. 'Perhaps. The point I'm trying to make is that Portia was a golden opportunity that Logan simply couldn't walk away from.'

'He wanted her father's financial backing.'

'Right, but he discovered that Farquhar was no pushover and had to concede that he'd met his match, which probably rankled more than I'd realised. Logan doesn't like to lose.' He thought of Frank's story about their younger days, when Logan had taken the girl that Frank wanted simply because he could, and then carelessly discarded her. He decided against enlightening Callie. It wasn't his story to tell. Besides, she'd already got Logan's measure. 'I've cut him too much slack over the years, I can see that now. This is my fault. I've been too damned trusting.'

'Seems to me you're guilty of nothing more serious than loyalty to your friend.'

Jack smiled at her. 'You have a big heart, Callie Devereaux.'

She blushed when he continued to focus his gaze on her face, and she was the first to look away. 'Perhaps it makes me feel a little better for being taken in by him if you were too. I mean, you actually *knew* him, I only thought I did.'

'How well do we actually know anyone?' Jack relaxed in his chair, sensing that she would play this game by his rules. All he had to do now was to decide what they actually were. 'Anyway, now's not the time to get all philosophical.'

'Do you think he's still in England?' Callie asked after a momentary pause.

'You're asking the wrong person, and the wrong question. The better question would be why now, when we were doing so well?'

'You think something or someone has spooked him?'

'I do. He's never been happy with Portia but used her and the kids to get what he wanted out of Farquhar, which happened sometimes. Having a wife who asks no questions and adores the ground he walks on gave him... sorry, but I was going to say the best of both worlds, which is insensitive.'

'Not if it's true.' Callie threw up her hands. 'Don't worry about my finer feelings. Logan's treatment has killed them stone dead, which is what I will likely do to him if I get my hands on him.'

'And get locked up?' Jack grinned. 'I have a better plan. Let's hit him where it hurts the most. What's his only god?'

'Money.' She ground her jaw. 'My money, and other people's as well, I expect. I'm sure I'm not his only victim. His performance was too slick for that to be the case. I honestly never suspected a thing. Anyway, he assumes I'll take the hit and keep quiet because he didn't wipe me out completely and because it would make me look foolish and desperate.' She shook her head. 'How little he understands what makes me tick.'

'He's a damned fool.'

Callie smiled. 'You don't seem that worried about your own situation. Given that he appears to have vanished from the face of the earth, he's hardly likely to have done so without helping himself from your company's coffers and left you high and dry. In your place, I'd be round to Portia's immediately, demanding to see the books.'

'I'll go first thing. One more day won't make any odds.' Jack lifted one shoulder, pretending a casualness he didn't feel. Inside, he was fighting mad, but he had learned to control his temper over the years and to let it cool before acting. Angry people made crap decisions they often lived to regret. Besides, he still struggled to believe that Logan would do this to him. Callie was right; his loyalty did run deep. Perhaps too deep. He would have to learn to keep an open mind where Logan was concerned. 'I probably won't be able to tell what's missing when I look at the books. He will have covered his tracks and accountancy isn't my thing.'

'It's Maisie's, though,' Callie replied, brightening. 'It's what she does. She's a fully qualified accountant and works from home, supporting her lazy husband and looking after their kids at the same time because he can't be arsed. She does my accounts.'

'You don't like her husband?'

'He's fine in social situations, but I've never thought he was right for Maisie. He's too up himself and won't deign to take any job that comes his way, claiming to be overqualified for most of them. I wouldn't say what I really think of him to Maisie and risk our friendship, although I think she has a fair idea. She's besotted and it's really none of my business.' Callie shrugged. 'If she wants to be treated like a doormat, that's her concern. But that's beside the point. She's a good and loyal friend to me, as angry as I am about the way Logan treated me and will, I'm sure, be delighted to go through the books on your behalf. If there's anything untoward to be found, rest assured she'll find it.'

'Thanks, I might well take you up on that and I will go round to Portia's, but not until tomorrow. It's getting late.' And the kids would be in bed, meaning that Portia would press him to keep her company and crack open a bottle. *Not happening.*

Callie glanced out the window. Although it was high summer and the days were long, the recent rain clouds still lingered, bringing with them the onset of darkness. 'I'd better get going,' she said, 'but I need to know that you'll let me come with you tomorrow... Damn, I can't. I have a full day of meetings for Saturday's wedding. I wonder if Jason would...'

'How about I bring the books over to you tomorrow evening. Unlike Logan, I will be more than happy to meet your friend Maisie and am not too proud to enlist her help. Will that work for you?' When she hesitated, he pressed the point. 'You can trust me, Callie. I want to find Logan as badly as you do and I will make it a personal crusade to ensure that he repays you in full, with interest, naturally.'

The sincerity in his expression appeared to convince her. 'Okay. Give me your number and I'll text you my address.'

They exchanged numbers, Callie sent the promised text and then picked up her bag. 'Thanks for rescuing me tonight,' she said. 'Sorry if I was less than gracious about it.'

'Under the circumstances, that's entirely understandable.' He walked with her to the door and fixed her with a smile. 'Sure you're okay to drive now?'

She nodded, failing to meet his eye. Jack would have given a lot to know what she was thinking. 'I'll be fine. All that water and coffee you fed me has washed the booze right out of my system.' She levelled her hands in front of him to prove that the tremor had gone. 'See you tomorrow. Let me know if you hear from him before then.'

'Right back at you.' He realised he'd said something stupid when her smile abruptly faded.

'I'm the last person he'll come anywhere near,' she said softly.

* * *

Callie jumped into Bessie, turned the key in the ignition, and reversed out of Jack's drive. Her satnav directed her away from the labyrinth of unfamiliar streets onto charted territory. She drove slowly, assessing what she'd found out that day and wondering at her readiness to trust Jack after everything that had happened to her.

She called Maisie on her way home, aware that she'd already missed two calls from her.

'I was getting worried,' Maisie said, answering immediately.

'I have a lot to tell you. Can you get away?'

'Is there an R in the month?'

'Actually no, but I don't suppose you'll let that stop you,' Callie said, smiling. 'I'll be home in ten.'

'Meet you there.'

It felt good to have a friend whose loyalty was beyond question, Callie thought, as she continued on her journey. Someone who had her back and was always there for her.

Maisie had beaten her to it and opened the door from the inside when Callie pulled up.

'I used my key,' she said, stating the obvious. 'And I brought wine.'

'Not for me,' Callie said, shuddering. 'I've already made an almighty fool of myself today and blame alcohol for that.' She walked into her hallway and threw her keys into the dish on the antique hall table that had always been there. It might be necessary to sell off some of the old pieces of her grandmother's furniture, she realised with a jolt of regret, in order to settle the debts that Logan had incurred in her name. That thought was almost enough to make her change her mind about the wine.

Almost.

She still had a slight headache and her mouth was dry. She poured herself a large glass of water, fed an indignant Jinx, who didn't like to be kept waiting for his creature comforts, and sat herself down in the lounge. Maisie had no qualms about drinking alone and had already poured herself a large glass of Merlot.

'The little monsters have been playing me up all day,' she complained, taking a healthy gulp, 'and Dan is about as much use as a eunuch in a harem. Roll on the end of the school holidays, that's what I say.'

'Why do people have kids and then do nothing but complain about them?'

'Because the demanding little devils aren't as angelic as the world would have you believe. But still, I wouldn't be without them. Well, probably not.' Maisie leaned forward. 'Right. Out with it. What did you find out?'

Callie felt implacably calm as she told an enraged Maisie about Logan's wife and kids.

'The bastard!' she cried, spewing wine from the corners of her mouth indignantly. 'But still, it makes sense, I suppose,' she added pensively. 'His unwillingness to meet your friends or to be seen with you in public. I did wonder.'

'Yes, well...'

'What's his partner like? Just as bad, I assume.'

'Actually, no.'

She went on to explain about their initial meeting, her storming off to the nearest pub and Jack rescuing her. Maisie roared with laughter.

'It could only happen to you.'

'It's not funny,' Callie protested, laughing anyway because Maisie's laughter was infectious and because it felt good to laugh. Nothing seemed quite as bad now that she and Jack had joined forces. 'Anyway, you'll get to meet him if you're willing to do me a favour.'

'Anything.' Maisie sat forward. 'What do you need from me?'

Maisie listened as Callie explained about the books.

'Right up my street!' Maisie rubbed her hands together gleefully. 'If the bastard's embezzling, there's nowhere for him to hide. Bring it on, sister!'

Callie laughed and clinked her water glass against Maisie's now empty wine goblet. 'That's what I thought you'd say.'

'What's wrong?' Callie asked after a brief pause, sensing a reserve about her vibrant friend's behaviour.

'It's Dan,' she replied, blowing air through her pursed lips. 'Unless he knuckles down to a job soon, I'm afraid we'll have to move somewhere cheaper.'

'No!' Callie leapt up and hugged her friend. 'I said I'd help...'

'But you no longer can. You have your own problems. Besides, I wouldn't have accepted your help anyway. Borrowing money from friends is the surest way to kill the friendship in question and your friendship means too much to me to risk it. Borrowing isn't the answer anyway. It's what we've been doing and it's in danger of spiralling out of control but Dan refuses to take the situation seriously. He keeps telling me that something will turn up, he has prospects, etc.' A single tear trickled down Maisie's cheek. 'My own work is what's keeping our heads above water, but there's only so many hours in the day and I'm struggling to keep up.'

'Oh, Maisie!' Callie pulled her friend into a hug. 'What can I do to help?'

'Getting Dan to help properly with the kids and stop giving in to their every expensive whim would be as good a place to start as any. He says it's not fair to deprive them of all the must-have gizmos that the others in their classes have. I say it's never too early to learn the value of money and that it doesn't grow on trees. Dan calls me a nag.'

'I'm going to kill him!' Callie cried, meaning it at that moment. 'Slowly and painfully. You have been holding that family together for months, years even, and he doesn't give you a tenth of the credit you deserve.'

'Yes, well, I've given him an ultimatum. Get a job, any job, and stick with it, or I walk and take the kids with me.'

Callie felt shocked and it probably showed. 'But you love him. You've never looked at another man.'

'Yeah, well, perhaps the blinkers have finally come off. Dan says he's a fully qualified structural engineer, which is true, that he sweated his guts out to qualify, and that's the only career he's willing to consider.'

'Selfish bastard!'

'Anyway, now you know.' Maisie let out a long sigh and refilled her glass. 'Keep an ear out. If you hear of anything... I know you mix with a whole raft of people at your weddings. You never know.'

'Of course I will, lovey. I have been so selfish, banging on about my own problems, when you had all this going on. You should have said something sooner.'

'There's nothing you could have done.'

'Even so, a trouble shared. Anyway, if the worst does happen and you feel you have to leave, if only to give him a wake-up call, you and the kids are welcome to camp out here. It will be a tight squeeze but all the time I can hold on to the cottage...'

'Thanks, hon, but let's hope it doesn't come to that. Dan's self-respect has taken a battering because he can't support his family, and so he takes it out on me. You always hurt the one you love and all that.'

Callie swallowed down the response that sprang to her lips. 'I'm here for you. You know that.'

'I do, but I should hate to cramp your style.'

'Ha, if you mean romantically then there's no style to cramp. I really have learned my lesson with Logan and won't get caught out again.'

'Getting laid now and again doesn't equate to a lifetime's commitment. We all have our needs.'

Callie smiled. 'Not me,' she insisted. 'It's simply not worth the angst.'

Maisie left soon after that, swearing that if the kids weren't in bed by the time she got home then someone wouldn't live to see the dawn.

Callie had a full schedule of commitments the following day, but she had a tough time concentrating. Her mind flitted between her own problems, the wisdom or otherwise of putting too much faith in Jack – could she really trust him? – and the state of Maisie's crumbling marriage. Why hadn't she noticed that her friend was suffering? It had taken all the self-control she possessed not to slag Dan off, aware that Maisie was still deeply in love with the only man she'd ever looked at twice, even if her eyes had been opened and she now accepted that he'd never grown into his responsibilities.

'What's eating you?' Jason asked, when Callie gave conflicting instructions for the third time. 'You're not yourself. Is the hunk responsible for turning your brain to mulch?'

'The hunk, as you so inaptly describe him, is history,' Callie replied shortly.

'Ah, I'm sorry. I thought the two of you had something good going.'

'Then you thought wrong. Seems his wife and kids have first claim on his affections and, frankly, they're welcome to him.'

'The bastard! I knew there was something off about him. He seemed too good to be true.'

'Didn't prevent you from drooling after him, and encouraging me to go for it,' Callie said accusingly.

'You needed to have some fun.' He turned when someone entered the hotel banqueting room where they were busy putting the final touches to table decorations for the next day's wedding. 'Hello! Things are looking up.' Jason gave Jack's person an assessing once-over and fluttered his lashes.

Callie, accustomed to Jason's theatrics, wiped her hands and walked across to join Jack.

'What are you doing here?' she asked.

'I have the books in the truck and thought you'd want to take a look-see with me. How much longer do you need to be here?'

'I can finish up.' Jason, who had been listening unashamedly to their conversation, walked up to Jack, hand outstretched. 'I'm Jason and you're delighted to meet me.'

'Behave!' Callie insisted, smiling in spite of herself. 'This is Jack and I am going to leave you to finish here. Call me if there are any problems with the bride's mother, but I don't think there will be. She's one of the easier ones, if there is such a thing.'

'Sure,' Jason said, clearly bursting with curiosity. 'Have fun, children.'

'Sorry about that,' Callie said as she walked away with Jack, conscious of Jason watching them leaving, his tongue almost hanging out in appreciation of Jack's physique.

Callie couldn't blame him. She might be off men but that didn't mean she was impervious to his tough, rough-round-the-edges appearance. Especially because, unlike Logan, he didn't put on an act. What you saw was what you got with Jack. Callie barely knew him, but was convinced she'd got that much about him right.

Once again, his hair was tousled and the small scar she'd noticed on his cheek the previous day was more prominent now. He wore jeans that were sculpted to his body, but not the skinny variety that Jason thought essential. Clearly, Jack was not a fashion victim, for which Callie was grateful. Following trends like a herd of sheep, even when the trends suited almost no one, was not a course of action that Callie had ever subscribed to.

Jack smelled of soap and the outdoors, not the expensive cologne that was Logan's signature. He looked distracted and Callie gave herself a kick for ogling him when, potentially, the problems created for him by Logan were at least as severe as her own. Perhaps even more so. At least Callie still had a means of making a living and would overcome the financial setback. If Logan had stolen from his own company, Jack might well go under, or worse, be prosecuted when he, as far as Callie was aware, had done nothing wrong.

'Don't let it worry you.' Jack lifted one broad shoulder in a casual shrug. 'I didn't mean to create problems for you in your workplace.'

'Oh, Jason won't cause problems. He's a bit of a law unto himself, and terminally nosy, but he understands the meaning of loyalty.'

'Good to know. How long has he been with you?'

'A little over a year and I already don't know how I managed without him. He's a whizz at placating irate mothers-of-the-bride.'

'Is that part of his job description?'

Callie smiled. 'That *is* his job description. Anyway, I take it you've found anomalies in the books,' she said.

'Not sure. Like I said, accounts are like a foreign language to me. I hoped your friend would take a look at them and it's kinda urgent. If he is on the fiddle, I need to know about it and I need to know now. That's why I tracked you down. You were right to say last night that it shouldn't be left to chance.'

8

Logan left his car tucked into a multistorey a short distance from his home and walked the rest of the way, sticking to the side streets, crossing over if someone approached from the opposite direction. He was paranoid about being recognised, even though he'd made a point of not mixing with his neighbours. He wore a baseball cap pulled low over his eyes and sunglasses, even though there was no sun to speak of and rainclouds threatened a deluge. He cut down a path between the houses and stopped short of his own, cursing when he noticed Jack's truck on the drive.

'What the hell?'

He didn't seriously suppose that his fraud would have been discovered yet. The annual audit was several months away and Jack never looked at the accounts. It was more likely that Portia had summoned him and he'd trotted along to reassure, just like the tame little lapdog he could be. Every man associated with Logan pandered to his wife's needs, with the notable exception of Logan himself. It irritated but hardly seemed important now.

What was significant was the fact that Portia was home at that hour of the day.

The sound of childish laughter coming from a nearby garden reminded him that he hadn't seen the usual parade of traffic ferrying hordes of little angels to school, clogging up the roads and creating havoc. He hit his forehead with the heel of his hand when it belatedly occurred to him that it was still the fucking school holidays. Damn it, would nothing go right for him? He had been *so* careful, or thought he had, not leaving a single detail to chance, with the possible exception of scamming Callie. That hadn't been planned, but the spoils had simply been too rich to ignore.

What the hell should he do now? Pull up in the Porsche once Jack left and front it out, or wait for Portia to go out, then slip inside? He remained concealed behind a tall hedge, watching his own home like some sort of apprentice burglar unable to make up his mind, getting more frustrated by the second.

Logan lost track of time and was unsure how long he stood there, hoping no one would notice him loitering. The hedges were tall, the houses spaced out and not many people walked about in his high-end neighbourhood, but still...

As he was about to leave and return later, the door opened. Portia kissed Jack's cheek and Jack said something that was most likely placatory. He then climbed into his truck with something tucked under his arm and his dog leapt onto the seat beside him. Logan strained his eyes and felt nauseous when he recognised the company books.

'How the fuck...'

Those books had been in a locked drawer in his home study and Logan had the only key. How had Jack got to them? Well, obviously, he'd picked the fucking lock. Jack grew up in the school of hard knocks where learning to pick locks was a rite of passage. What the hell else did Logan have hidden away in that drawer? He strained his memory but nothing incriminating sprang to mind. He wasn't quite that stupid, although right now he felt like a prize chump. What did Jack want with the books? He couldn't possibly have found out what Logan was up to. He simply didn't have the nous.

Or there again, perhaps he did.

Obviously, Logan had royally underestimated his partner, who was accustomed to Logan's occasional walkabouts and didn't fret about them. Except, Logan reminded himself, he'd missed out on an important investors' meeting and that would have set alarm bells ringing. But would that have led Jack to consider the state of the company's finances? He shook his head, attempting to convince himself that it simply wasn't possible. Not this quickly.

Another truck pulled into the driveway before Jack left. This one bore the name of a local locksmith, who set about changing the front door locks.

'Holy fuck!'

Logan felt fit to bust a gut. He sensed his damned father-in-law's hand behind this amateur attempt to keep him out of his own house. Except, of course, it wasn't his house, he reminded himself, gritting his teeth so hard that his jaw protested. Oh no, Daddy dearest owned the house and Logan had never been permitted to forget it. The Princess of Wales's marriage wasn't the only one that had been overcrowded.

Part of him wanted to follow Jack and see where he went with the books, but his car was almost a mile away, so he'd forfeited that opportunity. There seemed little point in hanging around and watching the locksmiths, who seemed to think they could prevent him from entering his home. Things had got a little out of hand, thanks to the growing demands of the loan sharks, but

Portia would still be putty in his hands if he spun her a line and paid her a little attention.

He briefly considered paying off part of his debt with the funds he'd borrowed from Callie to buy himself some time but as quickly dismissed the idea. They would barely cover the interest on a loan that he'd never intended to repay anyway. A loan that it wouldn't have been necessary for him to take out if his father-in-law had a little more faith in his abilities.

The rest mist descended and he fumed as he recalled the man's dismissive attitude when Logan had outlined his plans, calling them too ambitious, poorly researched and fraught with risk. Well, of course they bloody well were! Nothing worth having came *that* easily, otherwise the world and his wife would want a part. Real entrepreneurs recognised good opportunities and had the balls to go for them. Farquhar was too petty-minded to ever be the success that Logan himself planned to become.

He was in a tearing hurry but knew better than to rush things. One step at a time. If Jack took the books to his home, then Logan would simply break in and make them disappear. The possibility of him taking them anywhere else seemed remote. Now that the mist clouding his brain had receded, he'd got over the initial shock and thought things through a little more calmly. Jack was no fool and if he did suspect fraud then he would realise that he himself would be implicated if the missing funds came to light.

Oh no, Jack would want to keep this quiet.

If it came to it, Logan would make an anonymous call to the old bill and point them in his partner's direction. That would take the heat off Logan, at least for the time being.

He walked back to his car, whistling and in control again, after a fashion.

* * *

Jack noticed differences in Callie today. For starters, she was sober and in work mode; an area in which her confidence shone impressively through. He had watched her directing operations before she realised he was there and couldn't deny that he'd enjoyed the view. She was the first woman in a while who'd attracted Jack's interest, which was ironic, given that he couldn't make a move on her, even if he'd felt so inclined. She was a compelling mixture of anger, determination and underlying vulnerability – definitely not a ball-breaker – proving it was possible to be feminine and an achiever without the need to act tough.

Yeah, he liked what he saw and could understand why Logan had been tempted. The reminder that Logan had been there already was enough to kill off any thoughts of making a move on her. She still didn't trust him and anyway, they needed to find Logan without getting distracted.

'Shall I follow you?' he asked, when they reached the hotel carpark. He'd pulled his truck up beside her distinctive little yellow car and stood by the driver's door, unsure if in the cold light of sobriety she'd want Logan's partner anywhere near her precious cottage. Part of him wouldn't have blamed her if she'd had a change of heart.

'Sure. It's about twenty minutes away, give or take.'

Relieved by her response, Jack fired up his engine and trailed Callie's little car as they drove along narrow country lanes. Eventually they entered a picturesque village with a pub and not much else and arrived at an equally picturesque cottage with well-tended gardens, a sloping roof and small windows painted a cheerful shade of green. It was hidden away, with no neighbours close enough to able to identify Logan if pressed. Jack shook his head, feeling renewed anger at his partner's willingness to rip off a trusting woman. Had he always been so ruthless, and why had Jack not noticed?

'Very nice,' Jack said, nodding as he glanced approvingly at the cottage. 'I can understand why you like it so much.'

'And why I am determined not to lose it,' she replied, an edge to her voice.

'You won't lose it. I'll make sure of that.'

'I appreciate the sentiment,' she replied absently, 'but it would probably be best not to make promises you can't keep.'

She unlocked the front door and a ball of fur exploded from the hallway, hissing at Odin, who had jumped from the truck but now skidded to a halt behind Jack's legs, whimpering. Callie burst out laughing.

'Your dog doesn't have a lot of courage, does he? Jinx, stop that at once. We have guests and you are not to bully poor Odin.'

Much to Jack's astonishment, the cat stopped hissing and arching his back. Having established his authority, he stalked off into the garden, swishing his rigid tail, as though he had more important matters to attend to than terrorising a dog four times his size.

'I'll be damned,' Jack muttered.

'It's safe to come out now, Odin,' Callie said, tugging at one of the dog's ears.

Jack followed Callie into a hall with uneven flagstones and a handsome old console table, onto which Callie tossed her keys.

'Through here,' she said, leading the way into a kitchen that was in even greater need of a makeover than his own. He could tell from the collection of cookery books – no internet recipes in this household, it seemed – and the odd assortment of kitchen utensils that Callie enjoyed cooking. 'Sit down,' she said, indicating worn stools around a tall island. 'Beer?'

'Please.'

Callie produced one from the fridge – his brand, he noticed. Coincidence or had she made a special effort? From her neutral expression, it was impossible to know. He waved the offer aside when she asked him if he needed a glass. At least she no longer seemed to want to kill him, and an element of cautious trust had sprung up between them once they'd crossed the threshold. Jack suspected that Logan had once sat where he himself was now ensconced and wondered how that made her feel. He chuckled inwardly, thinking that he sounded like an out-of-work shrink.

'How did it go with Portia?' Callie asked, pouring herself a modest glass of wine and sitting across from him.

'Not well. She's in a right old state, not helped by the fact that it's the school holidays. She claims, and rightly so, that Logan has never been out of contact for such a long period of time before. I called her father when I couldn't calm her down and he's taken control.'

'She hadn't already been on to him?' Callie lifted one brow as she traced patterns with her forefinger around the base of her glass. 'From what you've told me about her, I find that hard to believe.'

'She had called him, several times, but Portia tends to exaggerate. Every time Logan does something to upset her, she runs to her father and expects him to sort it out and even I can see why that pissed Logan off. Unsurprisingly, Farquhar doesn't want to come between husband and wife and assumed this latest crisis would sort itself out as well.'

'But when you expressed equal concern, he decided otherwise.'

'Right.' Jack picked up his beer bottle and took a swig. 'He came round while I was there. I've never seen him half so angry.'

'I hope you didn't mention me.'

He sent her a look. 'What do you take me for?'

'Sorry, but I don't really know you and I'm guessing that your first loyalty is still to Logan, at least until you know where your business stands. Dropping him in it will have ramifications for you.'

'Farquhar didn't know I'd gone round there to take the books. I can't guarantee that Portia won't mention it, but I saw no reason to enlighten him.' Jack threw back his head, closed his eyes and pinched the bridge of his nose. 'Anyway, Farquhar's taken Portia and the kids back to his *and*, here's the significant bit, he's changed the locks on Logan's home.'

'Bloody hell!'

'My thoughts precisely. I wouldn't want to be in Logan's shoes if he comes back. Farquhar has a lot of connections and isn't the sort of man to cross on a whim; especially not when it comes to his precious daughter's peace of mind.'

Callie leaned an elbow on the table and rested her chin in her cupped hand as she sent Jack a speculative look. 'A daughter whom he palmed off onto Logan as quickly as he could, by the sounds of things.'

Jack waggled a hand from side to side. 'Logan went after her with all guns blazing, admittedly because he wanted the connection to Farquhar. He's never made a secret of that fact; not to me. Anyway, the poor kid didn't stand a chance. She was besotted in no time flat and determined to have him. What Portia wants, she ordinarily gets. Still, I won't deny that Farquhar probably embraced the opportunity to absolve himself from his parental responsibilities.'

'Even so, he's never stopped looking out for her by the sounds of things. It must be lovely to have someone who cares that much, even when you're an adult with kids of your own.' She sent him a rueful smile. 'Sorry, didn't mean to sound envious. Besides, he didn't look out for her *that* well if he let her marry Logan.'

'Well, like I say. Portia knows her own mind. Until she doesn't.'

Callie glanced at the ledgers, which Jack had laid on the table between them. 'Isn't that an outdated way of keeping accounts?' she asked. 'Everything's digital nowadays.'

Jack shrugged. 'I guess so. I never really thought about it. Logan did mention once that he preferred the old way of doing things. Said the internet is too easy to hack and I have to say, he's got a point there.'

'You're defending him!' she cried accusingly.

'Trust me, I'm not. Just trying to be fair.'

'Well, don't. It isn't helpful.'

Jack chuckled. 'You're thinking that he hasn't been fair to us.'

'If Logan was cooking the books...' She groaned at her unfortunate choice of words. 'My point is, if he was, then keeping the records this way would have made it a hell of a lot easier.'

'I have no way of telling what he was up to.' Jack spread his hands. 'I've taken a brief look but it's like a foreign language to me.' He paused and sent her a curious look, keen to make her smile. 'What is accelerated depreciation, anyway?'

'Idiot!' It had the desired effect and her face was illuminated with the briefest of smiles. 'Tell you what,' she said, her expression neutral and wary once again, 'I'll throw together something for us to eat and by the time we're done then Maisie ought to be here. I'll give her a call now and make sure she hasn't had an emergency of the child-minding variety.'

Jack sipped his beer, watching Callie as she moved round her cluttered kitchen with her phone pressed to her ear. She hung up after a short period of time and started rummaging in her fridge. A fridge that looked like it had been manufactured in the sixties and made a worrying variety of noises when the door was opened, which didn't seem to bother Callie.

'Maisie's in sleuthing mode and can't wait to get started,' she said, attacking an onion with a paring knife.

'Good to know. Anything I can do to help?'

'There's a bottle of Merlot in that rack.' She pointed with the handle of her knife. 'You can open that and let it breathe. Bottle opener in the drawer beneath.'

'Think I can manage that.'

Jack found it oddly domestic as he made himself at home in Callie's kitchen. Having opened the wine, he set about making a salad to go with the chilli that Callie prepared with an economy of speed and obvious dedication. Odin stuck so closely to her, sniffing appreciatively, that Jack was surprised she didn't trip over the dog. When her cat reappeared through the flap, Odin quickly retreated. Laughing, Callie fed Jinx and then found something for Odin, placing it well away from the cat's dish. The enticing aroma was sufficient to tempt Odin, who gulped the offering down in two mouthfuls and quickly retreated again.

'It's my turn to ask you where you learned to cook,' he remarked. 'You clearly enjoy it.'

'My grandmother.' Her eyes grew moist. 'This was my haven during my formative years. Well, it became my home once I reached my teens. My mother was a drug addict, in and out of rehab, incapable of looking after herself, much less a child.'

'What happened to her?'

Callie tensed and Jack knew he'd struck a nerve.

'Sorry. That was insensitive.'

'No, it's okay. I just haven't spoken about her for years now. Anyway, I have no idea what happened to her, or even if she's still alive. Nor do I care. Gran took me in and gave me all the love I'd never known before.' She wiped her cheek with the back of her hand. 'And that's one of the reasons why I'm determined not to lose this cottage. I have so many happy memories of times spent in this kitchen with her, learning to cook at the knee of an expert.'

'It shows,' he said softly.

They ate soon after that and it was superb. Quite the best chilli that Jack had ever tasted and he said as much.

'You're welcome,' she replied, waving the compliment aside, but he could see that the praise had pleased her.

They had only just cleared the plates away when the back door opened and a woman with an abundance of russet curls with freckles to match walked in as though she'd done so many times before.

'Hey, chilli.' The woman, presumably Maisie, sniffed the air. 'I hope you saved me some. You know I can't resist your chilli. Hello, darling.' She kissed Callie's cheek.

'Sorry,' Callie replied. 'I assumed you would have eaten already.'

'Always room for your chilli.' She patted a rotund stomach, then noticed Odin and patted him too. 'Hello, pooch. Still, perhaps it's just as...' She glanced up and appeared to notice Jack for the first time. Her words trailed off but her eyes widened in apparent appreciation. 'You must be Jack,' she said, holding out a hand. 'Maisie Montague, financial sleuth extraordinaire, awesome friend and revenge specialist at your service.'

Jack laughed as he took her hand in a firm grasp. 'Jack Carlisle, financial incompetent,' he said.

'We all have our strengths and should play to them.' She unashamedly gave him an exacting once-over with an extravagant sweep of her eyes. 'And I'm betting that your talents lie between very different sheets.'

'Maisie!' Callie looked horrified but Jack laughed off the compliment, if that was what it had been designed as.

'I speak as I find, darling, you know that.' She half turned away from Jack but he still noticed her lolling tongue and was pretty sure that she mouthed the words, 'Is he for real?'

'Behave yourself and get to work.'

Maisie obediently pulled up a stool and looked with amusement at the ledgers. 'Very eighties,' she remarked. 'And a fraudster's best friend. Fiddling the taxman, or one's too-trusting partner for that matter, is much harder with computerised accountancy.'

Callie put a glass of wine in front of Maisie. She absently took a sip but quickly became absorbed in the books and the only sound in the room for quite a while was the occasional turning of pages and Maisie's fingers tapping the keys of a calculator, Odin's panting from where he lay on the floor between Jack and Callie, and Maisie's frequent tuts.

'What have you found?' Jack asked after about ten minutes and a steadily rising number of tuts.

'It's too soon to be sure,' she said, 'but I think Logan has been at it for years. I will have to go back further and see all the receipts but, if pressed, I'd say that he's been manufacturing inflated receipts.'

'How is that even possible?' Callie asked.

'Anything's possible, sweetie,' Maisie replied. 'Especially nowadays when anyone can knock up a half-decent blank company invoice with just basic computer skills, especially if they have an original to copy. Or else, there are plenty of dodgy printers who'd do it for a price, no questions asked.'

'But the books are audited annually. Surely the anomalies would have shown up?' Jack said.

'They ought to have.' Maisie chewed the end of her pen. 'I suspect that he started off small, like most fraudsters do. When he got away with it, he turned up the heat. But this latest year...' She looked up at them both, her expression unnaturally serious.

'Unless materials have more than doubled in price then he'd obviously decided to milk you dry prior to scarpering.'

'Shit!' Jack muttered. His heart sank as a combination of anger at his own trusting nature and incandescent rage at Logan's willingness to rip him off fought for domination inside his aching skull.

'How would he have done it?' Callie asked.

'Simple. Do you ever look at the company bank accounts, Jack?'

He shook his head, feeling like a chump. 'Not very often, because…'

'You trusted Jack,' Callie and Maisie said together.

'You're not the only one,' Maisie added alone, fixing Callie with a sympathetic look.

'Well, you must have access online.'

'Yeah, but I never bother.'

'So pretty, yet so innocent.' Maisie let out a dramatic sigh, clearly enjoying herself. 'Pull the accounts up and let's take a look-see.'

Maisie rolled her eyes when Jack delved into his wallet, extracted a piece of paper that bore the access codes, and then went into the banking app on his phone.

'What?' he asked, grinning. 'It's in code.'

Maisie shared a look with Callie but made no comment. Jack's fingers were clumsy on the small keys, but he eventually got the business account up and passed his phone to Maisie. 'Go on, then,' he challenged. 'Make me feel even more stupid, why don't you?'

It didn't take Maisie long to find what she was looking for. 'There.' She placed the phone on the table so that they could all see the screen and pointed to an entry. 'That's this supplier, agreed?' She showed them an invoice.

'Agreed,' Jack said. 'We use them all the time. They're cheap but reliable.'

'But the amount paid to them is only just over half of the amount shown on the invoice on file,' Maisie said, sticking her pen behind her ear. 'Now look at this amount.'

'It's the balance,' Callie said, 'but where's it gone to?'

'Somewhere offshore. I can try to find it, but you can bet your life it's been moved on to a place where they aren't too strict about the banking code of conduct.'

'He's got offshore accounts?' Jack probably looked as shocked as he felt. 'How long for? When did he...'

'Only this year, far as I can see,' Maisie said, flipping back through the account. 'That's why it seems obvious that he planned to scarper imminently. He knew this would get picked up at audit.'

'And topped off his pension fund with my sodding money!' Callie cried, clearly frustrated and on the brink of tears.

Jack wanted to take her hand, to hold her, to apologise, when he personally was guilty of nothing more than being too trusting. 'I've been such a damned fool!' he said, glowering at the ceiling like he bore it a grudge.

'If he's disappeared to some small banana republic, or wherever it is he's keeping his loot,' Maisie said with a sigh, 'I'm afraid we'll never catch him.'

'Oh, I'm not so sure about that.' Jack reached for the bag that he'd brought the books in, extracted a passport from it and waved it in the air. 'He won't get far without this,' he said, feeling partially vindicated when both women looked at him with renewed respect.

9

Logan had tried his limited contacts in a futile attempt to procure a fake passport pronto. No dice. Holed up in a cheap hotel room that smelled of cigarette smoke and unwashed bodies, he wondered irritably why the current generation took no pride in a job well done. Even the crooks had upped the ante and wouldn't get out of bed for less than a couple of grand. The outright exploitation was enough to give criminals a bad name.

Someone had grudgingly offered Logan a passport for ten grand and made it sound as though they were doing him a favour. Ten grand! Had the world gone stark raving bonkers? They wanted cash too, but pride prevented Logan from stumping up. Someone had to make a stand against such rife dishonesty, he thought, failing to fully appreciate the irony underlying his moral objections. But then again, he wasn't a criminal, not really. It was every man for himself in this dog-eat-dog world and broken promises had forced him to help himself to what was rightfully his anyway. Well, his if he discounted the bonus that he'd taken from Callie.

His father had thought that his standing as an old-school man of substance would offer him a safety net. He could still hear his voice booming inside his head.

'Standards have to be maintained. Gentlemen stick together and help one another out. Never forget that, boy.'

Ha! The gentlemen that the old man put so much stock by had run for cover like the proverbial rats from a sinking ship the moment Logan's pa had lost his dosh. He'd been too arrogant to realise that when something appeared to be too good to be true, it inevitably was. All he was left with was a mountain of debts and severely damaged pride. He'd ended up living in the gatehouse, losing his marbles and requiring round the clock care. The majority of the estate had been sold to a city whizz-kid. Logan, who saw his expected inheritance disappear into the ether, was left with two choices. He could get a nine-to-five job like all the other worker drones, or he could show his father how to make a success from nothing in the modern world.

Not the type to work for anyone else, there was only one way he could go, and at first he did well, if only on a small scale. But Logan's ideas were big, and impressive, guaranteed to put his family back where it belonged and earn him the old man's gratitude and respect.

But it didn't work out that way. He was held back by his partner's caution and his father-in-law's broken assurances. Logan had been reduced to... well, this. He swung round in the small room, almost toppling over onto the bed when he collided with it and bashed his shin, his anger briefly clouding his vision.

Farquhar owed him big time for taking his flaky daughter off his hands, and both men knew it, so he would only have himself to blame when Logan quit these shores and left Farquhar to pick up the pieces. And there would be pieces, Logan thought gleefully. Portia would fall apart when she realised he'd gone for good, and Farquhar would have to step in, which was less punishment than he deserved for failing to keep his promises.

No firm assurances had been offered regarding the helping hand that Logan had needed to get his ambitious plans off the ground. Even so, there were circumstances in which his father's gentleman's agreements had a place. Logan had stupidly assumed that nothing needed to be spelled out; that Farquhar was a man of his unspoken word. Logan now knew that the opposite was true and that Farquhar was even more ruthless than Logan himself. But Logan was determined to have the last word and would achieve that ambition when he took off for pastures new. Farquhar would know that he'd been bested, even though he would never admit it, not even to himself.

But still… he would know.

He glanced out of the hotel room window. It was getting dark and the kids would be in bed. Time to call upon his wife and make nice – for an hour or two. He owed her that much. After all, he'd never see her again and she would be devastated. She'd most likely never recover, and her old man would have to commit her, which is what he should have done anyway, rather than palm her off onto him.

Portia seemed normal enough to the outside world, when things were going the way she wanted them to. But no one knew how many pills she had to consume on a daily basis in order to remain on an even keel. No one knew that she saw a shrink twice a week and had done for as long as Logan could recall. No one knew that she stamped her foot and threw tantrums that the worst behaved child would be hard pressed to better when she didn't get her way.

There was the public perception of normal, and then there was Portia, who was most decidedly off her trolly, but no one was allowed to say so. Not even Logan.

Especially not him.

And yet when the shit hit the fan, *he* was the one who'd be branded a villain.

Logan smiled at the pretty receptionist as he left the hotel, his ego stoked when she blushed and followed his progress with her gaze, ignoring the elderly couple standing at the desk, waiting to check in. He reclaimed his car and drove the short distance to his house, pulling up on the drive beside Portia's car that she never bothered to garage. At least she was at home and had no visitors.

'Honey, I'm home,' he muttered, as he took a deep breath and climbed from his car.

Only then did he notice that the house was in complete darkness. He didn't let it bother him. The kids would be in bed and Portia often sat in darkness when she was in one of her depressed states, which was frequently. He tried his key which, as expected, failed to work. Feeling his anger in danger of igniting once again and doing his best to fight off the onset of the red mist, he took a deep breath and rang the bell to his own house.

Then he rang it again.

'Damn it, Portia!' He hammered his fist against the oak door. 'It's me. Let me in.'

Nothing. No noises at all from inside. In fact, it was eerily quiet. Too quiet. Which is when the penny dropped. They'd gone back to Farquhar. With that knowledge came the realisation that Logan had well and truly burned his bridges and he felt a moment's panic. This was supposed to be happening on his terms and in an orderly fashion. Now he felt as though he was being pushed out.

What to do? He *had* to gain entry. Although the closest house was a good distance away, the front of his could still be seen from an upstairs window if anyone was looking out. The way his luck was running, he couldn't afford to dismiss the possibility. Not wanting to draw attention to himself, he moved to the side gate, the lock to which hadn't been changed, he discovered when he tried his key, and slipped into the back garden. There were no lights coming from the kitchen either, but he could see inside and it was spotless, confirming his suspicions.

'Jack isn't the only one who can pick locks,' he muttered. He returned to the front, rummaged in his car and came up with a thin screwdriver with a hooked end – an official lockpick available from all good online retailers. That retail opportunity caused him to chuckle. He'd never been a boy scout but believed in being prepared, which is why he'd purchased the implement and learned to use it, even though he hadn't had reason to put his skills to use before today.

He returned to the kitchen door and felt pleased with himself when he had it open in less than a minute. The alarm beeped a warning but he strode to the control panel in the hall and switched it off, correctly assuming that no one would have thought to change the code. The quiet after the loud screeching was calming and Logan felt a moment's regret when he looked round at the opulence he would be leaving behind.

Then he reminded himself of the opportunities that lay in wait for him and his momentary doubts evaporated.

He entered his study, annoyed that Jack had seen fit to break into his desk. There was no such thing as loyalty nowadays, not even after all that Logan had done to improve Jack's standard of living. Without his innovative thinking, Jack would still be working as a brickie, or something equally mundane. The drawer where the books had been kept was locked and there was no sign of any disturbance. Even so...

He opened his wall safe and stuffed the bundles of cash into the bag he'd brought with him for that purpose. His need was greater than that of his wife and children, who would live in luxury with Farquhar. He groped about in the safe, looking for his passport, recalling at the last minute that he'd thrown it into the same drawer as the books when he'd returned from his last jaunt abroad, meaning to put it in the safe later and never getting around to it. He produced his keys, opened the drawer and found...

Absolutely nothing.

'Shit! Fuck it! Shit, shit, shit!' He kicked his desk so hard that he began to think he'd broken his foot and hopped around on one leg, turning the air blue with his language as his vision turned a deep shade of crimson – a worrying sign. It was a long time since his demons had overcome him quite so comprehensively. 'Fucking Jack. Who the fuck does he think he is?'

Except, he reasoned, Jack might not have the passport. Why would he bother to take it? It was much more likely to be in Farquhar's possession. The vindictive bastard was attempting to keep Logan in this country and clearly didn't realise even now that Logan was perfectly capable of outmanoeuvring him at every turn.

Leaving the kitchen door unlocked and not bothering to reset the alarm, Logan opened the front door from the inside and left it on the latch.

'Burglars, it's your lucky day,' he said aloud as he got into his car and drove off, thinking he'd have to stump up ten grand after all if he was to stand any chance of leaving the country.

He noticed a dark car with tinted windows and the engine running loitering further up the road as he pulled out of his driveway. His heartrate hitched up a notch. The car didn't belong to his neighbours and if it was a visitor, it would have pulled up on their drive. He knew instinctively that the car's occupants had been watching him. What was less certain was why they hadn't accosted him when they saw him arrive. There again, the car hadn't been there then. Had they come along on the off chance or...

'Damn it!' He thumped the steering wheel so hard that the car swerved and almost crashed into a lamppost. 'They must have put a tracking device on the fucking car.'

The sharks had given him a week to stump up what he owed them and had made it clear what would happen to him and his family if he didn't make the repayment. Clearly, they also wanted him to know that he was being watched and he'd got the message loud and clear. Not many people scared Logan, but these people didn't piss about.

He'd ditch the car somewhere for the time being and take a cab to the forger. He absolutely didn't want these people to know that he planned to leave the country.

Ever since she'd discovered the scale of Logan's perfidy, Callie had felt as though she'd been living in a parallel universe, looking down on events happening to someone else from a great height and rolling her eyes at their naiveté. Not that there was anything otherworldly about Jack, as evidenced by Maisie's reaction to him. It had felt right and natural to have him in her kitchen and that bothered her.

It bothered her a lot.

She trusted him because they had both been shafted by Logan, and because... well, because he'd have to be a graduate from RADA if his reaction to Logan's activities had been faked. He was a victim too, with potentially more damaging consequences. Even so, she wasn't about to let him get too close. She had learned her lesson and now accepted that when it came to men, her judgement was definitely completely skewed.

Then again, she'd spoken to him, a relative stranger, about her mother and that was a subject she seldom let out of its box. It still rankled. He was too damned easy to talk to, that was the long and the short of it. Callie would need to be careful until she was absolutely sure that he wanted to catch Logan as much as she did and that he wouldn't forgive and forget if Logan repaid what he owed to their company. The two of them went back a long way, Logan was excellent at spinning a convincing lie, as Callie had good reason to know, and it would be in Jack's best interests to put the matter behind them.

It would be stupid for her to depend upon Jack to help her get her dosh back. If this business had taught her nothing else, at least now she knew that she couldn't depend upon anyone other than herself.

And Maisie.

'What made you take his passport?' Maisie asked before Callie could.

'Not sure. It was just... well, there, in that drawer with the books. Absolutely nothing else was and I figured that if he's planning to leg it abroad, which seems the most likely option, then we'd make it harder for him.'

'Fake passports are easy enough to come by, aren't they?' Callie asked.

'If you know where to look, I guess anything's available, at a price,' Jack replied. 'But they're not as easy to fake as they once were.'

'Well, unless he already has a fake, I think it's safe to assume that he's still in the country,' Callie said. 'Why are you so sure that he would actually go abroad? I mean, if he does then he'll have well and truly burned his bridges. There won't be any coming back from that.'

'He made his decision when he embezzled from the company

and upped the ante,' Jack replied, firming his jaw. 'He knows that anomalies on that scale won't fly beneath the radar.' He shook his head, looking furious as he absently pushed the hair away from his eyes. 'He's been planning his getaway and I didn't suspect a fucking thing. What a chump he's played me for.'

'Not only you,' Maisie said with a significant nod in Callie's direction.

'True.' Jack's tightly clenched fists slowly unfurled, and his expression softened as he glanced at her. 'Anyway, if he's planning to do a runner, he will have to go abroad. If he stays in England then Farquhar will find him and I wouldn't want to be in his shoes when he does. Farquhar, when he's angry, redefines the meaning of ruthless.'

Maisie's phone rang. She checked the display and rolled her eyes. 'Yeah, Dan, what is it?' She listened and did another expressive eye-roll. 'What do you expect me to do about it?' Another pause. 'How hard can it be to catch an escaped rabbit? Oh, for goodness' sake! I'll be there in ten.' She threw her phone in her bag and sighed. 'Sorry, children, domestic duties beckon.' She glanced at Jack. 'Do you want me to delve deeper? I'll have to take the books with me if you do. It's not a five-minute job.'

'Please. And I'll pay you the going rate for your time, obviously.'

Maisie flapped a hand. 'We'll work something out. Bye, hon.' She hugged Callie and whispered in her ear, loud enough for Jack to hear. 'Have fun and don't do anything I wouldn't do.'

'Sorry about that,' Callie said once Maisie had gone, embarrassed by her friend's larger-than-life character and lack of an off button. 'She's a bit of a law unto herself, but a good friend so I let her get away with it.'

'I'm just glad that she's agreed to find out how bad things are,' Jack replied, running a hand through his hair. Callie watched as the thick locks fell across his forehead in curly disorder. Logan's hair was sculpted to within an inch of its life and he wouldn't dream of running his hand through it, just in case he messed up the style. He was incredibly vain, she realised now, wondering why it hadn't occurred to her to mind.

Perhaps because he'd swept her off her feet and she'd been pathetically grateful to be noticed by him. God, how feeble, how irresistibly easy to manipulate she must have seemed to a man of Logan's ilk. Well, no more, she decided, looking away from Jack, refusing to acknowledge that he was a very different proposition, at least insofar as vanity went. He was a ruggedly handsome man who didn't pay much attention to his appearance. But even so...

'What is it?' Jack asked. 'You look like you're away with the fairies.'

'Sorry.' She pulled herself together, acutely aware of the fact that she was alone with Jack again. It hadn't seemed uncomfortable before Maisie arrived; now there was an air of expectancy that could be a product of her imagination, but which she chose to ignore. 'Another beer before you go?'

'I'll go right away if I make you uncomfortable.'

'Stop being so reasonable,' she said, laughing and fetching him the beer that he hadn't actually said he wanted.

'Thanks.'

He took the bottle from her and plonked his backside against a windowsill. With ankles casually crossed, he took a swig of beer and assessed her over the neck of the bottle with unnerving stillness, looking totally at his ease. She would give a great deal to know what thoughts occupied him, already having pegged him for being the quietly intelligent type who didn't rush to conclusions.

There were those, like Logan, who wore their intelligence like a badge of honour. Jack, she suspected, wasn't even aware that he was clever and probably felt like an idiot for letting Logan get away with daylight robbery. As far as Callie was concerned, his only crime was trusting his best friend. She was in a good position to know because she'd trusted him too, despite being suspicious when he made a play for her, which only went to show how good he actually was at what he did.

'You not joining me?' he asked. 'I don't like to drink alone.'

'Best not.' Callie poured herself a glass of tap water. 'Big wedding tomorrow. I have to be up earlier than the bride, just to make sure that her big day goes like clockwork. They almost never do. Despite all the forward planning, I can practically guarantee that a gremlin or two will creep in below the radar.'

When she sat down, Jack moved to the chair across from hers, close to where Odin was stretched full-length in front of the empty fireplace. Jinx had disappeared but Callie suspected that her cat would appear again soon, just to make sure that Odin wasn't getting ideas above his station on Jinx's territory.

'Do you enjoy it?' he asked. 'It must be a highly stressful job.'

'I enjoy creating order out of the chaos, but I don't enjoy doing battle with brides' mothers, who never seem able to make up their minds.'

'You mean the brides, surely?'

'Nope. As a rule, they're easy to handle. It's the mothers who feel they have to interfere at every turn.' Callie took a sip of her water. 'I don't come cheap, so I often wonder why they use my services and then try to countermand decisions that we reach together at the early stages when it's too late to change them, but there you have it. Jason, who you met earlier, is my secret weapon. He can charm the most irascible of mothers. I really don't know how I'd cope without him, but don't tell him that. His ego is already disgustingly inflated.'

Callie abruptly stopped talking, wondering why she felt the

need to prattle on. She considered a glass of wine to settle her nerves but resisted. She recalled what had happened the last time she drank in Jack's presence and decided that it would be better to keep her wits about her.

'What about you?' she asked. 'Did you always intend to go into partnership with Logan?'

'Nah. I did City and Guilds NVQs in construction when I left school because it seemed like a logical way to go. I was never going to take a desk job. I mean, no disrespect to my intellectual superiors, but the world and his dog appear to go to university nowadays, or what used to be polytechnics, and come out with degrees in areas that don't offer employment opportunities. Performing arts, social studies, whatever that is, and... well, you get the picture.' Callie nodded as he leaned back in his chair and crossed one foot over his opposite thigh, looking totally relaxed and absolutely gorgeous. *Stop it! Don't go there.* 'But try getting a plumber at anything under fifty quid at hour...' He spread his hands. 'It seemed like a no-brainer. Besides, I like getting my hands dirty and forging friendships with the other guys on the site. There's a sort of camaraderie that springs up between blokes who work outside in all weathers. We have one another's backs, no questions asked, and it feels good. Well, not so good now that I have one foot in management and one with the guys...'

'Which is where your loyalties lie.'

'Unquestionably.'

'Logan enticed you away?'

'He did. Once he finished his degree and realised that his father had lost most of the family's money, it was one hell of a shock. He had such expectations, and plans. Anyway, he didn't mope for long, I'll give him that, and instead sold me the idea of going into partnership. I'd be the brawn and him the brains.'

'Hardly,' she said softly.

'Well, you would say that,' he replied with a soft smile that Callie reacted to somewhere entirely inappropriate. She wasn't about to get her fingers burned for a second time, she reminded herself, even in the unlikely event that Jack was interested in her personally, but it seemed her head and her heart were struggling to get on the same page. 'The fact is, I was a blind fool. I knew how badly Logan wanted to make a name for himself, how willingly he'd cut corners if I let him, but it never once occurred to me that he'd embezzle company funds and leave me to carry the can.'

'He fooled us both. That's an established fact.' She sent him a challenging look. 'All we have left to decide is what to do about it. I don't know about you, but I don't intend to let him get away with it. Someone has to make a stand, but the question is, do we both want the same outcome?'

10

Jack put his empty bottle aside and stood up. On the point of leaving, her challenge had stopped him in his tracks.

'What do you mean by that?' he asked, unable to prevent himself from scowling but careful to keep his voice neutral. He had picked up on her truculence, for which he couldn't entirely blame her, but he wasn't about to be accused of colluding with Logan's criminal enterprise without fighting his corner.

'I didn't mean that the way it sounded,' she said, waving a half-hearted apology.

'Then what did you mean, Callie?' Jack struggled to keep his temper in check. 'Let's clear the air here. If you think I'm in this with Logan then come right out and say so, 'cause the way I see things, I could finish up doing time for something I knew nothing about.'

'I know. I've said I'm sorry. What I meant was that we have different agendas. I want revenge, and my money back if absolutely possible, but I'll settle for Logan being publicly exposed for the scumbag that he is. At least that way he won't be able to con anyone else. But you... well, as you yourself just pointed out, you could be implicated, especially if Logan has devised a way to make it look as though you were in on the fraud, which I wouldn't put past him. Naturally, you will want to cover your own back, even if that means sweeping this business under the rug.'

'You think that's what I'll do?' He shook his head. 'You really don't know me at all.'

'Well, let's be honest, I don't. We only just met.'

'I'm not Logan,' he said, his temper abating. 'I can see why you might think that way and I know I have to earn your trust.' He sat down again. 'But yeah, if you'll have me, let's work together and bring the bastard down.'

'Sorry if I insulted your integrity.' She sent him a placatory smile. 'I have trust issues at the best of times, which is why I'm still kicking myself for letting Logan into my life.'

'Don't beat yourself up over it. I've seen him in action. He can be very persuasive and plausible.'

'Thanks for trying to make me feel better about myself.'

'You're welcome.' He smiled at her. 'Is it working?'

She waggled one hand from side to side. 'Some.' She glanced down at her lap. 'Any idea how to trap him? You know him better than I do. A lot better. What would he be unable to resist?'

'The chance to make a quick buck,' Jack said, without hesitation. 'He's never stopped trying to impress his father. And Farquhar, too, but he never could.'

'Perhaps they both saw through him.'

'Perhaps, but in Farquhar's case that only happened after he enticed Logan into marrying Portia.'

'He could have pulled the rug if he thought Logan was no good for his daughter.'

'You're forgetting that Portia wouldn't have stood for it. She can teach a mule a thing or two about stubbornness when her mind's made up. But now that he's abandoned her, he will know that he's burned his bridges with Farquhar, so he must have something else lined up. Somewhere to go; another money-making scheme.' Jack absently rubbed his jaw as he thought it through. 'But why now?'

'Right, that's what we need to find out. If we know what forced him to move now, then we...' Callie planted an elbow on her knee and leaned forward with her chin supported in her cupped hand. 'We know that he'd upped the ante by no longer covering his tracks when it came to taking cash from your firm and by conning me. He knew me well enough to realise that I'd hunt him down and make one hell of a fuss if he stayed in England. Has anything happened recently to force his hand?'

'That site!' Jack clicked his fingers as a possibility occurred to him.

'What site?' Callie looked confused.

'He was pushing hard to develop a site that I was pretty sure we wouldn't get planning permission on. It's a brownfield site outside of Portsmouth. You know what that is?'

'Yeah, I think so. It's urban land that's been previously used but has become derelict. The government are keen to encourage their use rather than greenbelt, right?'

'Yep, derelict or contaminated sites give the planners a hard-on. But because of the possibility of contamination, the local authorities have to ask for preparatory regenerative work before they give permission for any redevelopment. Even so, it's often easier to get the required permission because they've become eyesores and locals embrace their redevelopment, whereas building on green sites has all the environmental objectors coming out the woodwork, waving placards, tying themselves to trees, then getting in their gas-guzzling cars and driving home.

Anyway, Logan acquired an option on a brownfield and reckoned it would be the big one. I've never seen him so excited. He just needed investors and targeted Blakely. He's a well-known supporter of urban regeneration, amongst other things, and puts his money when his mouth is.'

'I met Logan at his daughter's wedding,' Callie said softly. 'Blakely must have liked what he saw in him, otherwise he wouldn't have been there. I take it the deal didn't go ahead?'

'Nothing had been agreed.'

'What about Farquhar? Wouldn't he have gone for it?'

'Apparently not. Logan was convinced that he would and was fuming when he turned him down. But... I don't know, there was something not right about that site. Logan didn't want us to do the usual surveys, which would have drawn attention to our plans. He wanted it kept under the radar, then abruptly told me to forget it for the time being. I never knew why. Couldn't get a straight answer out of him but he could be like that. If he got something wrong, he would never admit it, or talk about it.'

'Was this recently? Perhaps he'd already decided to cut his losses and scarper.'

'A few months ago.'

'Did he purchase the site?'

Jack shook his head. 'If he did then it wasn't in the books.'

Callie sat forward, her eyes glistening as a possibility clearly occurred to her. 'Then he probably bought it himself and intended to cut you out, but something went wrong.'

'Blakely probably pulled out and he couldn't get anyone else,' Jack replied. 'But it should be easy enough to discover if the site was recently sold and if so who to.'

'Local authority records?'

'Right. I'll get right onto it tomorrow.'

'Would Logan have used his own funds if he made the purchase?' Callie asked. 'Well, funds embezzled from elsewhere.'

'Hard to say. He never has before but he was obviously up to something I knew nothing about.' Jack paused. 'Even if he did buy it, that doesn't help us much. We can't contact him and even if we could, how would knowing about that land be enough to entice him back?'

'If you'd fallen upon a rich potential investor...'

'Hmm, possibly.' But Jack probably looked as dubious as he felt. 'But Logan's no fool. He'd smell a rat.'

'He's not the only one who can be devious. Greed will prove to be his downfall, you just mark my words. You wouldn't ring him, but we could perhaps think of someone convincing enough...'

'You're reaching,' he said softly. 'Besides, Logan's long gone. I can sense it.'

'Yeah, perhaps that wouldn't work. Even so, don't be so defeatist. He can't have got far without his passport.' She sat forward, full of enthusiasm that he didn't have the heart to quell. 'Now, his phone's switched off but you can bet your life that he turns it on occasionally and picks up his messages. It was his lifeline when I knew him. He never ignored it, not even when we were...' She blushed and allowed her words to trail off.

'Were what?' he asked, grinning.

'Shut up!' She threw a cushion at him.

'If you were to leave a message saying that someone's been in touch about the site, wanting to purchase... if he's bought it and got lumbered, I'm betting he'd bite. Like I say, greed is his god.'

'Unless he's left his affairs in the hands of a lawyer.'

'Ah, I didn't think of that.' Callie frowned. 'Would he, though? I mean, if he wants to disappear, would he feel comfortable having anyone in this country knowing how to get hold of him? I know lawyers are sworn to secrecy, but still, leaks occur, especially if bribes are involved.'

'One thing at a time. Let me find out about the land first.'

Callie gave an absent nod. 'It would be useful to know what scared Blakely off. He and Logan must have been on the same page at one point. I mean, he invited Logan to his daughter's wedding. I saw Logan included in Blakely's inner circle, knocking back ruinously expensive brandy before the dancing started.'

Jack grunted. 'Sounds like Logan.'

'If he's such an astute entrepreneur, Blakely that is, we need to know what turned him off from Logan's scheme. You said yourself that he was a pretty astute judge when it came to opportunities.' Callie's expression turned bitter. 'I'm a perfect case in point.'

'Blakely won't take my calls,' Jack said, resisting the urge to assure Callie that Logan wouldn't have hit on her with thoughts of stealing from her in mind. He would have done so simply because he liked what he saw, as Jack himself did. But he knew that now wasn't the right time and wondered if it ever would be. She was still raw, and angry, and being ultra-cautious. Working alongside her and proving that he was cut from very different cloth to his ex-friend would have to be enough for him.

For now.

'He was pretty pissed with Logan over something or other; that much I do know. I heard Logan's end of a call with him. Logan was attempting to calm him down, to convince him of something. I got called away, so I don't know anything more than that and Logan wasn't saying anything other than that Blakely had pulled out.'

'He'll probably talk to me. I can say there's been a problem with the wedding accounts, a double invoice or something, and that I need to see him in person to sort it out. We got along quite well, so it might work.'

Jack thought it highly unlikely. Blakely was too important to spare any time for such a trifling matter and would likely palm her off onto one of his assistants. Even so, she looked so enthusiastic, so keen to be proactive, that he didn't have the heart to discourage her.

'Well,' he said, 'I'd best get out of your hair. I'll look into the land business first thing... Hell, I can't, it's Saturday.'

'Won't it be available online?'

'I have absolutely no idea and even less idea how to find out.'

Callie tapped her fingers impatiently against her thigh. 'We can't afford to waste a couple more days. It could be the difference between catching Logan and him getting away.' She bounced on the edge of her seat and pushed herself to her feet. 'Stay where you are. I'll get my laptop. I'm absolutely sure that the land registry is available to all and sundry.'

She scurried off and returned with her computer already fired up. Her fingers flew over the keys. She tutted, pressed a few buttons and then punched the air.

'I'm in!'

Jack stood to look over her shoulder, enjoying a view that had nothing to do with the contents of the screen.

'Give me the address of the property,' she said.

'Clydesdale Mews. It's a small row of houses bordering what used to be a recreation ground.'

'Ah, I see. I think.' She glanced over her shoulder at him, scowling. 'It's the old rec that caught Logan's attention, I'm betting. He hoped to redevelop the houses and spill onto the waste ground.'

'Something like that. Well, in fairness, it's a blot on the landscape right now and a haunt for drug users and prostitutes. The area does need to be regenerated.'

'So, if Logan did purchase the run-down houses, he couldn't

expect to gentrify them and flog them off for telephone number prices if they face a drug den, so why...' She paused, absently tapping her lips with her forefinger. Jack wished she wouldn't. It drew his attention to her full mouth and plump lips, which was not helpful. 'Blakely, presumably, has contacts in all the right places, which is why Logan needed him on board.'

'Smart girl! I told him it was a non-starter, but he was having none of it.'

'Well, those houses have been sold, and recently too.' Callie scrolled through a couple of pages. 'Damn! They've been sold to an offshore company.' Her shoulders slumped. 'That will be Logan, I'm guessing. That's where he's stashed his ill-gotten gains.' She shut her machine down and sighed. 'He's one step ahead of us all the way. It's hopeless. We'll never trace that company and even if we do, we'll still hit a brick wall.'

'We do have an edge in that Logan can't possibly know that I'm onto him. He thinks I trust him, which of course is the truth.' He moved to sit beside her and grinned. 'Don't give up now. We both have a vested interest in catching him or, in my case, at the very least proving that I'm not a party to his scams.'

'Of course.' She picked up her mobile.

'What are you doing?' he asked, watching as she scanned through her contacts.

'I'm going to ring Blakely and try to wangle an appointment.'

Impressed by her determination, Jack nodded his approval.

'Blakely,' a voice snapped, clearly audible to Jack because Callie had put the call on speaker.

'Mr Blakely, it's Callie Devereaux.'

'Who?'

'Your daughter's wedding planner.'

'Ah, yes.' The impatience left his voice, but it was clear that he didn't welcome the distraction. 'What can I do for you?'

'I wondered if you could spare me a few minutes of your time to discuss something important. Naturally, I will come to you and I promise that it won't take long.'

'If this is to do with the wedding costs, there is a procedure. I don't need to be involved.'

'No, it isn't. It's personal, relating to a mutual acquaintance. It's sensitive and not something I can speak about on the phone.'

'I have no personal connections to you, Miss Devereaux.' But his tone was now curious rather than borderline hostile.

'Actually, I need your help. Don't worry, it isn't financial or personal to you, as far as I am aware.'

'I can give you ten minutes tomorrow evening,' he said after a short pause. Callie's brows shot up and she again punched the air. 'Come to my house. You have the address.'

'I have to hand it to you,' Jack said, not trying to conceal how impressed he was as Callie disconnected the call. 'I really didn't think he'd bite. And you managed to get him to do so without revealing anything of substance.'

'I didn't really think that I would either,' she admitted, 'which makes you wonder. Anyway, men don't reach his position without treading on a few toes, perhaps even breaking the odd law, or at least circumventing them. You said yourself that he has contacts. I figured that if he thought I had something on him, he would want to know.'

'Well, I'm coming with you.' He held up his hands to prevent her from protesting. 'No arguments. We're in this together.'

'Okay. I'll be at the wedding venue that you came to today but should be able to get away by six. I know the village where Blakely lives. It will take about half an hour to get there.'

'I'll pick you up and drive you.'

'There's no need.'

'Safety in numbers.' He sensed her objections were more to

do with logistics. 'I'll drop you back to pick up your car afterwards. Better yet, I'll buy you dinner and we can discuss what we learn, if anything.'

'I don't know...'

'No strings,' he said softly. 'He really hurt you, I know that, but I'm not Logan.'

She smiled up at him, just as her cat appeared from the kitchen, stalked up to Odin and bashed his nose with its paw. Odin whimpered, making them both laugh.

'Jinx, behave!' she admonished.

'I think that's our cue to leave,' Jack said, gathering up his mobile and patting his pockets, looking for his keys. 'See you tomorrow at six.'

She walked him to the door and there was an awkward moment when Jack wondered how to make a graceful exit. Should he kiss her? Would she be expecting it, or recoil if he attempted to? He settled for a brief peck on the cheek.

Callie walked slowly back into her sitting room, breathing in Jack's earthy masculine aroma that still lingered. She slumped back into the seat she'd just vacated, absently stroking Jinx's sleek back when he jumped onto her lap, attempting to make sense of her oscillating emotions. Everything she'd strived to achieve had been taken from her by a smooth operating conman – Jack's long-time friend and partner – and yet she was fatally attracted to Jack.

How was that even possible?

'Human emotions are weird things, Jinx,' she told her cat. 'Be grateful that you don't have to wrestle with them.'

Her phone rang. Callie picked it up with a resigned sigh, assuming it would be a last-minute crisis regarding the following day's wedding. but a glance at the display showed that it was actually Maisie calling.

'Is *he* still there?' she asked.

'If by he you mean Jack, then no. Why would he be?'

'Honey, that man is sex on legs. Don't judge every member of the male species by Logan's slimy standards.'

'Logan was sex on legs too and look where that got me. Besides, I can't be absolutely sure that he isn't in this with Logan.'

Maisie chuckled. 'You're sure.'

Callie conceded the point with a slow nod, even though Maisie couldn't see her. 'Perhaps, but I have other priorities. Did you find the rabbit?' Callie asked, keen for a change of subject.

'I think Dan was the one who let him out. Gave him an excuse to get me back here. Soon as I walked through the door, he went through it in the opposite direction. To see a man about a job, or so he said.'

A horrible thought occurred to Callie. 'Surely you don't suspect him of playing away?' she asked, aghast.

'Well, sweetness, he sure was all dolled up for a casual meeting in a pub,' Maisie replied, with a little too much bonhomie. 'And he's had a lot of secret meetings recently that he's never properly explained. He doesn't even bother to make excuses. It's like he wants me to know and be the one to raise the subject, so obviously I'm keeping schtum.'

'Oh, Maisie, why didn't you tell me? You know I'm here for you.'

'I'm probably imagining things. Dan wouldn't dare. He knows I'd cut off his balls with blunt scissors if he tried it.'

'I'm a crap friend. It's been all about me recently.'

'With good reason. Anyway, I'll take an in depth look at those books over the weekend and let you know what I find.'

'Thanks, sweetie.'

'What are you and the hunk going to do next?'

Callie explained, omitting to mention the dinner invitation. Callie wasn't sure how she felt about that, or why she'd accepted.

But Maisie would put two and two together and come up with seventeen.

'Well, be sure and let me know what you find out.'

Callie promised that she would, cut the call and took herself off to bed. Tomorrow would be a long day.

11

Logan was between a rock and a hard place. He'd just flogged his beloved Porsche to a dodgy dealer willing to pay him in cash on the spot – far below the market value, needless to say. Damn Portia for forcing him into this position. Why did she have to go whining to Daddy dearest? After all he'd done for her, he'd expect a small display of loyalty. Logan stomped away from the car dealer, feeling like the world in its entirety bore him a grudge and feeling the pain in his ribs from the humiliating beating he'd taken a few days previously. A beating that had forced him to change his plans on the hoof.

He abruptly stopped walking when he realised that he had no idea where he was going, causing the hooded youth going in the same direction to cannon into his back.

'Watch it, granddad,' the kid said, giving Logan's shoulder a hefty shove as he passed him.

His ribs howled in protest when he stumbled forward but that was the least of his humiliations. Being followed to his own home by those heavies was in another league, the more so since it hadn't occurred to him that he would be. He was losing his edge and no longer felt in control. The incident had spooked him into a kneejerk reaction and he already regretted parting with his car, even though he'd known it would have to go, and go soon.

His thoughts turned to temporary shelter and from there to the various women he'd had flings with, wondering which of them to shack up with until he could get his passport sorted. Problem was, they were all married. All except one – the one whom he'd most like to idle a few days away with – but that ship had left port when he screwed her over.

Pity.

It started to rain – of course it did! Logan turned up his collar, his foul mood increasing with every stop he took. He could go back to his own house, he supposed. Portia would remain with Farquhar for the foreseeable, but if any of the neighbours noticed activity, they just might report it. Besides, it was the first place that his creditors, and others, would look for him.

He glanced at a nearby bus stop and emphatically shook his head. He hadn't fallen quite *that* low. His keys jangled in his pocket as he raised a hand to hail an empty cab, which sailed past him, soaking him with the standing water it stirred up, and leaving him stranded on the pavement. He swore violently, drawing an affronted look from an older woman who happened to be passing, as he thoughtfully fingered his keys. Today was Saturday and Callie was bound to be out all day at one of her weddings. He happened to know that she was solidly booked for weeks in advance. He still had the key to her place that he'd copied and he very much doubted whether *she'd* changed her locks.

Nah! He shook his head to dispel such a suicidal thought. Best find another cheap hotel, then grovel to the passport forger. He'd feel better once he had a means of escape and would be on the first plane out of here that he could procure a seat on once he did.

It didn't matter where it took him. The world was a small place and once he was clear of England, he would be able to breathe more freely, and get started on his ambitious plan for the future, unhindered by vengeful fathers-in-law and a business partner who lacked the ability to think big.

Logan finally caught a cab that took him into the city. There was anonymity in crowded cities, even cities as small as Chichester. He found an equally anonymous hotel, checked in using the credit cards he already had in the name of Ed Fuller, and threw the small carry-on bag with the only possessions he intended to take with him onto the bed. He then switched on his three phones, one at a time, to listen to the messages. He wasn't sure whether to be worried or pacified when there were none from Portia and her father. Either Farquhar had persuaded his daughter to give up on him or he had something else planned by way of retribution. Logan shuddered, suspecting the latter.

There was nothing from Jack either and Logan was obliged to accept that he'd somehow learned the truth. But there were several increasingly threatening ones from his creditors, demanding a meeting later that evening.

'Damn!'

Logan knew he would have to go. They'd been most specific and weren't the sort of people he could afford to openly cross. Besides, they'd implied that there might be a way for him to work off his debt and it would set alarm bells ringing if he didn't jump at the chance. He knew very well that if they even suspected he intended to run then... well, his legs would be broken at best, making movement of any sort impossible.

Feeling as though the entire world was against him, Logan used the third of his phones to call the passport man and agreed to his terms. Terms that had now increased to twelve thousand in cash in advance. By going back to him, Logan had proved his desperation and both men knew it.

* * *

Callie could finally relax. The wedding had gone off almost without a hitch, which was unprecedented. Now the dancing had started, the bar was doing a roaring trade and her duties were almost at an end.

'That usher has been giving me the come-on all day,' Jason said, sending the guy a speculative look and a little wave. 'Shame he's not my type.'

'He's breathing, isn't he?'

'Hush your mouth! I'll have you know that I'm highly selective.'

Callie chuckled. 'Of course you are.'

'Now, for instance, if that gorgeous hunk of masculine perfection who was all over you like a rash yesterday were to be looking at me like that Neanderthal has been all day, it would be a very different matter.' Jason eyes gleamed with curiosity. 'Come on girlfriend, dish. Who is he and what's happened to the other Adonis? These gorgeous men are a bit like buses, aren't they? None for ages and then two come along together. But still, I didn't have you down as a two-timer.'

'He's working on something with Maisie,' Callie said, stretching the truth to diaphanous lengths.

Jason gave her a look that said he wasn't buying it. 'Tell me to mind my own business, why don't you?'

'I would if I thought you'd listen.'

'You've dropped a few pounds, darling,' Jason said, in one of his lightning changes of subject, giving her person a swift once-over. 'The look suits you. Just shows the power of *lurve*.'

Hardly, Callie thought. She'd been close to falling for Logan but hadn't lost an ounce. The prospect of losing her beloved home, however, had sent her waistline into reverse gear.

'Thanks,' she said.

'And talking of *lurve*,' Jason added. 'Looks like Maisie needs more help.' He indicated the doorway with his eyes, where Jack was already engendering interest from a few well-oiled females. Not that a woman would need to be tipsy to appreciate the figure that Jack cut, standing there in all his muscular glory and not appearing to notice the attention he was getting. He'd made an effort and wore a smart shirt hanging loose over new-looking jeans. Callie didn't allow herself to wonder if he'd done so to impress her or for Blakely's benefit. 'You go, love, and have fun. I mean, make sure His Gorgeousness meets up with Maisie. I'll hold the fort here.'

'You sure? The usher might get to you without me having your back.'

'Well... I suppose he is here and not *that* bad looking.'

Callie laughed. 'You're impossible.'

Jason glanced in Jack's direction and waggled his fingers at him. 'Pots and kettles spring to mind, darling. Now scram, and enjoy yourself. You deserve it. But,' he added, his habitual teasing giving way to a concerned expression, 'my price for holding the fort is that you tell me what's really going on when you can. I know there's something. You haven't been your usual efficient self recently.'

Touched by his concern, Callie promised that she would and made her escape before he pressed the issue, reminding him that she would be at the end of her phone if needed.

'Hey,' she said, joining Jack, much to the obvious irritation of several women who had less than subtly drifted towards him. 'You scrub up well.'

'I was about to say the same about you,' he said, smiling with his eyes.

'Mustn't let the side down. I seem to drum up a lot of advance business at my weddings.'

'Good to know.' He waved towards the door. 'Shall we?'

'Let's.'

'Oh, where's the truck?' she asked when he led her towards a top-end BMW.

'That's for the day job.'

Odin, who was in the car, poked his nose through the open window and wagged furiously when he recognised her. She climbed into the passenger seat when Jack unlocked the car and opened the door for her. She thanked him and squirmed beneath the neck wash she received from Odin's backseat position.

'How did the wedding go?' he asked, as he fired up the engine and reversed out of his parking spot.

'Suspiciously well, which has me worried.'

'Why? It's all over now, bar the drinking. Your work is done and word of your legendary efficiency will spread.'

'Let's hope so.'

They completed the drive to Blakely's residence more or less in silence. Callie felt on edge but determined, convinced that Blakely must know something to point them in the right direction.

'How are we going to handle this?' he asked, indicating to overtake a slow-moving van.

'I think we need to play it by ear. It will be humiliating to admit the truth, but if he's as astute as I suspect then I don't suppose he'll fall for any half-measures. You okay with that?'

Jack nodded. 'I guess.'

But she could see that the prospect of admitting to Logan's

crimes unsettled him, and so it should. He had a hell of a lot to lose, with no guarantees that Blakely would be able to help him.

She watched Jack handle the car with casual efficiency, one strong hand resting on the steering wheel, the other on his thigh, and felt an overwhelming urge to take that hand in her own and assure him things would be okay. Since she had no way of knowing whether they would be, and because it seemed important to keep her relationship with Jack on a friends-only basis, she resisted, and the moment passed.

'It's hereabouts somewhere,' he said, when they drove into a quaint village. 'Look for signs to Outlander. I gather that even Logan was impressed by the place. It's up a track somewhere.'

'I know,' she said, smiling when Jack rolled his eyes. 'The names some people think are a good idea.'

They drove through the village without seeing a house large enough. Callie knew without needing to be told that Blakely's would be the largest house in the village. Just as they drove out the other side, Callie noticed a long driveway with a discreet sign.

'There!' she said, pointing.

Jack reversed up and took the winding drive, past fenced-in paddocks and woodland that presumably belonged to the property, rather like an old-fashioned estate. Callie half expected a gamekeeper with a shotgun broken over his arm to appear at any moment and demand to know their business. There were sheep in one of the fields and a pheasant strutted across the path in front of their car, forcing Jack to brake sharply. The day was dull with heavy clouds that threatened more rain. Callie, already impressed, imagined how much more spectacular it would look when the sun shone.

'Very Jane Austen,' Jack remarked.

They eventually reached wrought-iron gates that were closed, with a video camera and bell to one side. Jack opened his window and pressed the button but when a disembodied voice answered, Callie leaned across him and gave her name. The gates swung open on silent hinges, leaving them to negotiate another long gravel driveway surrounded by beautifully manicured gardens in full bloom and extensive lawns that were bowling-ball smooth. No self-respecting moles would have the temerity to invade this little corner of paradise, Callie decided.

Feeling a little intimidated, she was relieved when they eventually came to the house itself – a starkly modern structure with plenty of glass and balconies – and Jack pulled his car up beside a spotless Land Rover.

'One man and his wife live here,' Callie said. 'I wonder if Blakely has the time to appreciate it.'

'It's a status symbol,' Jack replied. 'Tangible evidence of what he's achieved. The sort of thing Logan would aspire to.'

Callie nervously swallowed and then nodded, aware it was true and that she herself would find it daunting, not to mention a nightmare to maintain. 'Come on then,' she said. 'He's just one man and this ostentatious display of wealth doesn't intimidate me.' She grinned. 'Well, not very much.'

They left Odin in the car with the window half open and approached the front steps. The door opened before they reached it and a man who appeared to be a servant – perhaps a modern-day butler – gave them an imperious look.

'Miss Devereaux?' he asked.

'Yes,' Callie replied. 'And this is Mr Carlisle.'

'Mr Blakely wasn't expecting two of you. Wait here. I will see if he's willing to receive you both.'

'This is starting to piss me off,' Jack said, tapping his fingers against the arm of a chair in the entrance hall, where they had been told to wait. 'What the hell does Blakely think all this pretension will achieve?'

'I have no idea, but he's the only man I can think of who might be able to help us,' Callie replied. 'Hold that thought. I don't like being spoken down to any more than you do but we'll just have to suck it up.'

'Wise words,' Jack replied. And the tension left his shoulders.

'This way.'

The butler, if that was the role he fulfilled, looked disappointed because he hadn't been told to turn them away.

'Thanks, Jeeves,' Jack said, earning himself a scowl from the man and a dig in the ribs with her elbow from Callie, who didn't quite manage to contain a giggle.

They were led past a bewildering series of rooms, all lavishly furnished and looking as though they were strictly for show. There wasn't a discarded magazine, a rumpled cushion, a blaring television, or any sign of occupation. It was a show house of massive proportions but definitely not a home. Callie thought longingly of her cosy, not especially tidy but definitely lived-in cottage and felt a fresh surge of determination to hold onto it by whatever means necessary.

Jeeves, as Callie would now forever think of the man, stopped in front of ornate double doors and knocked.

'Come.'

'Miss Devereaux and Mr Carlisle, sir,' the butler said, seeming to think that announcing them was one of his duties. Very likely it was.

Callie stepped into a booklined room that had a very different feel to the rest of the house. It was most definitely put to frequent use and was Blakely's private domain. Judging by the row of computer screens along one wall, he ran his entire empire from here. Callie wished now that she'd done more research and found out how exactly he'd made all his filthy lucre. Jack had mentioned that property development was one of his many interests and she wondered what the others were.

She gasped when she glanced through the full-length glazed doors that led to an atrium set out with expensive outdoor furniture arranged around a swimming pool. There was foliage everywhere, thriving beneath the glazed roof. But it was the magnificent view that held her attention; the first thing about this house that really impressed her. Even on a dull day, it was spectacular. How did he get any work done with that sort of distraction to hand, she wondered?

'I must say, you have a nerve coming here, Carlisle.'

The sound of Blakely's clipped, angry voice recalled Callie's attention from the view. The owner of this mausoleum had stood up from behind his desk whilst she'd been distracted and fixed Jack with a look of pure vitriol. Jack looked confused and stood his ground. If that look had been directed at Callie, she would have worried about self-combusting. What did it mean? Had Jack lied to her? Had he and Logan somehow defrauded Blakely?

She shook her head to dispel that thought. If that was the case, he would hardly have offered to come here with her and would have tried to convince her that it would be a waste of time coming herself.

'Excuse me,' Jack replied, an edge to his voice. 'We haven't met before so it's hard for me to know what I've done to offend you.'

Blakely looked at Jack for a protracted moment, then appeared to reach a decision. 'Perhaps you don't know. I'll give you the benefit of the doubt.' He paused. 'For now. Sit.' He indicated the two chairs in front of his desk and resumed his own. 'Why did you want to see me, Miss Devereaux?'

'Call me Callie,' she replied. 'I asked Jack to join me today because we are both in urgent need of your help.'

'What makes you suppose that I'd have any interest in helping you? You arranged my daughter's wedding and were well paid for your efforts. That, as far as I'm concerned, is the extent of our purely business relationship.'

Callie glanced at Jack, wishing now that they'd decided upon a strategy before coming, rather than playing it by ear. Blakely was fighting mad about something and was unlikely to be talked round with half-truths and allegations. He was nobody's fool and was expecting a response. She glanced again at Jack, doubting whether Blakely's patience would prove limitless, especially since he'd made it clear that they were intruding and had most likely only agreed to receive her out of a sense of curiosity. He was most definitely not delighted to see Jack.

'Your call,' Jack said softly, understanding what she'd been asking him with that look.

'Very well.' She sat a little straighter. 'I've been an idiot, Mr Blakely, fallen for the oldest line in the book, even though I should have known better. Anyway, it's resulted in my being defrauded out of a vast sum of money.'

'I'm sorry to hear it.' His attitude thawed a little. 'But I fail to see what it has to do with me, or how you think I can help you to regain your cash.'

'I trusted a man who I thought had feelings for me. I had absolutely no idea that he was a married man with a family – you must take my word on that. Perhaps, in retrospect, I should have suspected. He was almost too perfect. Anyway, I just discovered that he took out a large mortgage on my cottage *and* maxed my credit cards out.' Callie swallowed. 'I met the man at your daughter's wedding.'

'He is an associate of mine?' Blakely frowned. 'And you expect me to recover your losses, or somehow hold me responsible for them? Excuse me, but I find it very hard to believe that any of my friends would stoop so low. Without wishing to sound patronising, your estate would be small change to the majority of people I know. Have you consulted the police?'

'I can't.' She spread her hands. 'I can't prove any of this. Logan forged my signature.'

'Logan!' Blakely sprang from his chair, knocking it backwards. 'Your partner?' He pointed an accusing finger at Jack. 'You *do* know what he did to me! I admire your nerve in coming here, in that case, assuming I'd be out for revenge, but you're mistaken. I take care of my own problems in my own way.'

Jack shook his head in bemusement as the two men stared at one another. Callie could taste the aggression flowing between them.

'Jack is Logan's victim too,' she said.

Her voice cut off the staring match, and Blakely returned his attention to her. 'What do you mean by that?'

'He's disappeared off the face of the earth,' Jack said succinctly, 'and taken a big chunk of our company funds with him.'

Something about the anger in Jack's expression and the sincerity in his brief statement appeared to strike a chord with Blakely. He resumed his chair and moderated his tone.

'You should take more care in the choice of your partners – both of you.'

'You were considering going into business with him, I'm told,' Callie said, 'and although it's obvious in hindsight that Logan had been laying his plans to leg it for months, years even, he only took off when the deal he was attempting to cut with you fell through. That being the case, we wondered if you had any idea where he might be hiding out.' She spread her hands. 'It's a long shot, I know, but we're desperate to prevent him from leaving the country and prepared to try anything.'

Blakely leaned back in his chair and steepled his fingers

beneath his chin, appearing to consider his response. 'You have absolutely no idea where he can be?' he asked, fixing Jack with a probing look. 'Presumably you've asked his wife.'

'She plagued me with calls when she couldn't get hold of him,' Jack replied. 'I didn't think anything of it at first, then Callie came looking for him, told me what he'd done to her, and I realised we had a serious problem.' Jack narrowed his eyes to slits, scowling ferociously. 'I trusted him, more fool me, and now I'll be left holding the can, unless we can track him down before he leaves England, which I am convinced he plans to do. I have his passport, so he'll have to get a false one, but I don't suppose that will prove to be too much of a problem.' He lifted one broad shoulder. 'Perhaps he already has one, if he planned as meticulously as we think he did. It's impossible to know.'

Blakely allowed a significant pause and neither Callie nor Jack felt compelled to break it.

'Armitage and I didn't fall out over a business deal,' he eventually said, a clipped edge to his voice. 'Our association came to an end because I came home unexpectedly early from a business trip and found him in bed with my wife.'

12

A stunned silence was broken by Jack's groan, backed up by a few choice swear words.

'Of all the ridiculous...' He glanced at Callie's stricken features and cut off what he'd been about to say. 'You okay?' he asked, reaching over and giving her hand a squeeze.

'It makes sense, I suppose,' she said in a dazed tone. 'But I agree with you, Jack. It was unbelievably arrogant and stupid. Isn't that what you were about to say?'

'Not quite so politely.'

'I am very sorry, Mr Blakely.' She managed a weak smile. 'No one likes to be played for a fool. Take it from one who knows,' she added bitterly.

'No apologies are necessary,' Blakely replied. 'And please call me Robert. It seems all three of us have an axe to grind when it comes to Armitage.'

'Where is your wife now?' Callie asked.

'Gone.' His expression hardened. 'She was the one who insisted on marriage. I knew I was too old for her, but she wouldn't have it. She wanted the life, of course,' he added, waving an arm expansively around the elegant room. 'I never fooled myself into thinking otherwise but did warn her that I wouldn't tolerate infidelity. Seems she thought she could fool me and have the best of both worlds. Now she knows differently. I cut her off without a penny, in accordance with the prenup she signed.'

That, Jack thought, would explain the unlived in feeling in this barn of a house.

'I'm sorry,' Callie said. 'I am sure you had feelings for her and treated her well, but I did notice her watching Logan at the wedding, a bit like a predatory cat. It's my job to notice these things, being the planner. I have seen fights break out once the alcohol flows and people forget who they're married to. It happens more often than you'd think and I try to pre-empt brawling. It's all people remember the next day and tends to be bad for business.'

'Your sympathy is noted but unnecessary. I should have known I was asking for trouble when I married a woman my daughter's age. I work so hard and she reckons she felt neglected.' He waved the suggestion haughtily aside. 'She didn't mind spending the fruits of my labours, though. I dare say my ex-wife is laughing herself silly,' he added, with evident disinterest in the woman's feelings. 'Needless to say, what I've told you stays between us.' He fixed each of them with a threatening look. 'I shall not be best pleased if the world learns I've been played.'

Jack nodded, even though he thought that much would be obvious when the world in question learned that he'd ditched his trophy wife after less than a year of marriage.

'Of course,' Callie said.

'What did you do about Logan?' Jack asked.

'Cut off all dealings with him.' Blakely flexed his hands. 'Amongst other more physical retributions.'

That explained why Logan had been in some pain the last

time Jack had seen him, he thought. He said he'd walked into a door and although Jack had suspected it was a lie, he hadn't bothered to call him on it.

'I understand he purchased that row of houses in Clydesdale Mews ahead of our signing the agreement, which was remarkably stupid of him. Now he's stuck with them and will never get planning permission without my help.' Satisfaction fuelled Blakely's expression. Forcing him to take a financial hit seemed like a more enduring form of revenge than reverting to violence, Jack thought. 'The soil's contaminated.'

The fact that Blakely would have covered that fact up and pushed a planning application through, had he not fallen out big time with Logan, wasn't lost on Jack. Ethically, he didn't think there was much to choose between Blakely and Logan, but he kept his opinion to himself. He suspected that this man could help them to find Logan before he did more damage, which was now Jack's primary objective.

'Anyway, it seems we've all been shafted by Armitage, in our different ways,' Blakely said. 'What's less clear is what you expect me to do about it. As far as I'm concerned, the score is now even and, truth be told, he probably did me a favour by exposing Delia's true nature before she'd had an opportunity to get her claws into more of my wealth.'

'Well...' Callie spoke before Jack could and so he left her to it. 'We now know why Logan was forced into bringing his plans forward. I suspect that he was waiting for the profits from the Clydesdale Mews development to come rolling in before he helped himself to them and took off.'

'It would explain why he went ahead and purchased the site before it went to auction,' Jack added. 'You won't be surprised to learn that I knew nothing about it, damned trusting fool that I am.' A sudden thought occurred to him. 'I hope to God that he didn't put my name on the contract. I wouldn't put it past him.'

'Well, if he did then I guess you could sell it for whatever you can get for the houses,' Blakely said. 'They will get regenerated by someone somewhere along the line but the ground across from them won't get redeveloped unless someone knows someone...' He sighed. 'Anyway, get your legal people to do some digging and play the bastard at his own game.'

'I might just do that,' Jack replied, thinking that he didn't actually have any legal people. Blakely lived in a rarefied world and took such things for granted.

'You and I are both too trusting, Jack,' Callie said. 'But that's what Logan is so good at. When you're with him, it's impossible to imagine that he's anything other than the real deal.' She turned to look at Blakely. 'When he was playing fast and loose with your wife's affections, Robert, he was also hanging out with me. When things went wrong, I assume that's when he decided to help himself to what he could get from me. It would also explain why it was so clumsily done. He was in panic mode and didn't plan ahead insofar as I'm concerned, whereas he covered his tracks well with Jack, until the last few months when he got greedy, careless and probably desperate.'

'He will have had to borrow the money to purchase that site,' Jack said, 'and he didn't take it from the company. Even I would have noticed if that large a sum went out, but he might have assured whoever he borrowed it from that as his partner I was party to the deal. That's what concerns me. Logan has no track record as a businessman in his own right but together we've done okay.'

'And you don't deserve to have it all taken away,' Callie said softly.

'Who would have lent him over a million quid to buy the

site?' Jack asked. 'It sure as hell wasn't anyone legitimate or they would have audited the books, I assume, and Callie and I both know that the books wouldn't have stood up to that sort of scrutiny.'

'Would his father-in-law not have funded him?' Blakely asked. 'He was always banging on about how supportive he was.'

Jack shook his head. 'He and Farquhar were at odds. Besides, if he'd gone to him, it couldn't have been kept from me. I would have insisted upon an official company loan and we'd have both been required to sign the papers.'

'If he borrowed it off the grid then it's little wonder that he's desperate to leave these shores,' Blakely remarked, seeming to cheer up no end at that prospect. 'The people who lend that sort of money aren't to be messed with. I find it hard to imagine that they would have loaned that much to a nonentity but, like you say, he can be persuasive. Anyway, if they did, they will have kept a close eye on your partner.'

'They won't turn to Jack for repayment, will they?' Callie asked, sounding endearingly alarmed at the prospect.

Blakely shrugged. 'Can't rule it out,' he said.

'Shit!' Jack muttered, shifting uncomfortably in his seat.

'If they're watching Logan, he won't be able to leave the country,' Callie said, 'so what I had in mind just might work.'

'And what is that?' Blakely asked.

'Well, Mr... Robert, I think he will be desperate to cut his losses, to offload that site, even at a loss. So if you could find it in yourself to lure him into a trap, once we have him, we can get the law involved. If I can prove that I didn't take that mortgage out on my house, then I won't be liable for it. As to Jack, if he can prove that he didn't embezzle funds from his own company, or get involved with undocumented loans, then he won't risk jail.' She bit her lower lip. 'I know you've had your revenge and don't have any reason to get involved, but I did hope that you would agree to at least make contact and pretend to want to restore negotiations over the site,' she added, with a winningly persuasive smile. Jack knew that if it had been directed at him then he would have fallen in with her crazy plan because he wouldn't have been able to help himself.

'Perhaps.' Blakely returned her smile, proving to Jack that he was as susceptible as the next man to a little feminine coercion. 'But will he play?'

'I would imagine so,' Jack said without hesitation. 'If he's still in the country and can't get away. His ambition got him only so far, but his greed will be his downfall. And when it does, I intend to be in the front row, leading the applause when they take him away in handcuffs.'

'A pretty boy like him, banged up with all those hairy Neanderthals.' Blakely flashed an evil smile. 'It hardly bears thinking about.'

Jack chuckled. 'But you can't help thinking about it.'

'I'd be less than human if I didn't. I still think I let him off too lightly, which is why I am willing to consider your proposition.'

'Well, then.' Callie leaned forward, her eyes sparkling with anticipation. 'We're sure he must regularly pick up his messages, even though his phone is turned off.'

They discussed the matter for another half hour. Blakely ordered refreshments for them all, which were served by a highly incensed-seeming Jeeves.

'I don't think your man likes me,' Jack remarked, when he left the room and closed the door quietly behind him.

'Could be something to do with the fact that you called him Jeeves,' Callie replied with a sweet smile.

'Oh dear.' Blakely actually chuckled. 'Davidson's pride will never recover. He was my wife's idea, in case you are wondering, and now I'm stuck with him. But still, at least he runs the house efficiently, so I keep him on.'

Eventually, Blakely held up a hand to cut off Callie's latest persuasive pitch. 'You have me, Callie,' he said, flipping through his phone and dialling a number. 'Armitage,' he said, having put the phone on speaker and talking when invited to leave a message. 'Blakely here. Let's put our personal feelings aside. I think you did me a favour, as it happens, so I'll not let the matter intrude on my business dealings. Anyway, call me if you want to go ahead with Clydesdale Mews. I might be willing to invest.' He cut the connection and smiled at Callie. 'There, will that do it, do you think?'

'I am absolutely sure that it will. The man lives to make a quick buck. Thank you so much.'

'Oh, don't thank me. I'm actually having fun.'

Callie and Jack both left their numbers with Blakely and he promised to get in touch the moment he heard from Logan.

* * *

'That went surprisingly well,' Callie said, as Davidson escorted them from the premises.

'Thanks to you.'

'Not really.' She made a big fuss of Odin when Jack opened the car's door and the dog launched himself at them.

'I think what he said is true,' he added, sliding behind the wheel and firing up the engine. 'He isn't heartbroken to be rid of his trophy wife but will enjoy bringing Logan down to size.'

'We'll see.'

'Now then, I promised you dinner and I know just the place.'

Callie's stomach rumbled at the mention of food, making Jack smile and her cringe with embarrassment. 'I haven't had a chance to eat much today,' she said by way of justification.

'Well, that's a situation we can easily remedy.'

'What about Odin? We can't take him into a restaurant.'

'We can where I have in mind.'

Odin barked from his backseat perch, making them both smile.

'I swear that dog knows when he's being talked about. Or, more likely, it was the mention of food that got him all worked up.'

Callie fell silent as Jack drove her to a small restaurant buried deep in the countryside just outside of Chichester. He felt ridiculously nervous, having taken a massive gamble in bringing her here. She was skittish, still not sure whether to trust him completely, and could get entirely the wrong idea.

Odin dived through the door ahead of them as soon as Jack let him out, wagging up a storm.

'Goodness,' Callie said, glancing up at the welcoming façade of the restaurant – welcoming even on a damp summer's evening. Only half the tables on the terrace were occupied due to the inclement weather, but the space was strung with fairy lights and the pathway down to the river at the bottom of the garden was also illuminated. 'He does know where he is, doesn't he?' She turned in a circle, taking it all in. 'And this place is magical. I often drive this way but had no idea about this little gem.'

Before Jack could respond, a large woman hurtled through the front door and launched herself at Jack, almost knocking him from his feet. Everyone at the tables turned to watch, with the exception of one couple who appeared to be totally absorbed by one another.

'I thought you'd forgotten where we live,' Jack's sister Elsie said, planting a smacking kiss on his cheek. 'It's been ages since you graced us with your presence.'

'You exaggerate, as always. Now let me go before you squeeze the life out of me and I'll introduce you to my guest. Callie, this is my sister Elsie. Elsie, Callie.'

'Your sister?' Callie looked from one to the other. 'I don't see the resemblance.'

'No one does,' Elsie said cheerfully, shaking Callie's hand as she assessed her. 'My baby brother is the runt. I think the postman knows more about his conception than he's ever let on. Anyway, come along in. It's a bit chilly out here.' She glanced at the groping couple. 'Although you could be forgiven for thinking otherwise. Anyway, we're full inside because of the bloody weather but we'll squeeze you in somewhere. Jim's in the kitchen, obviously, but he knows you're coming.'

'Er, where did Odin go?' Callie asked.

'Oh, he'll be loitering with intent near the kitchen, which is how Jim will know Jack's here. Don't worry, Odin won't get anywhere near the food preparation but that won't stop him from trying.'

'Perhaps because your soft-hearted husband takes pity on him,' Jack suggested, throwing an arm over his sister's shoulders.

'Well, if you fed him occasionally, he wouldn't have to.'

'That damned mutt eats me out of house and home.'

'How long have you known this reprobate, Callie?' Elsie asked as she led them to an intimate table in a small corner booth. Jack refrained from rolling his eyes, surprised that it had taken her this long to start the interrogation. 'You must be *the one*.' Elsie indulged in an exaggerated eye-roll. 'Jack never brings his dates here.'

'Oh, this isn't a date.' Callie's cheeks flooded with colour.

'Right.' Elsie fixed her with a probing look, her tone implying that she didn't believe a word of it. 'Okay, specials are on the board. I'd recommend the duck, if you're not a veggie, Callie. No one does duck cassoulet as well as my husband. Well, perhaps Jack once did, but he's too grand to get his hands dirty in the kitchen nowadays. I'll leave you with the menus. What can I get you to drink?'

Jack ordered a bottle of wine, most of which he intended to let Callie drink since he was driving, and a beer for himself.

'I'll be right back. Play nice without me, children.' She leaned towards Jack but didn't bother to lower her voice. 'She's nice. I like her. Don't screw it up.'

Jack laughed in spite of himself and shook his head. 'Sorry about that. She doesn't mean to embarrass, it's just the way she's always been.'

'Not a problem. I like her.'

'I can't think of anyone who doesn't. She's ideally suited for this type of work.'

'It sounds as though you are too.' She grinned at him, a little less wary. 'I knew you could do more than scramble an egg.'

'Busted,' he said, smiling.

Elsie reappeared with their drinks and took their orders. They both accepted her recommendation and ordered the duck.

'So, tell me about it,' she said, taking a sip of her wine and sighing with pleasure. 'Clearly, the culinary gene runs in your family.'

'Yeah, Mum liked to cook, which she did for the Armitages whenever they were entertaining. My dad reckoned she did just as good a job as professional caterers for half the price and called them tightwads. He was most likely right. Anyway, Elsie and I both got into it. Elsie went to catering college, which is where she met her husband. Jim's a pretty inventive chef who likes to push boundaries. That's why this place is always jammed. Michelin star standard without the prices.'

'Bet he hasn't told you that he made it possible,' Elsie said, passing their table with someone else's plates but apparently listening in on their conversation.

'What did you do?' Callie asked, pulling apart a warm roll, slathering a piece with thick butter and popping it into her mouth.

'It's no biggie. Jim couldn't get recognition on his own terms because he couldn't afford to open up shop, so when I started to make a few bob, I...' He spread his hands, feeling embarrassed.

'You set him and your sister up here.' She smiled across at him. 'That says a lot about your generosity.'

'Don't get carried away. I'm a sleeping partner as well as a hard task master and take my cut every month.'

'Don't believe a word of it,' Elsie mouthed as she walked past them again, clearly intending for Jack to see her. They constantly argued about Jack not taking back his investment now that they were doing so well. He couldn't seem to make Elsie understand that he had everything he needed and that seeing Elsie and Jim succeeding was reward enough. With his dad now dead and buried, his sister and her family were his only remaining relations, and family mattered.

'Just for the record, why did you bring me here?' Callie asked, after her starter had been placed in front of her and she tucked in, closing her eyes in appreciation at her salmon tartar. 'Elsie mentioned that you don't often bring strangers.'

'Two reasons. You mentioned that Logan hid you away, like he was ashamed to be seen with you.'

'That isn't precisely what I said.'

He waggled his hand from side to side. 'The implication was there.'

'Perhaps, but Logan and I were in a relationship.' She scowled. 'At least I thought we were.'

Jack felt deflated. The mention of Logan's name had caused a veil to descend over Callie's eyes. He wondered if she wished they still could be an item, despite the way he'd screwed her over. He must be a sensation in bed, Jack decided, because something about him caused women to forgive him time and again, no matter how badly he treated them. It irritated the hell out of Jack, especially when he saw a compassionate and sensitive soul such as Callie's being so callously trampled over and he was left to pick up the pieces, a poor substitute for the man she'd probably prefer to be with. She would eventually find a way to blame herself for what Logan had done to her too, he reckoned, which infuriated him.

Perhaps she already had.

'Well,' he contented himself with saying, 'I'm not ashamed to be seen with you.'

'Thank you.' She reached out and touched his hand, smiled and the regret left her eyes. 'That means a lot.'

'You also mentioned something about never having known family life,' Jack said, keen to steer their conversation away from Logan. 'I just wanted you to see that it's not all a bed of roses.' Jack winked at her as he raised his voice so that Elsie, who appeared to find dozens of reasons to hover around their table, would overhear.

Callie laughed. 'I can see that you and Elsie hate one another.'

Jack refilled her glass and enjoyed watching her slowly unwind. 'As sisters go, she's not all bad.'

'I heard that,' Elsie objected, no doubt aware that she was supposed to. 'Logan was in here a few weeks ago,' she said, clearing their starter plates. 'Came in with some stick-thin creature who nibbled on a lettuce leaf and offended Jim's finer feelings by ignoring his food.' Elsie patted her ample midriff. 'So up herself that she likely needed a torch to find her way. Nothing between her ears but then, I don't suppose Logan dated her for her conversation. When does he ever? Anyway, I felt like charging her double and would have, if she'd been paying. As it was, I didn't feel I could charge Logan anything.'

Jack glanced at Callie. 'You always give him freebies?' he asked.

'Sure. Why wouldn't we? You and he have always been joined at the hip. He kept my little brother out of trouble, or so he insists, so I guess I owe him.'

She wandered off, leaving them with that little nugget to chew over.

'He doesn't miss a trick, does he?' Callie said in a brittle tone.

Elsie returned with their main courses and the wonderful aromas made Jack salivate.

'He's history,' he said, when Elsie had left them again, returning to their conversation about Logan. 'Don't let him spoil things. Not tonight. It would be a sin to be down when we have this gorgeous food to eat. Food, in case you were not aware, is a religion. Well, Jim's is and ought to be dutifully worshipped.'

Callie smiled. 'Then we shall worship it.' She took a bite and savoured it slowly, closing her eyes and nodding her approval. 'Jim went to catering school. Where did you learn to cook?'

'No one taught me. I just copied Mum, watched what she did, picked a few things up along the way.'

'Right.' She leaned towards him when they were halfway through their duck, looking suddenly unsure of herself. 'Do you think this business with Blakely will work?'

'If Logan's still in the country, then there's a very good chance that it will. I reckon that he would have been here with one of his women in an effort to impress, aware that he wouldn't have to pay.'

'The cheapskate!'

'Right, but my point is, he can never resist an opportunity to exploit any given situation, as you yourself know to your cost. We're pretty sure he bought that site and won't be unable to unload it for what he paid. We also suspect that he borrowed a large sum from some dodgy people to finance it and will want to recoup his losses before he loses the ability to walk unaided.'

'Do loan sharks really break legs?' she asked, pausing with a forkful of duck halfway to her mouth. 'I thought that was all Hollywood glitz.'

'The sort that lend those amounts do. They will have needed some persuasive assurances before stumping it up, and you can be sure that they've been keeping an eye on him, which is another reason why I think he must still be in England. Anyway,' he said, pushing his empty plate aside, 'what did you think of the food?'

She indicated her own plate, almost scraped clean. 'I think that does all the talking for me.'

'Glad to hear it.'

'Jim!' Jack stood and shook a man in chef's whites warmly by the hand. 'You haven't lost your touch and got fat and lazy.'

Jack introduced Callie and the three of them spent a short amount of time in conversation before Jim felt obliged to do the rounds of the rest of the tables, accepting plaudits with grace and charm.

'Where's my dog?' Jack asked, when Jim passed their table again.

'Somewhere where the health inspectors will never find him.'

'Just so long as he's not in your freezer.' Jim chuckled but Callie looked appalled. 'Don't worry,' Jack told her, 'Odin is the restaurant's unofficial taster. Everything has to get past him before it goes anywhere near a table. He takes his duties very seriously.'

Callie smiled. 'I am perfectly sure he does.'

'Dessert?' Jack asked.

'Thanks, but no.' She patted her stomach and stifled a yawn. 'I couldn't eat another thing.'

'Come on, you've had a long day. The wedding must have taken it out of you.'

'What wedding?' Elsie demanded to know, zeroing in on them with greater accuracy than an Exocet missile. She narrowed her eyes at Jack. 'What are you not telling me, brother dear?'

'Not what you're thinking, more's the pity. Callie is a wedding planner.'

'You are…' She pointed an accusatory finger at Callie and her jaw dropped open. 'You're Callie Devereaux. *The* wedding planner.'

'We've met before?'

'They did a spread about your extravagant wedding venues in the local paper a few months back. Everyone who's anyone goes to you.'

'I'm not so sure about that, but thanks.'

'I've been trying to persuade Jim to offer this place up as a wedding venue. It would be perfect, if the weather cooperates.'

Callie thought of the lovely terrace, the river sparkling at the end of the garden, and had to agree. 'If Jim agrees, I'll come back and have a proper look some time.'

'That would be wonderful!' Elsie hugged Callie as though she'd known her for years. Her generosity was spontaneous, and Callie instinctively hugged her back. 'Make it soon.'

Callie promised that she would and offered Jim a less exuberant goodbye when he came to see them off too. Jack had to whistle twice before Odin came scampering from the direction of the rear garden, licking his lips.

'That's the back door to the kitchen,' Jack explained, rolling his eyes. 'That mutt doesn't miss a trick.'

'Well, you won't recoup your investment, Jack, so your dog does it for you,' Jim said, grinning.

Callie laughed as she tugged at one of Odin's ears with her right hand and waved to Elsie and Jim with the left. There was now just one couple left at the tables on the terrace; the same couple who had appeared more interested in eating one another than Jim's wonderful food. The man happened to look up when Odin loped past their table and his gaze clashed with Callie's. He did a double take, looked shocked and immediately averted his gaze.

But not so quickly that Callie didn't look equally astounded. Clearly they knew one another.

'What's the matter?' Jack asked, as he unlocked his car and opened the passenger door for her. 'Sorry if I've offended you and you'd rather I didn't open the door for you. I'm old-fashioned that way.' Callie opened her mouth but no words emerged. 'You're worrying me,' he added, as she slid wordlessly onto her seat. He swung round to the driver's side, let Odin in the back and then took up his place behind the wheel. 'I know Elsie can be full on, but she has a good heart and...' He knew good and well that her suddenly being lost for words had nothing to do with Elsie and everything to do with the man on the terrace. 'Who was that guy?' he asked softly.

Callie swallowed, looking dazed, angry and disbelieving. 'It was Dan,' she said in a hollow voice. 'Maisie's husband.'

13

'Shit!' Jack didn't start the engine but instead turned towards Callie with a look of deep sympathy that almost floored her.

'Why are all men such bastards?' she demanded to know.

'Not all of them,' Jack replied, and Callie realised even through the mist of her disillusionment that he was very likely right. Any lingering doubts she'd harboured about his morals had been almost eradicated following their time with Robert Blakely. Seeing him with his sister had convinced her. No one could pretend that sort of closeness. Jack Carlisle was just as much a victim of Logan's heartless ambition as she had been and equally keen to achieve retribution.

'Perhaps not.' She let out a long sigh, close to tears. Jack caught her hand and squeezed it. It felt good and she didn't try to snatch it back. 'Poor Maisie,' she said, shaking her head. 'I remember how crazy about each other they once were, like they could conquer the world together and didn't need anyone else. I felt a bit envious of their perfect love. Okay, so real life and two boisterous kids have taken the edge off but even so... Maisie is still crazy about Dan, even though she knows he has feet of clay. She constantly makes excuses for him and works her socks off to hold her family together, and yet he...' She waved a hand in the direction of the terrace, too angry to formulate a coherent sentence.

'Does she suspect?'

'Yeah, she poured her heart out to me the other day but I told her she was imagining things. She and Dan have been together since the beginning of time and neither has ever looked at anyone else.' She paused. 'Well, obviously one of them has. What I don't understand is how Dan can afford to take his floozy—'

'Floozy?' Jack's lips tipped up into an amused grin.

'If the cap fits.'

'I take your point. Presumably a meal for two would cut into Maisie's family budget.'

'What budget? Dan hasn't worked for months. Maisie just about keeps their collective heads above water and that's how he repays her.' She took her hand back, reluctantly. She might trust him more now, but she wasn't about to lean on him. 'What do I tell her?'

Jack raised a brow. 'You're going to tell her?'

'She's my best friend.' She gaped at him. 'Of course I'm going to tell her.'

'Sure about that?' He canted his head and sent her a probing look. 'She may not thank you for it.'

Callie took a deep breath, aware that he was playing devil's advocate. 'I might have hesitated in the way that she refrained from sharing her suspicions about Logan with me, but I don't see how I can.'

'Would you have believed her if she had warned you off?'

'Well...'

'Exactly. She knew you wouldn't listen and that it might drive a wedge between you.'

'Right, but this is different. She told me she suspected Dan, and Dan knows I saw them together, so presumably he will say something to her before I have to.' She glanced at him, biting her lower lip, feeling conflicted. 'Is it cowardly if I leave him to do the heavy lifting? He's the one who's a cheating rat, after all.'

'Nope. You want what's best for your friend but because you're not emotionally involved you're bound to see things very differently to her. Sleep on it, if you want my advice, and see what tomorrow brings. One thing's for sure, if he intends to leave Maisie, then your seeing him with his date will have forced his hand. Best remove the sticking plaster quickly rather than prolonging the agony.'

'The scumbag!' Callie screwed her eyes tight shut, threw back her head and growled. 'I've known him for years. I thought they adored one another. They have spectacular fights but equally passionate reconciliations. Things changed, priorities shifted as they inevitably do when children come along but still, I never would have believed him capable...'

'All men, and women for that matter, are capable of cheating. No one else knows what goes on inside a marriage.'

'I suppose not.' Callie let out another deep sigh. 'Anyway, don't worry about me. Just drop me off at home. I'll take your advice and sleep on it.'

'Your car?'

'Jason picked me up this morning because I knew I was going on with you.'

'Right.'

Jack fired up the engine and turned his car onto the road. Callie cursed Dan for putting a damper on their evening. An evening that she had thoroughly enjoyed. Jack had been right to suggest that being embraced by his family gave her a fresh perspective. It had been almost as comforting as being back with her grandmother.

Now Dan and his philandering had spoiled it all.

'I'm sure I've seen the woman he was with somewhere before,' Callie mused. 'I only briefly saw the back of her head and her profile but I'm absolutely sure I know her.' She shuddered. 'God forbid that she's a friend of Maisie's. Maisie told me the other day that she'd go after Dan's balls with blunt shears if she found out he was cheating on her. What she would do to the other woman doesn't bear thinking about.'

Jack shuddered as well and instinctively dropped a hand protectively into his lap. 'Brutal,' he said.

Callie grinned. 'You'd better believe it. Dan ought to know better than to mess with my friend, but I guess he's doing his thinking with an organ situated south of his brain.'

They arrived back at Callie's cottage sooner than she was ready to let Jack go. Comfortable with her own company as a general rule, tonight she didn't want to be alone.

'Will you come in?' she asked.

'Don't tempt me.' He cupped her face with one large hand and smiled. 'Best not. Your cat terrifies Odin.'

She laughed. 'Odin needs to learn to stand up for himself. Jinx is really... well, just a pussycat.'

'With claws.' His expressed softened. 'Hey, don't look like that. I'm trying to be noble here and trust me, it ain't easy.'

'You're right. Let's keep this professional.' She tossed her head, glad that it was too dark for him to see her burning face. 'I don't know what I was thinking. It must be the shock.' She opened the door and pushed it so hard that it bounced back on its hinges. 'Let me know if you hear from Blakely and I'll do the same. Thanks for dinner. Night.'

'Callie, I...'

She felt humiliated to have been rejected, even though she'd had no intention of propositioning him, which is what it must have sounded like.

Which is what it was, she accepted, mortified.

'What's gotten into me?' she asked aloud, as she took three attempts to insert her key into the lock.

'Here, let me.'

She hadn't heard Jack get out of his car. For a big man, he moved with remarkable stealth. He took the key from her hand and unlocked the door with ease. Odin slunk cautiously through it ahead of them.

'Come here.' He kicked the door closed and pulled her into his arms. Callie went willingly, wanting to forget about... everything.

He kissed her hard, deep, and with passion.

'I've been fighting the urge to do that all night,' he said in a husky voice when he finally let her up for air. 'You have no idea.'

Callie, feeling reckless and wanting to lose herself in mindless sex, wrapped her arms around his neck and tangled her fingers in hair that touched his shoulders. 'Then why stop?' she asked provocatively.

'You sure about this?' He released his hold on her. 'It has to be for the right reasons. I know you're upset about Logan, your friend's husband and... well, everything. I don't want to be used,' he added, making her smile. 'I'm no slut.'

'Speak for yourself!'

Jack chuckled, then howled when something sharp attached itself to his shin. 'Goddamn it!'

'Jinx, stop that!' Callie bent down and detached Jinx from Jack's leg. She carried her cat into the kitchen, where she fed him a belated supper. 'There are less aggressive ways of getting my attention,' she told him.

Jinx sent her a reproving look and applied himself to his dinner.

'Sorry about that.' Callie returned to her sitting room and found Jack examining his injuries. 'He can be a bit protective.' Odin, cowering behind the sofa, whined. 'Did he draw blood?'

'I'll live.' Jack laughed. 'It's kinda funny, when you think about it. I hope he did that, and a lot worse, to Logan.'

'I had to lock him out when Logan was here. He hated him.' Callie hugged her arms across her torso. 'Perhaps my cat is a better judge of character than I realised.'

'Hey, he just attacked me too.'

'Oh, that was just a friendly little scratch because he'd missed his dinner and likely blamed you. You'd know if he didn't like you. Trust me.'

'Good to know.' Jack opened his arms and Callie went to him. 'Now, where were we?'

Without waiting for an answer, Jack kissed her again. Ten minutes later, they were naked and in her bed. She couldn't help thinking about all the times she'd shared it with Logan and how she'd had to convince herself that she felt fulfilled.

Jack didn't leave her in any doubt in that respect.

Logan dressed in preparation for his meeting with the loan sharks, terrified of enduring another beating or worse but aware that he'd have to go or things would get even worse for him. It was hard to envisage what could be worse, but he knew they were vicious bastards who enjoyed inflicting pain. At least they'd told him to meet them in a high-end hotel, and would have chosen somewhere less public if he was in for a drubbing, wouldn't they? Their top dog, a suave individual by the name of Denning who dressed in designer Italian suits and turned heads everywhere he went, wouldn't be seen dead in an alley, Logan reminded himself. He left that sort of thing to his minions. Even so, the fact that the meeting was at the Grand implied that Denning would be there himself, so perhaps he really did have a proposition for Logan.

That possibility filled Logan with optimism. He hadn't come across a situation yet that he was incapable of exploiting. If Denning had a problem that required guile rather than brawn, then Logan was his man, no question.

He decided to check his messages before leaving. Having found nothing of interest on the first two phones, he switched on the third and felt his heart lurch when he heard Blakely's suave tone. He instinctively touched his ribs, which were still giving him hell. He felt a fresh wave of humiliation when he recalled how the older man had floored him with a single blow and then set about him with the toe of his boot.

In Logan's own defence, he'd been caught unawares. They'd been in the summerhouse in the grounds of Blakely's estate, where Delia's friend Davidson was supposed to warn them if anyone was likely to catch them at it – specifically if it was Blakely doing the catching. But the system had failed and Logan had been so shocked, not to mention erect and naked, when Blakely burst in on them. He'd beaten seven bales of shit out of Logan, who hadn't got in a single blow.

Delia, with her constant demands upon Logan's time, hadn't even been worth it. She'd been a lifeless lay, especially when compared to Callie's athletic inventiveness between the sheets. He'd got involved with her because he saw an opportunity. Blakely was wavering about involving himself with Logan's redevelopment plans and he thought that Delia would be able to persuade him. He only discovered after he'd taken up with her that Delia had no part in her husband's business affairs – she was strictly arm candy – and that it would seem highly suspicious if she suddenly took an interest in any of them. But by then it was too late. Delia had got her claws into him and wouldn't let go again until she was good and ready.

Would he never learn?

The silly bitch had actually assumed that when her husband ditched her, she and Logan would become an official couple. As if! It wasn't as though Blakely had let her take any of the family silver when he kicked her into touch. He'd had the sense to tie up their prenup good and tight in his favour. Delia, the fucking little gold digger, had just assumed that Logan would pick up the slack. He'd mentioned Portia and the kids, but she simply told him to walk out and let her daddy take care of them.

Now Blakely had his business brain back in gear, just in time to save Logan's arse. He'd always believed in fate, which is perhaps why he'd not been able to find his passport. If he had, he'd have scarpered by now and missed this opportunity to build bridges with Robert Blakely, who could do a damned sight more for him than his skinny soon-to-be-ex-wife ever had.

Life suddenly looked a hell of a lot brighter.

He wouldn't return Blakely's call quite yet. It had only been left a couple of hours ago and it would be a mistake to look too keen. He'd go to the meeting with Denning first, see what he wanted, buy himself some time and then get back to Blakely.

He was whistling for the first time in what seemed like forever as he left his dingy hotel room, walked out into light drizzle and hailed a cab to take him into the city.

* * *

Jack lay flat on his back, one arm draped around Callie's shoulders as he waited for his breathing to return to normal.

'That was brutal,' she said, leaning up on one elbow and kissing his shoulder.

'Hey, did I hurt you?'

'Absolutely not!' Her smile was wide and self-satisfied. 'That was by way of a compliment.'

'In that case, right back at you,' he said, smiling as well. 'I really didn't mean for that to happen, but I can't lie and say that I'm sorry it did.'

'You did try to resist.'

He chuckled. 'Not very hard.'

'Thanks,' she said, her expression turning serious. 'It was the perfect end to an almost perfect evening.'

Jack knew that her thoughts must have returned to her friend's cheating husband. He pulled her closer and ran a hand gently over her generous curves, looking to distract her, wondering how any man could prefer a stick-thin model to the more voluptuous type.

He was about to say something to reassure her when his phone rang. He reached for his discarded jeans. 'Best get it,' he said. 'It could be Blakely.' He retrieved his phone and put it on speaker. 'Yeah?' he said.

'Mr Carlisle? Jack Carlisle.'

Jack didn't recognise the voice. He glanced at Callie, who shrugged. 'Yes, who's this?'

'DI Renton, local CID. I'd like to arrange a time to talk to you about your partner, Logan Armitage.'

Jack sent Callie another sharp, questioning look. 'What about him?'

'I'd prefer to see you in person.'

Jack looked at his watch and frowned. This didn't sound good. 'At half ten on a Saturday night?'

'It is rather urgent.'

'Logan's missing, but I dare say his father-in-law has already told you that. I have no idea where he is. I'm anxious to find him myself.'

'In that case, I'm sure you wouldn't mind if a colleague and I dropped by. Perhaps we can help one another.'

'Have them come here,' Callie mouthed. He nodded, seeing the sense in that, surprised but pleased that she no longer felt the need to keep her relationship with Logan confidential.

'Okay, but I'm not at home. I'm with someone, a lady, who is equally keen to find Logan.'

'We've come across one or two of them already,' came the dry response. 'But okay, if that's the way you want it. Where are you?'

Jack gave him Callie's address, Renton assured him he'd been there within half an hour and cut the connection.

'What the hell was that all about?' Callie asked, sitting up and running a hand through her tangled hair.

'I have absolutely no idea, but CID making house calls at this time on a Saturday night cannot be good news.'

'You think he's done something criminal.' Callie flapped a hand. 'Forget I said that. We already know that he has. I should have speculated upon the possibility of his having done something that can be traced back to him. The police wouldn't want to talk to you at this time of night if it's just a case of a missing person.'

'Come on.' Jack levered himself from the bed and tapped her thigh. 'Race you to the shower.'

The police arrived within twenty minutes. Jack let Callie shower first and had only just emerged from it himself, with wet hair and a worried feeling, when the doorbell rang. Odin had emerged from the kitchen and stuck to his side, a soft growl rumbling at the back of his throat. Callie let the detectives in and introduced herself. Renton was probably in his early forties and looked as though he'd been round the block a few times. He introduced his colleague as DC Pettigrew, a young woman who looked like she ought still to be at school. She was a very pretty Asian woman, with alert eyes, but her attractiveness was marred by a near perpetual scowl and an obvious desire to prove herself to her boss.

'How do you know Logan Armitage?' she asked aggressively.

Jack walked into the hall as the question was posed, wondering how Callie would handle it. He knew that he would have taken exception to her surliness and soon discovered that Callie was of similar mind.

'Please come in and sit down,' she said with exaggerated politeness. 'This is Jack Carlisle,' she added, pointing at Jack for emphasis. DC Pettigrew's surliness evaporated when her gaze landed on Jack. 'I understand it is him you've come to see, DI Renton, and I will decide if my connections to Logan are relevant once I've learned why you are here at this time of night.' She smiled at the DI, still ignoring the young woman, whose cheeks had turned scarlet. 'Now, can I get either of you any refreshments?'

The DI smiled and declined for them both as he lowered himself into an armchair. The DC stood at the back of the room, notebook poised. Did they still take notes by hand, Jack wondered, in this day and age? Presumably so. Callie sat on the settee and Jack took the place beside her. They were both clothed but to Jack the aroma of sex lingered in the air, if only in his imagination, and he assumed that an astute detective of Renton's calibre wouldn't have to strain his brain too much in order to decide what he'd interrupted.

'What's this all about, Inspector?' Jack asked politely.

The inspector answered Jack's question with one of his own. 'How long has Mr Armitage been missing?' he asked.

'Surely Farquhar enlightened you,' Jack replied, conscious of the DC's gaze lingering on him from the back of the room. He inwardly groaned. That happened a lot, especially when he wasn't with Logan, and it was something he could do without.

'Cards on the table,' Renton said, studying him and Callie and appearing to decide to trust them. 'We had no idea that he'd done a runner until we tried to track him down. He wasn't at his house, so we tried his father-in-law, who enlightened us but didn't seem particularly concerned by his abrupt disappearance.'

'They don't get along,' Jack replied.

'How long has he been missing?' the DC asked.

'Four or five days,' Jack replied. 'He hasn't been seen by his wife, or at any of his regular haunts during that time.'

'Could he have left the country?' the DC asked. Her quick grasp of the possibilities made Jack see why she had become a detective at such a young age. There again, perhaps she was a graduate on their fast-track scheme.

'I have his passport, so unless he's obtained a fake one...' Jack turned back to the inspector. 'What's this all about?'

'This is all going to sound highly implausible,' Renton said, 'so I must ask for your discretion.'

'You're assured of it,' Jack replied. 'I'm keen to find my partner and, in case you're wondering, I wouldn't need much convincing to believe him capable of just about anything.'

'I can't tell you everything, but I can tell you that we have a number of informants amongst the criminal fraternity. The no-grassing-up-your-mates rule is strictly for the movies. You'd be surprised what lengths a few lowlifes will go to for the price of a pint. Anyway, we've heard from several different sources that there's a turf war brewing which might well result in the murder of someone important.'

'Who?'

'Murder?' Callie said at the same time, looking incredulous.

Renton held up a hand. 'We're not at liberty to disclose the who, at least not yet. You'll just have to take my word for it that the intelligence is sound.'

'But what's that to do with Logan?' Callie asked, sharing a bemused look with Jack. 'He's very ambitious. A scumbag, in fact.' She briefly outlined her relationship with Logan and brutally admitted that he'd scammed her.

'Did you report this?' the DC asked, looking less than sympathetic.

'Would you have believed me if I had?' she shot back. 'I can't prove that I didn't take that mortgage.'

'Perhaps you did.' The DI sent the woman a warning look and she didn't finish articulating her thoughts.

'Suffice it to say that money is his god,' Callie said, 'but I can't see him committing cold-blooded murder. If he is involved, though, are Jack and I in any danger?'

'What the hell has Logan got himself involved with?' Jack ran a hand through his damp hair. 'Who put the contract out? At least tell us that much.'

'A legend around these parts. A man by the name of Denning. Ever heard of him?'

'Holy fuck!' Jack breathed.

'I'll take that as a yes, then,' Renton replied grimly.

14

Logan arrived at the meeting a few minutes late, wishing he hadn't left all his bespoke suits behind. He felt underdressed and disadvantaged in Denning's sartorial presence. As always, the man was impeccably turned out. His salt and pepper hair was swept back from his forehead, still thick and abundant, and he was freshly shaved. Denning, casually seated in a huge armchair in a quiet part of the hotel's foyer, looked up at Logan, swept his person with a scathing look, then indicated the chair across from him.

His two minders stood a little apart, watching everything and discouraging anyone else from getting too close. An elderly couple eyed the vacant settee on Denning's left, then met the eye of one of the minders and hastily turned away.

'You're late.' Denning picked up a brandy balloon, swirled the liquid around, then slowly swallowed it down. He clicked his fingers and a waiter materialised from nowhere to fetch him a refill. The fact that Logan wasn't asked if he would like a drink didn't bode well but then, he had known from the outset that this was no social call.

'Just a few minutes behind schedule,' he said. 'Sorry. There was nowhere to park.'

Denning's expression darkened, scaring the shit out of Logan, who now regretted indulging in such a pointless lie. Of course Denning would have been watching him and would know that he hadn't driven here. And if he had, the hotel offered extensive parking. Hell, Denning probably even knew the name of the scummy hotel Logan had been reduced to staying at. He told himself that he'd done so in an effort to remain under the radar but since he didn't believe it himself, there was zero chance of Denning falling for the lie.

'How can I help?' he asked, crossing one leg over the other and trying to appear relaxed and in control when his insides were literally churning with fear. He linked his fingers together, wishing he had a glass to hold. It would have given him something to do with his hands. Denning's dead fish eyes gave him the creeps. There weren't many men who truly terrified him but Denning sure as hell qualified in that regard. Logan knew it was important not to let his fear show and struggled to hold onto his dignity. 'You said something about working off my debt.'

'Right.' Denning's new drink arrived and he took his time savouring it, dragging the moment out and stretching Logan's nerves right along with it. 'You are acquainted with a man who is causing me a little inconvenience.'

'I am? Who would that be?'

'You hoped to go into business with him but screwing his wife put the kibosh on the deal, which is why you had to come to me, cap in hand.'

Logan had actually gone to Denning for a substantial loan before asking Blakely to invest. He knew that if he gave the impression of being able to afford the site before inviting investors to partake then it created confidence in his abilities. It was a ploy he had utilised before, albeit not on such a large scale. But still, he had thought it foolproof and had been so confident of Blakely's involvement that he'd been convinced he would be able to repay Denning within a fortnight.

He could see from Denning's scathing look that he thought Logan was an idiot for letting his libido take precedence over a lucrative business opportunity. Logan couldn't help but agree with him, especially now that he was in so deep with Denning that he couldn't see any daylight above his head.

'I'm no longer on Blakely's Christmas card list,' Logan said, attempting to make a joke of the situation. No one smiled.

'Even so, I hear tell you have a score to settle with the man.' He gave Logan's ribcage a significant look. Fucking hell, did anything get past him?

'I got careless,' Logan replied, with what he hoped would come across as an equally careless shrug.

'Are you aware that Blakely is branching out into money-lending, undercutting the current market leaders?'

'Fucking hell!' This time Logan said the words, rather than merely thinking them. 'He's obviously got a death wish.'

'My thoughts precisely.' A reptilian smile crept across Denning's face. 'I would go so far as to say, in the vernacular, that he's bang out of order. In actual fact, he and I go back a long way, but not many people know that.' Denning leaned one elbow on the arm of his chair and waved the long fingers of one hand in the air in an elegant gesture, revealing thin gold cufflinks set with what looked like Ceylon sapphires. 'We had a difference of opinion and went our separate ways, managing not to tread upon one another's turf.' He allowed a significant pause, his expression turning dark and forbidding. 'Until now.'

'You think he's broadened his horizons in a deliberate attempt to undermine you?'

'I am absolutely sure of it, and you are responsible.'

'Me?' Logan jerked forward in his chair and pointed an index finger at his own chest. 'How? Why...'

'Robert Blakely is not a man that it's wise to cross. I hate to admit it, but he's got as many ways of finding things out as I do. He will know by now that I loaned you the money to purchase Clydesdale Mews. A sweat deal that you fucked up by... well, by fucking his wife,' Denning added, his voice hardening. 'And Blakely now holds me equally responsible for the collapse of his marriage.'

'But you didn't...'

'No, I didn't and nor should you have done.' His expression radiated hostility. 'And so it's down to you to sort it out.'

'How?' Logan spread his hands. 'You know that I would never deliberately do anything to make your life more difficult, Mr Denning.'

'And yet you did, simply because you're incapable of keeping your prick in your pants. If Blakely gets away with muscling onto my turf, I will lose respect and others will move in. Weakness is infectious and that cannot be permitted to happen.' He leaned forward and jabbed Logan in the chest with his forefinger. 'So you will have to take Blakely out.'

'Me? Kill him?'

Logan's shoulders slumped as he let out a long breath. He had imagined that Denning wanted his nemesis badly beaten, in which case Logan would have obliged, even though violence wasn't ordinarily his style. But murder? He shook his head.

'I can't. I don't know how to kill a man.'

Logan knew that in making that admission he sounded weak, pathetic, in front of these hard men. He was almost wetting himself, now that he knew what they wanted of him and again laced his shaking fingers together.

'Besides, I wouldn't be able to get anywhere near him.' Except, of course, he could, he reminded himself, thinking of the message he'd just picked up. But Denning couldn't possibly know about that. Could he?

'Your lady friend can help you there.' Denning clicked his fingers at one of his minions. The man disappeared and returned very quickly with Delia Blakely, looking drop-dead gorgeous. She had a minder of her own with her.

'Hello, darling,' Delia said in her deep, husky voice that had once turned Logan on but now left him feeling as cold as he knew the woman herself to be.

'Delia. What the hell...' Logan half rose from his chair but at a look from one of Denning's minders, he quickly sank back into it.

'Delia holds you responsible for being thrown out of her comfortable home,' Denning said conversationally. 'And expects you to right matters.'

Logan knew it would be a waste of breath to point out that he hadn't wanted to screw Delia on home turf but she had insisted. He wondered now if it had been an elaborate set-up. He only had Delia's unreliable word for the fact that she hadn't expected Blakely home. For some obscure reason, perhaps she had wanted to be caught in the act. Why was less clear to him.

'Delia was my spy in the opposition's camp and you spoiled it all, causing me a great deal of inconvenience.'

Delia perched herself on the arm of Denning's chair, crossed her long legs provocatively, causing her short skirt to ride up even higher, and draped her own arm around his shoulders. 'Sorry, Uncle,' she said, pouting.

'Uncle?' Logan's eyes bugged. He had no idea that Denning *had* any family. He had certainly never married, or dated members of either sex, as far as anyone knew. Rumours abounded about his being asexual, but no one had the balls to ask him outright if it was true.

'Delia will arrange for Davidson to let you in,' Denning said casually. 'He's one of ours. How you do the deed is for you to decide. We'll supply you with whatever weapon you'd prefer to use and the rest is up to you.' Denning leaned forward, the planes of his face lean and hard. 'Do it right and we're even. Fuck it up and... well, don't fuck it up if you want to live to see another dawn.'

The teasing smile playing about Delia's lips caused the penny to drop. Delia had been cut off from Blakely without a penny, but they weren't divorced yet. Presumably, if he died before that divorce became absolute, she would be able to claim a share of his estate. Clearly, he had underestimated her, fallen for the dumb blonde routine, whereas she was almost as sharp and calculating as her uncle – and equally lethal. Denning had probably persuaded her to make a play for Blakely and then install her own people inside his domain. Davidson was still employed by Blakely, so he obviously didn't suspect a thing.

Clever.

He inclined his head in admiration as his thoughts turned to self-preservation. Warning Blakely of the danger, which had been his original intention, no longer seemed viable, unless they met in a public place. Logan was pretty sure that Davidson would have Blakely's study bugged in some way that was undetectable. Maybe he'd have to go through with it. It would be the perfect way to extract himself from the mire. His problem was that he didn't think he'd be capable of killing another human being without bottling it. Besides, if Davidson was in the house, on the spot so to speak, and Blakely trusted him, he was the obvious man for the job.

But Denning so enjoyed his games. This was his way of

teaching Logan that no one crossed him and got away with it. Well, there was only one thing for it. He'd have to grab his fake passport the moment it was ready and disappear. It was a shame that he couldn't meet with Blakely and resurrect their plans for Clydesdale Mews but on balance he'd prefer to remain breathing.

'We have a room booked here for you,' Denning told him. 'Charge anything you need. You'll only be here for a day or two at most. I think you will find the surroundings more comfortable than your current abode.' The suggestion of a smile touched Denning's thin, cruel lips.

A couple of days? How the fuck did they think he could devise a plan to murder a man and get away with it, much less carry it out, in a couple of days? Still, it didn't matter. A couple of days would be more than enough for him to collect his passport and take his leave of England for good.

'Oh, and by the way, one of my men will be keeping you company all the while.' Logan couldn't prevent the despair from seeping into his expression. Denning actually smiled, a cat taunting his prey. 'Montague here will take the first watch,' he added, jerking a thumb in the direction of the man who'd escorted Delia into the room.

'Aw, Dan, I had plans for us tonight,' Delia said, blowing him a kiss.

Logan barely heard the exchange. Instead, his blood ran cold. Dan Montague. He'd heard that name frequently and it wasn't a common one. Dan Montague was Callie's best friend's husband. They had never met but this couldn't be a coincidence. How the fuck had Callie managed such fast and brutal revenge? He never would have thought her capable.

* * *

Callie looked directly at DI Renton. 'I'm not sure what you expect either of us to tell you,' she said. 'But I would be interested to know why you imagine that Logan has reinvented himself as an assassin.'

'He borrowed the money to purchase Clydesdale Mews from Denning,' Jack said musingly before Renton could answer her.

'That is our understanding,' Renton replied. 'And because he isn't in a position to pay it back, Denning owns him.'

'Are you attempting to find Logan in order to prevent the murder or to have him grass Denning up?' Jack asked.

Renton acknowledged the astuteness of the question by inclining his head. 'Naturally, we are keen to prevent any laws being broken but I won't deny that Denning has been on our radar for years and we've never been able to get him for anything. Not even a parking ticket, since he never drives himself. But he is single-handedly responsible for a great deal of the organised crime that goes down in this neck of the woods. If we can get him, then the rest of the criminal fraternity will...'

'Jump in and fill the void,' Jack said, flapping a hand. 'Hardly seems worth the effort.'

'I was about to say, they'll be disorganised, but I take your point. However, we have to try to shake them up.'

Jack nodded. 'Well, you would. You're paid to keep us safe.'

'I don't see how we can help if you aren't willing to tell us who the target is,' Callie said. 'Is it anyone we know? Not that that's likely, but still...'

'The problem is, we don't actually know ourselves,' Renton admitted. 'Denning is too careful to talk in front of anyone other than his inner trusted circle, none of whom would turn on him. All our informant can tell us is that someone's pissed Denning off big time and he wants him out of the way, but that's all he knows.'

'You must have some idea,' Callie protested. 'Presumably, it's one of Denning's business rivals. Who are they?'

'We can't give that sort of information out to civilians,' DC Pettigrew snapped.

'And yet you have come here, asking for our help,' Callie replied in an even tone. 'How's that working out for you?'

'It was a long shot coming here,' Renton said, standing. 'Between you and me, I don't much care if the lowlifes kill one another off but my superintendent takes a different view, especially when a man of Armitage's calibre gets drawn in as a patsy. It sounds as if he's a bit of a player himself, given what he did to you, Ms Devereaux. Even so, if you hear from him, please be sure to let us know.'

'Here's my card, in case you need to talk to me about anything,' DC Pettigrew said, thrusting the card in question into Jack's hand.

Callie found the situation amusing and didn't bother to hide her smile. 'I'll show you out,' she said.

She returned to the sitting room once the detectives had left and shot Jack a disbelieving look.

'Curiouser and curiouser. What the hell are we supposed to make of that?' she asked. 'I don't believe they expected us to know where Logan is.'

'Probably not. They wanted to be sure that we weren't in it with him, or should I say they wanted to make sure that I wasn't up to my grubby neck in Logan's shenanigans. They didn't know about your involvement with Logan until you enlightened them.'

'No, I guess not.'

Jack took her hand and squeezed it. 'In spite of everything,' he said, 'I didn't think Logan could fall quite as low as Renton just implied.'

'If you go to bed with thieves...' Callie sighed. 'It sounds as though he's between a rock and a hard place and I hope he's enjoying the view. I'd be less than human if I didn't revel in his current circumstances.'

'Yeah, but I feel like a prize fool for being taken in by him for so many years.'

'Why didn't you mention our deal with Blakely?' Callie asked.

'I thought about it, but I figured that if we can pull that meeting off quickly then we can take Logan in ourselves and prevent him from actually killing anyone. I know it would give me considerable satisfaction to turn him in and I'm sure you feel the same way. He'd do time and spend it looking over his shoulder, worried about the prospect of one of Denning's men getting to him. That would be a worse punishment in some respects.'

'Just so long as Blakely isn't his intended target.'

'I doubt it. As far as I'm aware, he's a legitimate businessman.'

'Would you know if he wasn't?'

'Good point but either way, Logan won't kill him if we're there. We won't give him the chance.'

'Are we unintentionally involving ourselves in a murder plot?' Callie asked with a worried frown.

'By going after Logan?' Jack shook his head. 'I doubt it very much. Logan has no stomach for violence. Anything he's doing, he'll have been forced into by Denning and as far as I'm aware, that person has no axe to grind with either of us. Even so, we need to be careful.'

'Right.' Callie hid a yawn behind her hand.

'Come on.' Jack took her hand and pulled her to her feet.

'Where are we going?'

'You're going to bed. You're beat.'

'Stay with me.'

Jack grinned. 'I thought you'd never ask.'

* * *

Logan felt like he was back at his despised boarding school, being disciplined by one of the bullies who went by the name of prefect for some perceived transgression of the rules. Being a good-looking kid had drawn all the sickos to him and he still sometimes had nightmares when he recalled what they'd done to him.

Clearly sensing his unease, Montague stuck close by his side, grinning. 'Not a nice feeling, is it, being played at your own game?' he asked.

'You're one to talk,' Logan snapped, standing back as Montague unlocked a room with the key card. He stepped inside, too worried to appreciate the opulence; opulence that until a week ago he would have taken for granted. The depths that he had fallen to in that short space of time weren't entirely lost on Logan and already his mind had gone into overdrive, trying to think of ways to save his skin. 'Okay, get lost,' he said abruptly. 'I'll take it from here.'

Montague's grin widened as he closed the door. 'You heard the boss,' he said. 'I'm your new best friend, at least until someone relieves me in the morning.'

'I don't need a babysitter. I'm not suicidal and know better than to cross Denning.'

Montague sat in an armchair, stretched his legs out in front of him and yawned, not bothering to respond.

'Seriously? You're going to spend the night in that chair?' Logan gaped at the man. 'Does Maisie know that you associate with gangsters?'

If he'd hoped to compromise the man by admitting that he'd recognised his name, Logan was to be disappointed.

'Given what you did to Callie, I'd be a little more careful about throwing around veiled threats, if I were you.'

Logan only just stopped himself from protesting that he'd always planned to pay Callie back because... well, because he hadn't. For the first time in his entire life, he didn't feel good about what he'd done. Even being asked to murder a man in cold blood didn't affect his conscience in the way that Callie's situation did whenever he allowed himself to think about it. Callie had got under his skin in a manner that still bemused Logan and she hadn't deserved what he'd done to her.

He hadn't needed to do it either, not really. And if he hadn't given way to temptation, he'd still have a bolthole that no one knew about in this, his hour of need. Stupid, stupid, stupid!

Without saying another word, Logan withdrew the only phone he'd brought with him from his pocket and headed for the bathroom, and privacy. Montague was on his feet, blocking the door, before Logan reached it.

'I'll take that,' he said, holding out his hand for the phone.

'I'm not allowed to make calls?' he asked, incredulous.

'Not in private. Feel free to call whoever you like from in here but I need to know who it is in advance.'

'I'm not desperate enough to turn Denning in, if that's what you're thinking.'

Montague pocketed Logan's only means of communication with the outside world, other than the hotel phone, and shot Logan a look of loathing. 'You really don't want to know what I'm thinking, not when it comes to you.'

'And yet you're no better than me.' Logan had had enough of being bullied and manipulated. 'You've got a wife and kids depending on you and yet you turn to a career with a criminal enterprise.'

Montague cocked a brow. 'How are your wife and kids doing?'

Logan didn't have an answer to hand so threw himself on the bed and switched the TV on, just to avoid looking at Montague's smirking face. He was up shit creek and he knew it, especially now that he had no means of answering Blakely's message.

He would have to find a way to get his phone back. Montague was bound to fall asleep at some point and then there would be an opportunity.

15

Callie woke early to the sound of someone moving around in her kitchen and the feel of a warm body in bed beside her. She sat up abruptly, momentarily alarmed, until she glanced at the slumbering and very enticing form of Jack lying flat on his stomach beside her. Who could be in the kitchen was less obvious.

'Wake up!' She gave Jack a nudge in the ribs.

He turned over and a slow, lazy grin spread across his face. 'Morning, gorgeous,' he said. 'Something I can do for you?'

'Not that!' she hissed. 'There's someone downstairs.'

The flirtation immediately left his expression. 'Stay here!'

He leapt naked from the bed, retrieved his discarded jeans from the floor and pulled them on.

'Do you think it could be Logan?' she asked.

'Only if he has a death wish. He'll have seen my car outside.' Odin, who'd been sound asleep on the floor, lifted his head and wagged his tail. 'You're supposed to be an early warning system,' Jack told him.

Callie jumped from her bed as well and pulled on an oversized T-shirt. Jack rolled his eyes and refrained from asking her to remain behind for a second time. Just as well because Callie was tired of having her space invaded and fully intended to go on the offensive. She picked up a baseball bat that had always lived by the side of her bed. She couldn't remember how it got there, or why.

Jack decided against stealth and ran down the stairs two at a time, with Odin ahead of him. He followed the sounds coming from the kitchen, as did Callie. As soon as she smelled coffee brewing, she inwardly groaned.

'Hang on!' she said in an urgent undertone. 'It's only Maisie. I don't want her to see…'

'Well, good morning!' Callie could hear the smile in Maisie's voice as Jack burst into the kitchen, bare-chested, with a classic case of bed-head. 'Hope I didn't disturb anything. I thought I was being quiet.'

'What are you doing here so early?' Callie asked, strolling into the kitchen and trying to seem nonchalant.

'Nothing as interesting as you two have been getting up to, obviously.'

'Grow up,' Callie said, grinning at her friend. 'Is the coffee brewed yet?'

'I thought the smell might get through to you. Nothing else did. I knocked, you know.' Callie and Jack both sent Odin an accusatory look. 'When no one answered, I used my key.'

'Of course you did.' Callie rolled her eyes as she took a seat at the table, wondering if now would be a good time to tell her about Dan. Would there ever be a good time? Was she being cowardly, wanting to break the news when Jack was there to cushion the blow? 'Thanks,' she said, when Maisie plonked a mug of coffee in front of her and repeated the process with Jack. 'You look chipper this morning,' Callie added, wondering if she would dare to burst the bubble.

'That's because Dan has finally got some gainful employment,' she said, joining them at the table.

Callie's gaze clashed with Jack's. 'That's great. Doing what?'

'Bodyguarding. I know,' she added, taking her turn to roll her eyes. 'It's not what he planned but it is well paid, and you have to admit that all that time spent in the gym hasn't been wasted. He's fit and strong and the martial arts are a bonus. Anyway, it's done no end of good for his self-esteem and for our marriage.' She grinned unselfconsciously. 'You're not the only one who got lucky this morning, Callie.'

Callie stuck her fingers in her ears. 'Too much information.'

'Well, I can't remember the last time he rose to the occasion so enthusiastically, so who am I to complain about his new career path?'

'Who's he guarding?' Jack asked.

'He's not allowed to tell me. Makes it sound like he's signed the official secrets act.' She leaned an elbow on the table and sighed. 'Anyway, that's where he's been going at all sorts of weird and wonderful times. They were trying him out and he was sworn to secrecy. He wasn't even allowed to tell me. It is *such* a relief to know that I've been worrying about nothing.'

Callie smiled and tried to pretend that she was happy for her friend. She glanced at Jack and he gave an imperceptible shake of his head. Callie was happy to defer the revelation but also felt cowardly.

'If you were enjoying yourself so much, why are you here at this ungodly hour?' Callie asked.

'You clearly don't have kids.'

'Good point.'

'Actually, Dan didn't come home until a couple of hours ago. I decided I'd had enough and that I'd tackle him on the subject of the other woman I was convinced he was seeing, which is when he told me about his new line of work. It explains so much.'

'Did he get paid yet?' Callie asked diplomatically.

Maisie's sunny smile faded. 'You don't think this is kosher?'

'Just playing devil's advocate.'

'Well, actually, he has been paid. I'd stopped checking our account, it was too depressing. Anyway, there's now a nice healthy balance on the plus side. It went in yesterday, which is when his employment became official.'

'Then I'm happy for you,' Callie said, attempting to summon up a smile. There was an outside chance, she supposed, that Dan had been employed to look after the woman they'd seen him with, although she couldn't think of any reason why she'd need a bodyguard. Especially not one who kissed his client in a public place and didn't seem to be paying a great deal of attention to her security.

Something definitely wasn't right.

'Anyway, I left him force-feeding the monsters their breakfast and came to tell you what I've found in your books, Jack.'

'That was quick,' he replied.

'Had to do something to distract my mind from what I thought of as Dan's shenanigans while I waited for him to come home.' She chuckled. 'I had a right go at him. Gave it to him with both barrels. I mean, he was out almost all night, didn't tell me where he was going and didn't answer his phone. It's not on and I told him so in no uncertain terms. Anyway.' She grinned. 'The make-up sex was phenomenal.'

'The books,' Callie reminded her.

'It's okay. I wasn't about to share all the gory details!' She glanced at Jack's rather impressive chest and grinned. 'Although, I will if you do.'

'Behave!'

Callie smiled as her friend as she spoke, thinking that Jack was right to suggest holding back on telling her about her husband's little *tête-à-tête*. Let Maisie feel good about herself, at least until they got to the bottom of things. One thing Callie would put good money on, though, was that whatever Dan was up to, it wasn't strictly legal. She was also aware that Dan had seen her and probably assumed that Callie would rat him out. Could that be why he'd come up with the story about bodyguarding? Except, if he'd been paid a hefty wage and it was in their bank account, there had to be some truth to his claims. Besides, Maisie hadn't said anything about Callie having seen Dan, so he was probably banking on the fact that she'd keep her mouth shut.

'Dan knows where you are, does he?' she asked casually.

Maisie shrugged. 'Where else would I go?'

'Good point.' She leaned forward.

'I'm sorry to say that Logan is more of a louse than I gave him credit for being, which is saying something. His accounting has become more creative and less plausible and significantly so over the past few months.'

'How much has he taken me for?' Jack asked in a surprisingly calm, resigned tone.

Callie blinked when Maisie gave them a ballpark figure. Jack swallowed and said nothing.

'Sorry,' Maisie said. 'Are you any nearer to finding him?'

'That's a hell of a wedge,' Jack said, 'but nowhere near enough to purchase that development site at Clydesdale Mews, so I reckon we're right to assume that he borrowed from some dodgy characters.'

Callie nodded, wanting to grasp his hand and take her turn to reassure him. She resisted the urge. Their relationship was still new, undefined, complicated, and she was determined not to repeat the same mistakes she'd made with Logan. Not that there was anything to compare between the two of them, but still, once bitten and all that. In the end it was he who reached for her hand and Callie was glad.

'Denning,' Callie said, nodding. 'It makes sense.'

'Who's Denning?' Maisie frowned. 'I've heard that name somewhere, and quite recently.' She threw back her head and closed her eyes. 'Dan!' Her eyes flew open again. 'I heard Dan on his mobile talking to someone by that name. I remember because he was being so deferential, which isn't like him.'

'Dan is working for a loan shark?' Callie asked, wishing the words back the moment they passed her lips.

* * *

Logan's frustration increased when Dan Montague finally fell asleep in his chair at about two in the morning, snoring softly. But he'd put Logan's sodding phone in his jeans pocket and there was no way in living hell that Logan would be able to get to it. There was an outside chance that he'd be able to use the landline in the room but he didn't know Blakely's number by heart. Montague had positioned his chair so that Logan would have to climb over him in order to get to the door.

It was fucking hopeless!

He threw himself on the bed, fully clothed, head thumping, hungry and very worried. It seemed Denning was deadly serious and really did expect him to kill Blakely. Logan had never fired a gun in his life and didn't think he'd have the bottle to stab a man, not even if it was a case of self-preservation, which this had every sign of becoming. He tried to sleep, hoping that a resolution would come to him, but gave up after half an hour of tossing and turning and went to the minibar instead. He helped himself to a scotch and downed it in one long swallow, enjoying the burn as it trickled down his oesophagus and pooled in the pit of his empty stomach. It made him feel light-headed but did nothing to resolve his problems.

He retained the majority of his ire for Delia Blakely. What a conniving bitch! It came as a severe blow to Logan's ego to discover that she'd set him up. She'd never stopped complaining about Blakely's miserly ways when they'd been together and dropped the odd suggestion about doing away with him so that they could be together and enjoy all his lovely wealth. Logan hadn't taken her seriously but understood now that she'd targeted him for that reason. As to sharing the spoils with him...

Logan shook his head, well aware that he'd been a means to an end. He'd seen the way she looked at Dan Montague as though she could eat him whole and, bizarrely, felt righteous indignation on behalf of Callie's friend. He almost smiled at the irony, increasingly frantic to get hold of Blakely and warn him. Denning had kept his family connections, such as they were, a closely guarded secret. Blakely wouldn't have known that the woman he married was his nemesis's niece, deliberately planted in his house to spy on him, and Logan had a feeling that he would pay handsomely for that information, and to know that Denning had taken a contract out on him.

All he had to do was find a way to reach him and a largely sleepless night had failed to provide him with any bright ideas in that respect.

A tap at the door woke Logan from a light doze. His head reeled as he sat up and glanced at the clock. Five in the morning. With the dawn came realisation of the obvious. Keep it sodding simple! All he needed to do was to make a call to Blakely and say that he was willing to let him have the Clydesdale Mews site at a bargain price. None of Denning's minions would cotton to the fact that Blakely wouldn't ordinarily give him the time of day.

None other than Montague, perhaps, but he'd just woken and opened the door to his replacement.

'Have fun,' he said, handing Logan's phone to the man. 'And watch him closely. He's a slippery bastard.'

'Yeah, yeah.'

The new guy, more brawn than brains from what little Logan had seen of him, settled into Montague's abandoned chair and yawned. He didn't bother to block the door but Logan wasn't about to try getting past him. Instead, he yawned as well and asked the guy if he fancied some breakfast. Davis was a long-standing and trusted member of Denning's crew, Logan knew, and a man who was capable of breaking another man's neck with his bare hands. He had probably performed that service for Denning on more than one occasion and Logan couldn't help wondering why he hadn't called upon him on this occasion too.

'Yeah, get the works,' Davis said, stretching.

Logan dialled room service and did precisely that.

The food arrived after about twenty minutes, at which point Davis came alive and did justice to the majority of it.

'You decided how to approach Blakely yet?' Davis asked.

'Give me a chance!'

'How long do you need? You've had all night to think about it. The boss will want to know. And he'll want to know how you'll explain Montague away when you take him with you.'

'You what?' Logan dropped the slice of toast he'd been toying with onto his plate. 'First I've heard of taking him.'

'I expect the boss was testing you. Blimey, he ain't stupid. He'd never have survived in his line of work for one minute if he trusted shysters like you. I mean, what's to stop you marching in on Blakely and grassing Denning up?' Davis scratched his stubbly jaw. 'Mind you, you'd have to have a death wish to do something that daft. Denning is a vicious bastard on a good day. Cross him and you'll wish you'd never been born.'

Logan was starting to feel that way already. 'Why Montague?' he asked.

David shrugged a beefy shoulder. 'No idea. The boss will have his reasons, I expect.'

Logan assumed that Denning must know about his fling with Callie, and what he'd done to her. He would also be aware that Montague was her best friend's husband, although how he'd found that out and managed to get Montague onto his payroll remained a mystery. Either way, he appeared to enjoy exploiting the animosity that had sprung up between the two men. Davis was by far the scarier but for some reason it was Montague whom he truly feared.

'I had no idea the boss had any family,' Logan said, fishing, 'or that Delia Blakely was his niece.' He forced a chuckle. 'Got to hand it to him, the man has balls of steel.'

Davis guffawed. 'You didn't believe all that uncle/niece crap, did you? Christ, you are gullible. Delia is one of the girls he used to run who showed a bit more nous than most. He reckoned she was wasted serving punters, even if she did charge a fortune, so he groomed her for greater things. Blakely liked what he saw when she passed through a hotel foyer apparently, which is when the boss came up with his brainwave.' Davis sent Logan a smug look, probably well aware that he'd been played by her too. 'You have to hand it to our Delia, she took to her new role like a duck to the proverbial.'

Logan hadn't even been aware that Denning ran a string of escorts but supposed he shouldn't have been surprised. The man had fingers in every lucrative pie in town.

'Tell you what,' he said. 'Let me have my phone and I'll simply call the guy. I can be plausible when I need to be, play on his greed. I'll put it on speaker so you can hear everything but he will need to see that the call's come from my mobile or he'll get suspicious.' It was a risky ploy, but Logan had to do something.

'Okay. I guess.' David produced Logan's phone from his pocket and passed it to him. 'No funny business, mind. The boss has told me to do whatever it takes to keep you in line.' He cracked his knuckles. 'Don't piss me off.'

'Shit!' Logan tried to switch his phone on but it was dead. 'Got a charger?'

'What do I look like, a helpline? Use mine.'

'I don't have his number. It's in my phone.'

'Well, then. We'd best go out and find what you need.' Davis hauled himself to his feet. He was a big man but the bulk was all muscle; not an ounce of fat on him that Logan could see. It would be pointless trying to leg it once they got outside. Davis would catch him, no trouble, and probably beat seven bales of shit out of him for putting him to the trouble. Besides, Logan had nowhere to go.

'There's a phone accessory shop round the corner,' David told him. 'Hurry up, we ain't got all fucking day.'

* * *

'I'm sorry,' Callie said when she and Jack were alone again.

'About what?' he asked, smiling at her, thinking how cute she looked in her oversized T-shirt, and absolutely nothing else. He felt himself getting aroused by the view.

'At Logan having shafted you, obviously,' she said impatiently. 'We ought to tell Renton what we now know, just to cover your backside.'

'In due course.' He sighed. 'Nothing Maisie told me came as a big surprise; not after the initial shock of discovering that Logan had been ripping the company off for years. I thought it might have been even worse, truth to tell.'

She remained at the table, leaning her elbow on it and her face on her splayed hand, her expression contemplative. Jinx came in through the cat flap, causing Odin to whimper and hide behind a chair. Callie smiled, tugged at the dog's ears and then got up, responding to her cat's loud demands for food.

'Delia Blakely!' Callie turned to face Jack, waving the fork she'd used to decant her cat's food in the air, looking triumphant.

'What about her?'

'That's who Dan was with. I told you I thought I recognised her, and I've just remembered why. She didn't make herself inconspicuous at that wedding.'

'Blimey.' Jack rubbed his chin. 'Are you absolutely sure?'

'Positive,' Callie assured him.

'Maisie's husband being involved with Delia Blakely worries me,' Jack said when Callie returned to the table. 'How the hell?'

'Me too. It can't be a coincidence, can it?'

'I very much doubt it. But why would Delia Blakely require a bodyguard?'

'Not telling Maisie what we saw was hard. I felt like a crap friend from keeping it from her, but I suppose there *could* be an innocent explanation, couldn't there?'

'Callie, they were practically eating one another's faces,' Jack pointed out.

'I know.' She sighed. 'It's getting scary.'

'Don't worry, we have Odin to protect us.'

'That's what's so scary.' They both laughed.

Callie got up again, rummaged in the fridge, and withdrew the ingredients for a fry-up. Jack watched her, thinking he could watch her graceful and economical movements all day.

'Maisie mentioned that Dan spends a lot of time in the gym. Do you happen to know which one?' he asked.

'The one down by the canal, I think.' In the process of cracking eggs into a bowl, she glanced over her shoulder at him. 'Why do you ask?'

'Because Denning owns a gym, out of which he deals in all sorts of stuff, and I think it's that one. In fact, I know it is. All his crew hang out there, so...'

'So, that's probably how Dan got involved with bodyguarding, or whatever it is that's he's really doing. Shit!'

'Seems that way.'

'How can you sound so casual?' Callie demanded to know, agitatedly waving a spatula at him.

'No point getting all steamed up, babe.' He winked at her. 'Well, not over Denning, anyway.'

Callie smiled, shook her head at him, and returned her attention to her frying pan. 'You have a one-track mind.'

'Didn't hear you complaining last night,' he replied, probably sounding as smug as he felt. He'd worried that his performance wouldn't match up to Logan's and that she'd be disappointed, but the opposite appeared to be the case and made Jack feel like he could walk on water.

'Looking for marks out of ten?' she asked, still with her back to him.

'Since you mention it, how did I do?'

'I guess you were adequate.'

'Adequate?' Jack crept up behind her and snagged an arm around her waist. 'Take that back at once, woman, or there will be consequences.'

She giggled but shook her head. Being a man of his word, Jack turned the gas off beneath the frying pan and lifted her, protesting half-heartedly, from the floor. Somehow she finished up flat on her back on the kitchen table and Jack set about proving his more than adequate abilities.

'Well?' he asked, breathing heavily as he pinned her arms above her head with one hand and agitated her clit with the probing fingers of the other.

'Okay, you're better than average. Better than a ten. Better than anyone I've ever had before. Now, please, finish what you started and stop being such a tease!'

'Well, since you ask so persuasively.'

Jack kissed her long and deep once it was over, then patted her backside and sent her off to the shower. He knew that if he joined her in it then there'd be a repeat performance and they'd never get anything done. He never seemed to be able to get enough of Callie, which ought to concern him. He wasn't ready for a commitment of any sort as things stood, at least not until he found out where he now stood financially and if he was likely to be prosecuted for something he had nothing to do with, for that matter. He barely had a penny to his name so couldn't sustain a relationship, even if he'd wanted to. But something other than common sense took over whenever he was with her. Perhaps it was just the gloss of a new date, but somehow he doubted it.

He'd never known a feeling like it ever before.

He took a quick shower once she'd finished, managing to get back downstairs again before her and rescue the residue of the fry-up. He had the eggs scrambled by the time she appeared and bread in the toaster.

'Sorry, I had to take a call about work.'

'No problem. Here, sit yourself down.'

'I could get used to this.'

'All part of the service, madam.'

They ate mostly in silence, with Odin watching enviously.

'Will he eat cat food?' Callie asked. 'The poor chap looks starving.'

'He'll eat anything.'

Callie got up and decanted the contents of a tin of cat food into a bowl. Odin had wolfed it down and was licking his lips before Callie had resumed her seat.

'Your dog has an identity crisis,' she said, smiling.

'Where food's concerned, he's species-fluid.'

'What do we do now? About Blakely, I mean, and Dan's connection to his ex?' she asked, her smile fading.

'Well,' Jack said, pushing his empty plate aside and delving into his pocket for his mobile. 'I guess we call him and arrange a meeting. This isn't the sort of stuff we can discuss over the phone.'

16

Logan's opportunity came unexpectedly. The hotel's foyer was crowded with conference attendees, all in costume. Some sort of themed exhibition, Logan assumed. All that mattered was that he and Davis got separated when a woman carrying a tray of coffees dropped them right at Davis's feet, causing mayhem in the foyer as everyone scattered. She screamed at Davis, blaming him for an accident that she had caused, waving her arms around and clearly embarrassing the big man.

Logan legged it, heading for the exit without stopping to consider the consequences. He heard Davis calling out to him but he was swallowed up by the crowd, whilst Davis appeared to have been detained by the woman's friends, who had taken her side.

Being in the heart of the city worked to Logan's advantage, since the streets were crowded on a Sunday morning. *Gotta love Sunday trading*, he thought. Logan knew the lie of the land well. He took off down a labyrinth of passageways, hearing the sound of Davis's feet pounding after him and his voice bellowing for Logan to stop. He didn't stop; stopping had ceased to be an option the moment he took off and so instead, he continued to run until his lungs burned and his breath came in disjointed spurts.

Logan, well aware that he'd burned his bridges with Denning, who would come after him with everything he had, leaned against a wall, panting as he recovered his breath and tried to think rationally. Sweat gathered and cooled beneath his layers of clothing. He could hear Davis swearing as he veered off in the wrong direction. Logan concealed himself in a grimy alcove and wrinkled his nose against the foetid smell.

'What the fuck have I been reduced to?'

Judging from the debris scattered on the ground, this charming location, damp and dingy, was a favourite haunt for hookers and junkies alike during the hours of darkness, and perhaps even before. Logan couldn't be seen but knew he was far from safe. Denning would have every man in his employ out looking for him once he learned of his escape. It had been suicidal to cross him but what choice did Logan have? Murder was above his pay grade and, he was prepared to admit to himself, he didn't have the balls to see it through.

He felt in his pockets for his phone, his lifeline, and turned the air blue when he remembered that he didn't have it. He had two more phones back at his hotel but that's the first place they would look for him so was off limits. He did still have his wallet, which was stuffed with cash and a fistful of credit cards. Would it be safe to use them? He assumed so. Even Denning didn't have the power to trace his card purchases, did he? He rattled the keys in his pocket, all of which were now useless.

With the possible exception of Callie's.

No one would think to look for him there, he decided, feeling fractionally better about things. He could return, full of remorse and with an explanation that would move her soft heart. He'd think of something plausible. He gave a mirthless chuckle. Being pursued by dangerous men to whom he owed money would definitely sound plausible, simply because it was the truth. He'd offer to return the dosh he'd stolen from her once his latest building project saw a profit. She would understand simply because she loved him.

The thought of her welcoming him back with open arms – she was *that* gullible – caused a modicum of optimism to bring a smile to his lips.

Davis hadn't come back this way yet, but he would eventually, and Logan couldn't afford to linger. He leaned out of the alcove but there was no sign of anyone in either direction. He darted out, pleased to breathe air that was a little fresher – anything would be – and joined the throng of shoppers flooding the street market.

He purchased a baseball cap and shades from a cheap stall, providing him with a cliched disguise – all that was missing was the false beard – and headed for a mobile phone shop. He shelled out for a pay-as-you-go, found a quiet corner in an otherwise crowded café, and ordered a coffee. The upturn in the weather had brought half the world out, which suited Logan's purpose. He saw some of the conference delegates, still in gaudy costumes that made them look as though they'd just arrived from an alien planet, making a lot of noise as they browsed. Most of the customers at this café had chosen to sit at the tables outside, blocking Logan from the view of anyone looking in.

He'd chosen a table close to a power point and waited impatiently for his new phone to have enough charge in it to be usable. Nowadays phones charged quickly and the wait wasn't that long, even though it felt interminable. Logan's nerves were frayed and his heart leapt every time someone walked into the café. He actually slid down in his chair, suffering from palpitations, when he noticed Davis, looking to left and right and pausing to give the café a long, considering look before moving on, wearing a thunderous expression.

With enough juice in his phone to make it serviceable, Logan set about installing all the apps he'd need to get him out of this jam. Technology was his friend in the normal course of events and right now he needed all the friends he could get. He remembered Callie's number by heart but knew that a phone call wouldn't cut it. He would have to confront her in person, grovel a bit – well, a lot – and plead his case. Finding Blakely's private number and scoring points with him was his only hope but he didn't have… well, a hope in hell of getting that number from the internet.

He closed his eyes and racked his brains. There had to be a way.

Of course! Email was the obvious answer. He'd installed his provider and pulled up his account, scrolling through until he found his exchange with Blakely. He swore aloud, more audibly than had been his intention, drawing curious glances from the occupants of nearby tables. He pulled his cap low over his brow and waited for the offended to look away again.

There were no personal contact details and the account was probably monitored by one of Blakely's minions, but he had to take the chance. He thought for a moment and then came up with:

You are in danger and not from me. My phone has been taken by those who wish to harm you. Your ex-wife is involved and is not who she appears to be. Call me. I want to help.

He added the number of his pay-as-you-go, re-read the message, and grimaced. It sounded like a line from a bad gangster movie but he couldn't think of a better way to express the urgency.

Now he would have to wait. But where? He couldn't risk checking into another hotel and definitely couldn't go home, or anywhere else where Denning would think to look for him.

Which left Callie; the one destination that he'd always wanted to settle for on a subconscious level, he accepted. But how to get there? She lived in the back of fucking beyond. He couldn't risk going back for his car, nor could he chance hiring another one. There was only one thing for it. He would have to stump up for a taxi.

Sighing, he paid for his coffee and cautiously left the café, trying not to look furtive or do anything to draw attention to himself. It had been half an hour or more since his impulsive bid for freedom. Would Davis have admitted to losing him yet or would he assume that he'd find him and that Denning need never know? Logan's money was on the latter. Denning was not a man anyone would willingly antagonise. He'd been indiscreet too in telling Logan that Delia wasn't Denning's niece. He would know that if Logan somehow got word to Blakely then there would be a turf war; the war that Denning had been hoping to avoid by having Blakely murdered.

How had it come to this, Logan wondered, feeling aggrieved as he reached the taxi rank and gave the driver the name of a street a good mile away from Callie's abode. It paid to be cautious. He ought to be in sunnier climes right now, counting his money and working on his tan. Instead, he ran the risk of crossing Montague's path, since he lived close to Callie – a gamble he would have to take.

It was funny in a non-humorous sort of way, he thought, as the taxi made slow progress through the narrow streets. He'd made excuses not to meet Callie's friends because... well, because they were sure not to be as gullible as her. Now he'd had the dubious pleasure of making Montague's acquaintance under the most dire of circumstances. And there could be no doubt that it was Montague; Logan had seen their wedding picture displayed in Callie's cottage often enough. If Montague went home and told his wife everything then Logan was sunk. He clung to the belief that his wife remained in the dark. She would not, Logan sensed, approve of her beloved running round doing a gangster's dirty work.

Walking a mile down country lanes in unsuitable clothing when the taxi dropped him at his destination might get him noticed. It was a calculated risk since it was unlikely that anyone would think to look for him in an area where he would be so exposed. He should have bought a change of clothes at one of those stalls, he now realised, thinking that hindsight was fucking annoying.

He paid his fare in cash when the taxi dropped him outside a terrace of cottages on the edge of the South Downs National Park. His driver had mercifully not been the curious type and hadn't uttered a word for the entire journey. He accepted Logan's money, nodded his thanks when told to keep the change, executed a U-turn and took off in a cloud of diesel fumes.

The sun had disappeared and the rain returned. A heavy downpour that soaked through Logan's thin jacket in seconds flat.

'Great, just great!' he muttered, turning up his collar, for all the good it did, and trudging off towards Callie's cottage.

He arrived soaked to the skin and in a foul mood. Thankful that Callie had no near neighbours, his mood lightened when he saw her little car on the drive. His joy was short lived, though, when he turned down the side of the cottage and encountered a BMW. A very familiar BMW.

'Holy shit!'

Logan sank to his haunches and groaned, impervious to the wet ground and the rainwater working its way into his thin shoes. How the hell had she and Jack joined forces? He had been ultra-careful not to mention her name in front of Jack, or anyone else. If Jack had somehow found the discrepancies in their company accounts already, the chances were he'd called the police in. It's just the sort of boy scout behaviour that came naturally to him. If Callie had gone to the police as well, it would explain how they'd hooked up. Logan, a worried man, quietly seethed, thinking all his escape routes were gradually being closed down.

It was so fucking unfair!

After all he had done to make a success of things, dragging Jack along for the ride. Jack lacked ambition and would be nothing without Logan's driving force, and this was how he repaid him. What was Jack doing here with Callie on a Sunday morning, he wondered? Jealousy ricocheted through Logan in virulent waves. She wouldn't! Callie was no slut. But then again, Jack had always been popular with the ladies, without having to put any effort into it. Logan resented the lazy, persuasive charm that came so naturally to him. He didn't put on a front and the ladies liked him for who he was, not for what he could do for them.

Logan had never been equally self-assured. He blamed a father who was disinterested and a mother who put him down but played on his upper-class background in an effort to impress. Unlike Jack, he was determined to be someone and despite these setbacks, he wasn't done for yet. He'd just have to wait for Jack to leave, then he'd confront Callie, work his charm on her, and go into damage limitation mode. One thing was for sure, he'd take his chances with her and Jack rather than Denning and his crew any day of the week. In fact, if he let slip what Montague was now doing to earn a crust, it might well go some way to digging himself out of the massive crater he'd fallen into.

Feeling slightly more in control, Logan concealed himself behind a bush, its wet leaves adding to the soaking that he'd already endured. Settling in, resigned to a long wait, he was rewarded when the door opened and Jack emerged. Fuck it, his hair was wet from the shower! He might as well take out a placard and tell the world what he'd been doing. And Callie was with him, looking radiant in the way that only a recently fucked woman ever could.

Logan had stood up without realising it and rapidly ducked down again. Callie, presumably alerted by the rustle of leaves, turned in his direction. She said something to Jack that caused him to look as well. Logan held his breath, hoping against hope that Jack wouldn't come to investigate. That damned dog of his was with him. It trotted up to the bush, sniffed and then lifted his leg, peeing all over Logan's already soaked shoes. He wanted to kick the damn mutt but didn't dare move, astonished that it hadn't detected his scent. At a whistle from Jack, it trotted back to him and jumped into the car when Jack opened the back door.

Callie slid into the passenger seat and Jack fired up the engine, causing Logan to seethe with jealousy when he leaned over to Callie and kissed her hard and deep. She laughed at something he said to her when he broke the kiss, then backed the car out into the road. Logan stood up, watching it go. Perhaps it was just as well that Callie had gone with him. If she knew even part of the truth from highly exaggerated accounts on Jack's part, there would be no talking her round.

Soaked to the skin, Logan withdrew the keys from his pocket and let himself into Callie's cottage, breathing in the essence of her and feeling as though he'd finally come home.

* * *

Jack sensed how conflicted Callie still felt over her friend's husband's career choice. Jack reckoned he had to be either desperate or too stupid to live. Either way, all Jack could do was watch Callie's back. He finished his brief call with Blakely, pocketed his phone and pulled her into his arms.

'Hey, it will be all right,' he said, dropping a light kiss on the top of her head. 'Montague's a big boy.'

'Yeah, but it will destroy Maisie if he does anything illegal. She is the most law-abiding person I know. I just wish I knew...'

'I get that.' He released her, trying to sound upbeat, even though he himself was worried about the way things were playing out. He didn't like coincidences and Maisie's husband just happening to involve himself with Delia Blakely was about as big a coincidence as he was able to imagine, especially given the fact that Logan had been there before him.

'Come on,' he said. 'Let's get over to Blakely's. He's anxious to see us.'

They left the house and Callie paused in the process of locking the door.

'What was that?' she asked, glancing at a bush. 'I thought I heard something, or someone.'

'Just the wind and rain. You're spooked and imagining things.'

'Yeah, I guess.' She glanced around. 'No one walks here and I don't see any strange vehicles.'

She watched as Odin ran up to the bush in question and lifted his leg before sliding into the car when Jack opened the door for her.

They repeated the now familiar drive to Blakely's more or less in silence. Callie stared fixedly out the window for the majority of the time, probably without noticing the scenery, and Jack left her to her cogitations. There were some things she'd just have to work through for herself.

The gate opened on silent hinges as they approached it.

'Blakely's keen,' Jack remarked.

'He probably wonders why we want to see him again so soon.'

'Yeah, most likely. I was vague on the phone, and he wouldn't be human if he didn't wonder what we've unearthed.'

'I'm still not sure about his motives, Jack.' She touched his forearm. 'Be careful what you say.'

Jack smiled and blew her a kiss. 'Right back at you,' he replied.

Blakely opened the door to them himself. Either the modern-day butler had the day off or Blakely had told him to make himself scarce. Jack was glad. He hadn't liked Davidson and harboured suspicions about his motives.

'Come in.' Blakely was dressed casually by his standards, albeit expensively, in chinos and a polo shirt bearing the logo of a famous French designer. His salt and pepper hair had recently been cut and was swept back artistically from his face. The man was vain, Jack decided, as well as ruthless. 'I didn't expect to see you again so soon. You sounded fraught on the phone.'

'With good reason.'

They entered Blakely's library and he swept an arm towards an array of chairs. 'Please, sit.'

'Excuse me, but is this room swept for listening devices?' Jack asked in an undertone, ignoring the startled look that Callie directed towards him.

Blakely frowned but whispered his response. 'Weekly. Why do you ask?'

Without giving Jack an opportunity to explain, which was just as well because Jack didn't actually know why he'd asked, Blakely extracted a gizmo from a drawer and waved it about like a wand.

'Spyware detection, available online,' he mouthed with a cynical shrug, clearly not expecting to find anything. 'Shit!' he added, when he swept the wand over a picture frame and it beeped continuously.

'Leave it!' Jack mouthed when Blakely went to remove the bug. He nodded instead towards the massive atrium complete with swimming pool and full bar accessed through folding glazed doors. His meaning registered with Blakely and he led the way, his expression fixed into a thunderous scowl. He closed the doors behind them and then made his way meticulously round the room with his detector wand.

'Clear in here,' he said in a normal voice, sitting down across from them. 'How the hell did you know?'

'I didn't, not for sure, but from what we've be able to learn, it made sense. Someone is out to get you,' Jack said, stating the obvious. 'That someone seems to know an awful lot about your plans and is one step ahead of you.'

'Who could have planted that bug?' Blakely asked, clearly talking to himself. 'I sweep the room at least once a week so it has to be...'

'Someone with regular access,' Callie finished for him.

Jack almost flinched at the ferocity of Blakely's scowl. 'Do you have high-powered meetings here at home?' he asked.

'Occasionally, but I always sweep the room beforehand and have never found anything before. Not ever.'

'Which implies that whoever plants the bugs is aware of your habits.'

Blakely spread his hands. 'Then why plant one when there's nothing to be overheard?'

'Your phone conversations?' Callie suggested. Jack suspected that Blakely would already have reached that conclusion for himself.

'I seldom talk about anything sensitive over the phone.' He elegantly crossed his legs, calmer now, even if the icy stillness of his disposition was almost as frightening as his anger.

'How sure are you of Davidson's loyalty?' Jack asked. 'He's in an ideal position to place the bugs and you did say that he came with your wife.'

'He's out on his ear,' Blakely said on a note of subdued menace.

'You might want to rethink that decision,' Jack suggested. 'Keep your enemies close and all that.'

Blakely grunted. 'Why did you want to see me?' he asked.

Jack succinctly outlined the details of the visit they'd received from DI Renton. Blakely sat forward in his chair at the mention of Denning's name.

'You clearly know the man,' Jack said carefully.

'Our paths have crossed but we aren't on one another's Christmas card lists. Quite the opposite, in fact. And now you tell me that Armitage has got himself in the mire with Denning.' He shook his head. 'The stupid bastard! He's playing way out of his league.'

'We reckon he borrowed the money to purchase Clydesdale Mews, thinking you would be sufficiently impressed to get on board with him. He'd then have been able to pay him back and get his project off the ground, with the help of your backing and connections.'

'I would likely have invested. The project had merit.' If he noticed Jack's disapproving expression, it didn't appear to bother him. Jack knew that Blakely would have had a soil survey faked in order that homes could be built on contaminated land, resulting in unexplained illnesses of the homes' occupants, or worse. That prospect clearly didn't give him sleepless nights. He thought only of the bottom line. Jack was reminded of all the reasons why he disliked the man's lack of moral conscience. 'However, Armitage was incapable of keeping his prick in his pants, so that was that.' He inclined his head towards Callie. 'If you'll excuse the vulgarity.'

She smiled in a perfunctory manner. 'No apology necessary.'

'It gets worse,' Jack said, going on to explain about Dan Montague and his affectionate connection with Delia. 'There was absolutely nothing professional about it. He's told his wife that he's working for Denning in a bodyguarding capacity.' Jack fixed Blakely with a penetrating stare. 'You and I both know what that means. Given that Renton warned us that Denning had a contract out on a rival businessman, we wondered...'

'If it could be me?'

Jack nodded.

'Very likely,' Blakely said, sounding remarkably unconcerned. 'We've been treading upon one another's toes recently. Denning doesn't believe in free trade opportunities and has a unique way of disposing of the opposition.'

'That's as maybe, but I understand Denning employs plenty of hard men. Jack and I are both having trouble seeing Logan as a cold-blooded killer,' Callie said, biting her lower lip anxiously. 'Frankly, he doesn't have the balls, but Renton didn't tell us everything he knows and seems confident that Logan has been pulled into the mess.'

'If Denning has given him an ultimatum, do as you're told or face the consequences then, trust me, he will have no choice.' Blakely yawned. 'Everyone is capable of murder, especially if it's a case of self-preservation and we all know that Armitage has an honours degree in putting himself first.'

'You don't seem especially concerned, given that you could be the intended victim,' Jack remarked.

Blakely responded with a mirthless chuckle. 'I've been threatened before and am not an easy person to reach. Besides,' he added, his expression darkening, 'I have one or two resources of my own.'

Jack fixed the anti-spy detector with a significant look and said nothing.

'Right, point taken.' His expression hardened. 'It has to be Davidson who's planting bugs. I can't imagine how my ex-wife engenders such loyalty. Or then again, perhaps I can. I clearly underestimated her.'

'You think she is somehow involved with Denning?' Callie asked, widening her eyes.

'Well, my dear, it would be something of a coincidence if she isn't,' Blakely replied calmly. 'Armitage and Davidson are both disloyal and she has her claws into each of them in different ways.'

'And Dan,' Callie muttered.

'Which is something we can use to our advantage. You don't want your friend's husband mixed up in Denning's murky world. I can find a position for a man of his calibre, one with legitimate career opportunities, always supposing he can convince me of his loyalty.'

Jack let out a slow breath.

'Get him to tell you what Denning has planned and you'll offer him well-paid, gainful employment?' Callie smiled. 'That's ingenious.'

'Except that will put Dan in Denning's crosshairs,' Jack pointed out. 'Grassing him up would be looked upon as the worst kind of betrayal.'

'If I am Denning's intended target then that will cease to be a problem.' Blakely's expression turned venomous. 'It will be me or him and I fully intend to be the one who survives. In that eventuality, your friend's husband will at least have secured himself gainful employment, which is more than will be said for the rest of Denning's minions. I have no need of the services of thugs.'

Jack knew that Blakely had just admitted to contemplating murder, almost as casually as if he'd been offering them refreshments. He wondered how he could live that way; collecting enemies in the way that others collected stamps, distributing his own form of retribution, always looking over his shoulder, living in a house that resembled a fortress. Never relaxing. Always wondering who would try to shaft him next.

'So, if you'll bring this man, Dan Montague, to me, I'll see what I can get out of him.'

'Hang on, won't Davidson see him and report back?'

'Good point.' Blakely rubbed his lips with the side of his forefinger. 'Perhaps, in that case, I could prevail upon you, my dear, to invite him to your home. I could see him there.'

'Out of the question!' Jack shouted, jumping to his feet.

'Of course,' Callie said at the same time.

'It's too dangerous, Callie. You'll get caught in the crossfire, to say nothing of potentially bringing yourself to Denning's notice.'

'I could probably get Dan to agree to visit if I imply that I want to talk to him about his relationship with Delia,' Callie said musingly, speaking over Jack's objections. 'He will come or risk me telling Maisie and clearly he doesn't want Maisie to know; otherwise he would have come clean already. He's probably wetting himself, wondering if I intend to tell her, so I can't see him blowing me off. Getting him to my cottage will be easy enough but getting him to come here's entirely another matter. Short of kidnapping him...'

Jack sighed, knowing when he was beaten. 'We'll see what we can do and be in touch,' he said.

'Which is all I can ask for.' Blakely stood up and led them

through the house to the front door, which he opened. 'I won't forget this,' he added. 'I reward loyalty.'

'We aren't doing this for you,' Jack replied, scowling. He didn't bother to add that if anything happened to Callie then he would hold Blakely responsible and go after him himself, fortress-type houses notwithstanding.

Blakely stood on the threshold of his opulent prison, watching as Jack drove off, his expression set in stone.

17

Logan felt calmer as the familiarity and welcoming warmth of Callie's cottage embraced him in the way that his own show home never had. He walked into her bedroom, breathing in her light floral fragrance. The bed was neatly made but the aroma of sex lingered in the atmosphere, spoiling Logan's momentary peace of mind.

A peace of mind that he hadn't known since walking out on Callie. She was a natural carer, putting his interests ahead of her own. Cooking for him, listening to whatever he had to say, believing in him in a way that no one else ever had.

That realisation stopped him in his tracks, forcing him to concede just how much his priorities had cost him. He could, he belatedly realised, have taken Callie with him when he embarked upon his new life. Her trusting nature and open adoration had got under his skin and refused to budge, and not only because his best friend had lost no time in moving into his territory. Now that there was little chance of his being able to talk her round, he understood just how much it would have meant to him.

'Damn it!' He thumped his fist against the surface of her

dressing table, causing the things on it to rattle. A perfume bottle fell over and Logan righted it, absently reading the label. He'd never heard of the brand. It obviously wasn't top range, otherwise he'd have known it, but he would recognise the aroma anywhere from now on and it would always make him think of her.

She who could have been *the one*.

She who thought he walked on water, never questioned his motives or made demands on his time and money. She was simply prepared to accept as much of him as he was prepared to offer her.

And he had let the best thing that had ever happened to him slip through his fingers.

'You never know what you've got till it's gone,' he said aloud, feeling ridiculously sorry for himself.

He lay on her bed, careful to keep to the side that she always occupied and dismissing from his mind the fact that his best friend had usurped his place in it. He laced his hands behind his head, startled into sitting bolt upright again when a sound disturbed him. Her damned cat, who had never liked him, stalked into the room, gave a disapproving hiss and left again, tail swishing.

He ought to have taken Callie into his confidence, he knew now, sold her the dream and asked her to mortgage her home short term to help him out of a hole. She would have done it, too, because she believed in him like no one else ever had. She understood his determination to make something of himself, even if she didn't know the underlying reason for his ambition.

No one did. Not even Jack.

Sighing, Logan closed his eyes. This old bed with knackered springs wasn't a patch on the huge status symbol that he and Portia had occupied and yet it was ten times more comfortable. With the chintz covers and matching curtains, old-fashioned mishmash of furniture and sloping ceiling, the small room had a cosy, welcoming feel that drew a body in. Logan felt himself relaxing for the first time in what seemed like forever. He had barely slept for days and closed his eyes for a moment, giving in to the seductive allure of oblivion.

Something woke him.

A noise. Voices. Logan sat up abruptly, dazed and disorientated. It took him a moment to recall where he was. He glanced at his watch and swore beneath his breath. He'd only intended to close his eyes for a minute and yet he'd slept solidly – more solidly than he had for weeks – for over two hours.

Callie was back, which was good. But the sound of Jack's voice most definitely wasn't. He was trapped here. He might well be able to talk Callie round. Well... possibly. But Jack would be a much harder nut to crack. He couldn't be found here. She was bound to come upstairs and there was nowhere in this small room to hide.

He called to mind the layout of the cottage. Apart from her bedroom and a bathroom, there was only one other room up here. Not much more than a box room, it contained all the tricks of Callie's trade and was her inner sanctum. Logan had only ever set foot in it once, pretending an interest because he'd still been grooming her at the time. She had been reluctant to let him over the threshold and he'd sensed her anxiety the entire time he'd examined her meticulously catalogued bridal books, floral catalogues, fabrics and God alone knew what else.

It would have to do. The chances were good that she wouldn't venture in there now, at least not whilst Jack was still with her. And once he remembered that he had a life and buggered off, Logan would have no reason to hide from her.

He moved stealthily, pulling the bed back together as best he could. Why couldn't she use a duvet, the same as the rest of the world, he wondered as he tussled with sheets and blankets which refused to return to their previous smooth state. Trusting to luck that she would assume it was Jack who had disturbed them, Logan moved on tiptoe to the door and listened. He couldn't hear what was being said but guessed they must be in the kitchen. The box room was directly above it, and he might hear better from there.

Recalling that the landing boards creaked, he walked on his toes and stuck to the sides, hoping that Callie and Jack would be too taken up with what was obviously an intense conversation to hear him.

He reached the box room out of breath, even though he hadn't exerted much energy getting there, relieved that no one came to investigate other than that damned cat. It wound itself around his legs, almost tripping him up, making a sound that could have been anything from a snarl to a roar.

'Get lost!' Logan hissed, shooing the bloody creature away with his hands. It sent him an imperious look and sauntered off down the stairs.

Logan breathed a little easier as he took stock of his surroundings. The room was smaller than he recalled, with just one small, padded chair in the corner to sit on. He caught sight of himself in a full-length mirror that Callie had hung on the back of the door and gave an involuntary groan. He looked terrible! There were bags under his eyes that looked as though they wanted to grow into suitcases and were a fair way along to achieving that ambition. His hair was tousled, despite being so short, and his jaw was covered with five-o-clock shadow, interspersed with a sprinkling of grey. The appearance of grey hair would have had him in a panic in his previous life. Today, he simply despaired at the overall picture. His looks were his fortune. Right now, they'd probably raise him a fiver, if he was feeling lucky.

Logan sat on the chair, then leapt up again and knocked over a tailor's dummy, lunging to catch it before it crashed into something else and caused an avalanche. Managing to do so, he set it straight and then examined the chair's seat in the hope of finding what bastard thing had attacked his backside. A damned innocent little pin glistened up at him. Logan picked it up, threw it across the room and sat down more cautiously.

As his heartrate returned to normal, he realised that he could hear Callie and Jack's conversation quite clearly.

And they were talking about him.

* * *

Callie made coffee for them both and threw together some sandwiches that she put on a plate in the middle of the table. Not hungry herself, she nibbled at one, distracted, whilst Jack made short work of the rest.

'How can a humble sandwich taste so good?' he asked, grinning at her as he consumed the final crust.

Callie knew he was simply attempting to subdue the tension that had sprung up between them when she insisted upon inviting Dan here and was grateful that he'd made the effort. She would have been disappointed if he'd tried to tell her what to do and was glad that it hadn't come to that. She gave herself a jolt when it occurred to her that Logan had dictated her every waking move when they'd been together. He'd done it so skilfully that he hadn't appeared controlling, and Callie was aware that she wouldn't have objected even if she had cottoned on. She understood now why it had been so important for him to have her right where he wanted her, waiting anxiously for his next call, his next visit, for any time that he could spare for her. He couldn't risk her finding out about his real life and she had fallen for it.

How pathetic had she been?

Well, no more. She liked Jack, more than liked him, but she wasn't ready to think beyond getting her revenge upon Logan, to say nothing of recovering her money.

She had learned to be cautious.

'You know I'm not going to let you see him alone, don't you?'

Callie smiled. 'It might be better if I do.'

'Not a chance! He's running with a rough crowd now. He'll be in damage limitation mode and there's no saying how he'll react. Or you, either, whenever you think of him cheating on your friend.'

'I've known Dan for years. I'm not his favourite person because I've never tried to hide the fact that I don't approve of his lifestyle. He has a wife and kids, responsibilities, and yet he's been content to let Maisie be mother and breadwinner for years.' She leaned the side of her face on her cupped hand, elbow on the table, and sighed. 'And the devil of it is that Maisie never complained; well, not until recently. But if I'd tried to point out his failings it would have threatened our friendship. I wasn't willing to take that risk so was forced to watch him exploiting her infatuation every step of the way.' She looked directly at Jack. 'And yet I realise now that's exactly how I was with Logan. I believed him because I wanted to. I was so stupid!' She slapped her palm on the tabletop for emphasis. 'And now I hate myself for being so gullible.'

'He makes a habit out of...'

'I know, but I won't ever let my guard down like that ever again. Once bitten and all that...' She paused. 'Anyway, as far as Dan's concerned, I think I can handle him.'

'Perhaps once, but his connection to Denning will have changed him.'

Callie nodded absently. 'I wonder what made him desperate

enough to go down that route?'

'Perhaps he does care that he isn't able to support his family. Despite the equality of the sexes, a lot of men still feel that's their responsibility.'

'If Dan feels that way then it's taken him a while to wake up. There have been dozens of opportunities for him to prove it, but he always said that he wanted to forge a career based on the degree that he struggled through, otherwise what was the point?'

'He struggled academically?'

Callie waggled a hand from side to side. 'I think so, reading between the lines. Maisie has never actually said. But still, he's a qualified structural engineer and there have been no shortage of vacancies in that field. He's been for enough interviews, often shortlisted, but never selected. Makes you wonder what the employers see that we don't.' Callie pushed out a long breath. 'Anyway, he argues that his CV won't be enhanced by a string of temporary jobs. Maisie could see his point, of course, whereas I reckoned it would demonstrate a good work ethic. Still, it's easy to be judgemental when you're not emotionally involved, I suppose.'

'I'm still not sure about you...'

'Don't worry, he's a big guy but he won't raise a hand to me.'

'No, he won't because I'll be here when you talk to him.' Jack's tone brooked no argument.

Callie threw up her hands. 'Okay, okay. I know when I'm beaten.'

'Smart girl!'

'I just wish we had some idea where Logan is now,' she said pensively.

'My money's on his having fled the country. He'd have shown up somewhere before now otherwise.'

'It's easy enough to hide in plain sight if you have the funds.' Callie sounded bitter, as she had every right to. 'And... I don't know, I just sense that he's still hanging around. He obviously didn't intend to scarper without taking his passport. He's planned too meticulously to make such a basic error. Something spooked him and so he's had to make up lost ground.' She sent Jack a speculative look. 'Do you think the lovely soon-to-be-ex Mrs Blakely is offering him bed and board?'

Jack flexed a brow. 'As well as Montague?'

Callie wrinkled her nose. 'You think she's the monogamous type?'

'Good point.'

Jack hated to see the veil that descended over her eyes whenever her thoughts turned to Logan. He gave in to temptation, pulled her into his arms and kissed her long and deep. They were both breathing heavily when he released her again.

'Callie, I know you have trust issues and given what that bastard did to you, it would be surprising if you didn't. But when this is all over, I intend to convince you that not all men are bastards and that it's okay to... Damn, I'm getting ahead of myself.' He ran a hand through his hair, not having intended to instigate this conversation, wondering when his thoughts had turned in the direction of a long-term commitment. But at least she was listening and hadn't run screaming for the hills. 'All I'm trying to make you realise is that I'm here for you and don't intend to go anywhere unless you kick me out.'

'I know,' she replied, tears sparkling on her lashes. 'And I do appreciate it. You have even more pressing reasons than I do to catch him.'

'Is that really why you think I'm—'

'Let's not go there now. It's not the right time.'

'Okay, but I'll just say this one thing. In case you're wondering, what you see is what you get with me. There's no Mrs Carlisle or kids waiting in the wings. I'm free and single, if not twenty-one any more,' he said, warming to the idea of commitment with every word he spoke.

They both smiled. Then Callie stood on her toes and placed a chaste kiss on his lips. 'Thank you,' she said softly. 'I guess I needed to hear that, and whatever else it is that you want to say, at some point. But first...' She extracted her phone from her bag. 'I have Dan's mobile number as an emergency contact when I babysit. Hopefully, he won't be anywhere near Maisie when he answers it. If he calls me by name, then...' She spread her hands and allowed her words to trail off as she trawled through her list of contacts. 'Here goes nothing.'

She dialled the number and put the phone on speaker.

'It isn't what it looked like,' Dan said, as soon as he answered. Jack shared a look with Callie, thinking that if ever anyone sounded guilty... 'I can explain.'

'This I have to hear. Come round now.'

'I can't get away. I...'

Callie hung up. 'He'll be here,' she said confidently. 'It's obvious that he doesn't want Maisie to know.'

Sure enough, less than ten minutes later, Montague's people-mover screeched to a halt outside. Well, screeching would be stretching it when it came to describing what Jack looked upon as a kiddies' bus. They didn't have much horsepower under the bonnet and screamed family man, a situation that had never appealed to Jack in the past. He glanced at Callie, wondering if being around her would change his point of view.

Damn it, it already had!

Callie opened the front door to Montague and they exchanged muted greetings.

'Are you going to tell her... hey, who the hell is this?' Montague stopped dead in his tracks, scowling. 'You didn't say anyone else would...'

'He's a friend,' Callie said, taking control in a curt manner that Jack admired, aware how nervous she actually felt. 'He was with me when I saw you eating Mrs Blakely's face and knows everything that I do.' She made the introduction but neither man offered to shake hands.

'Hell!' Montague fell into a chair and dropped his head into his splayed hand. 'It isn't what you think.'

'Hard to put another interpretation on it,' Jack remarked, leaning his backside against a counter and folding his arms.

'She came on to me. It just happened, and only the once. Someone... a man I work for asked me to babysit and well... she's a maneater.'

'Very chivalrous of you to put the blame on her,' Callie replied scathingly. 'From what I saw, you weren't putting up too much resistance.'

'Look, it wasn't like that. I didn't set out to... oh, fuck, what's the point? You're going to tell her, aren't you? You two have always been joined at the hip but I didn't have you pegged as deliberately vindictive.' He lifted his head and glared at Callie. He looked terrible, his features tired and drawn. 'You got me here to make me suffer but you've wasted your time. Just so that you know, you couldn't possibly make me feel any worse than I do already.'

Jack relaxed his rigid stance, accepting that he was being completely honest now; at least about his opportunistic shag with Delia Blakely. 'Then why?' he asked.

'She's a hard woman to rebuff – a close relation of... well, of someone it wouldn't be wise to cross. Maisie and I haven't been getting along and—'

'Oh, please!' Callie rolled her eyes and let out an exaggerated breath. 'She's been carrying you, holding your family together single-handedly for years, whilst you swan around looking for the perfect opportunity that never comes off. Have you ever stopped to ask yourself why that is?'

'You weren't getting any and then an attractive woman came along and offered it to you on a plate. You're only human...' Jack left his words dangling, ignoring Callie's look of deep betrayal.

'Something like that.' He turned to look at Callie. 'You're wrong about me not wanting to support my family. How much less of a man do you think it makes me feel when I can't do what's right by them? But taking delivery jobs, or cash-in-hand work... what good would that do? I needed something that paid better and had prospects. When this influential guy asked me to bodyguard Delia Blakely, I knew I was being tested. Keep her sweet and there would finally be an opportunity for me to be the man of the family, bringing in a decent wedge. Okay, so I wouldn't be using my qualifications to forge a career but...' He spread his hands. 'Times have changed since the pandemic, and we all have to change with them if we want to get ahead.'

'By throwing in your lot with a criminal?' Callie asked.

Montague's head shot up. 'What the hell do you know...'

'It doesn't matter how. All you need to worry about is that we're aware you're working for Denning and everyone knows he's got his fingers in just about every dodgy deal in the south.'

Jack stepped forward as he spoke, crowding Montague and filling the small kitchen with his musculature. He noticed Callie's eyes widen in the periphery of his vision, presumably because she'd never seen Jack when he felt the need to intimidate. Montague thought he was tough, but his bulk was the result of hours in a gym. He'd seldom got his hands dirty, Jack sensed. He, on the other hand, had grown up streetwise, more often than not fighting his way out of trouble. Since achieving maturity, he'd spent more time labouring than he had sitting behind a desk or, as Montague would put it, considering his options.

Montague's flexing biceps were pathetic and Jack would back himself if it came to a tussle any day of the week.

'Look, I'm doing what I have to do for the sake of my family.' Montague's tone had turned whining, which irritated the hell out of Jack. *Be a man, goddamn it!* Like Logan, he was a handsome guy and traded on his looks but didn't know how to stand up for himself when the brown stuff hit the fan.

'Where's Logan?' Callie asked, breaking the brittle silence with an equally brittle question.

Montague's head swivelled in his direction. 'What are you talking about?'

Jack leaned forward and slapped his hand against the surface of the table, causing Montague to flinch and draw back from him, which is when Jack knew he'd pegged him right. Tough men never, ever backed away from confrontations. It was a sign of weakness. His reaction had confirmed other suspicions too. Montague was running scared *and* he definitely knew where Logan was.

'The man was my partner,' Jack said in a mordant tone. 'Not only has he taken Callie for almost everything she had but he's helped himself from our company's coffers too, leaving me to carry the can. So, as you can imagine, I am none too happy and keen to have a very private conversation with my ex-best friend.'

'Maisie found the discrepancies in Jack's books,' Callie added, when Montague looked shit scared but didn't open his mouth. 'Would you like me to get her involved? I will ask her to confront you about that and a few other matters if necessary.' She fixed him with a resolute look. 'Never doubt it.'

'Okay.' Montague pushed his hands towards Callie, a defeated and weak individual with a pretty face. 'Okay, you've made your point.' He splayed his legs, leaned his forearms on his thighs and stared at the floor, as though seeking inspiration. 'I had no idea

Logan Armitage and Denning had any business going on. Turns out Armitage took out a massive loan. Can't understand why Denning fronted him so much, or at least I couldn't, not at first. Not that it was any of my business. I just heard about it from some of the guys who've worked with him for a long time. They couldn't figure it out either.' He paused. 'It's more obvious now.'

'Denning wants someone with no connections to him to bump someone off.'

Montague looked up at Jack as though he'd suddenly grown a second head. 'How the hell did you know that?' he asked.

'I'm not surprised that Maisie's tired, given the burden she has to carry.' Callie looked fit to explode. Jack's instinct was to calm her down, but he knew she had to get this off her chest. Perhaps letting some of the anger that ought to be directed towards Logan out on Montague would make her feel better. 'And she did it because she believed in your desire to carve out a career for yourself in which you could utilise that supposed intellect of yours. I don't think it was a career in the criminal underworld that she had in mind, though.' Callie paused mid-rant. 'You know she'll never stand for it. You'll have to make a choice, your family or your criminal friends.' She shook her head. 'What on earth were you thinking?'

'What sort of a man can't support his family?' he asked, taking his turn to shake his head. 'All that slogging away to earn a qualification that ought to have got me somewhere. I feel like a complete failure. I've lost all respect, couldn't bear to see the way that Maisie looked at me, so when Denning asked me to run one small favour for him and paid me way above the odds... well—'

'You were in over your head,' Callie said, nodding. 'Even so, you must have known that you were breaking the law, or skirting very close to its edges, otherwise why pay so well?'

'Where is Logan?' Jack asked, his glacial tone cutting through the ensuing loaded silence. 'And don't tell me you don't know because I'm not buying it. I also don't have limitless patience.'

'I don't know, as it happens.' Montague held up a placatory hand. 'I was told to take him to a hotel last night and keep watch over him.'

'What hotel?' Callie and Jack asked together.

Montague told them. 'But it won't do you any good. He isn't there any more. The guy who took over from me got sloppy and he escaped. He could be anywhere. Denning is not happy about it.'

Callie and Jack glanced at one another. 'Who was he supposed to knock off?' Jack asked, looking to Montague for confirmation.

After a long, tense pause, he spoke. 'Robert Blakely,' he said. 'And I think part of the reason for that, putting aside the fact that they're business rivals and can't stand one another, is because Delia asked him to arrange it.'

'What is she to him?' Callie asked.

'His niece,' Montague replied. 'Well, that's what she pretends anyway, but I'm told she was a high-end prostitute before Denning plucked her from obscurity.'

Logan pressed his ear to a gap in the floorboards and could hear every word spoken quite distinctly. It didn't make for pleasant listening. Any lingering hopes that Callie and Jack had found one another by accident dissipated and he fell back on his haunches, feeling desperate. Convincing Callie to believe he'd been boxed into a corner and intended to repay her was now a pipe dream. She'd never buy it.

His only option was to wait until Montague and Jack left. Hopefully Callie wouldn't go with them. She'd have Blakely's number somewhere because she'd organised his daughter's wedding and just like the efficient little planner that she was, she would have all the details filed safely away. She told him once that she kept them because marriages didn't last and she often got repeat business.

They'd laughed about it and then he'd brought her upstairs and fucked her brains out. Despite his dilemma, the memory caused him to harden. Shame she wouldn't be up for a repeat performance – well, not voluntarily.

He heard a commotion below. Someone was about to leave.

'Will you tell Maisie?' he heard Montague ask.

'Not if you rethink your career path,' Callie replied.

'It's not that simple. No one walks out on Denning until he's ready to let them go.'

'Stop whining!' Callie cried impatiently. 'You knew what you were getting yourself into. Man up and sort it out yourself.'

A long pause. 'Give me some time,' Montague said. 'Maisie and I are overdue a heart to heart. I'll find a way out of this mess.'

Footsteps, the front door opened and closed, and Logan waited to see if Jack intended to leave too. It was Sunday afternoon and he always visited his sainted mother on a Sunday. Not that she knew which way was up, but Jack wasn't deterred by her failing memory and never missed his regular visit.

'Fuck it!' Logan seethed when he heard Jack suggest to Callie that they retire to the living room to talk things through. He knew he was losing it when his alter ego threatened to take over and that could only spell trouble. He fought hard against the pull and his brain cleared. At least for now. 'Not happening,' he muttered, thinking hard of a way to get rid of Jack.

An idea occurred to him. It was risky but desperate times and all that. Confident that Jack wouldn't be able to hear him since they'd shut themselves in the living room, he picked up a piece of cloth. It was a wedding dress sample, he thought, as he covered his phone with it and dialled Jack's number, having first withheld his own.

'What is it?' Jack answered on the first ring.

'Nothing to be concerned about. Your mother took a little fall. She's at A&E and her carer gave us your number to call.'

'Is she all right?' There was anxiety in Jack voice, just as Logan had known there would be. He was *so* predictable about the welfare of an old lady who anyone with half a brain – which was more than could be said for the woman herself – knew would be better off out of it. She had no quality of life. Her time was long overdue. 'I can't hear you. It's a bad line.'

'She's confused and complaining about the fuss.' Logan felt sweat trickling down his back, convinced that Jack would recognise his voice, even though it was muffled by the cloth. 'She's asking for you, so... excuse me, we're swamped here. I must get on.'

Logan was shaking as he cut the connection. He'd taken the dosh that was his from the company without a second thought. It certainly hadn't troubled his conscience. In fact, he'd barely spared the dilemma he'd be leaving behind for Jack a passing thought. But this felt like a more personal form of betrayal, and he wished Callie hadn't forced him into it. This was all her fault, of course, for getting involved with Jack when she ought to be crying her eyes out over him. Woman were so fucking fickle! It made his alter ego's blood boil and this time Logan couldn't keep him at bay.

'Needs must,' he muttered, straining his ears.

He was rewarded when he heard muffled voices and movement into the hall. The front door opened, Jack and Callie exchanged a few words, then the sound of Jack's engine roaring into life was music to Logan's ears.

'Game time!' he muttered.

18

Callie sighed, wishing now that she'd asked Jack to take her with him. He spoke of his mother with great affection and she knew that watching her mind deteriorating must make him feel helpless. She could empathise because her own grandmother had lost her marbles too. It had been heart-breaking to watch from the sidelines and often be mistaken for a stranger by the woman who had meant so much to her. She wanted to help Jack deal with the gut-wrenching inevitability of his mother's cruel disease. But that would imply a commitment she wasn't ready to make, wouldn't it?

Callie didn't know her own mind and that was why she hadn't made the suggestion. Now she felt lonely and anxious for reasons she was unable to fathom. She returned to her living room and threw herself on the settee, thinking that things were moving apace. They now knew that Logan was still in the country, but that didn't help much because he could be anywhere. She had wanted to ring Blakely and warn him that Logan was coming for him... perhaps. But Jack had made her see there would be no point. They had left him tightening his security and she failed to see how Logan could break through it.

She had promised Jack that she would stay here and he'd come straight back as soon as he'd assured himself that his mother was okay. Then they would make decisions together. It annoyed her when she realised how much she looked forward to his return.

'Don't lean on him,' she muttered aloud, yawning as she lay back on the sofa and closed her eyes.

Jinx joined her. She stroked his sleek back as he curled up at her side and purred fit to bust a gut. It was too peaceful, too domestic. The lack of sleep caused by worry caught up with her and she felt herself dozing off.

The door opening woke her with a jolt what felt like five minutes later.

'That was quick.' She sat up and pushed the hair away from her eyes. 'How is... you!'

She jerked into a sitting position, her heart racing, her mouth hanging open in shock. It wasn't Jack's muscular bulk that filled the doorway. Logan stood there instead, very much less impressive physically, but far more dangerous. How could she ever have thought him to be a prime example of male perfection, she wondered?

'What the hell are you doing here? How did you get in?' She shook her head, trying to keep the fear out of her voice; a fear created by the cruel, rigid and determined set to his features. A moment's clarity of thought reminded her that he was desperate, on edge and probably as nervous as she was. A meticulous planner, he had been forced to act on the fly and would be out of his depth, especially since Denning was chasing him down. With that thought in mind, she went on the offensive.

'Stupid question,' she said disdainfully. 'Forget I asked. You're good at forging keys, aren't you?'

'Hello, darling,' he said conversationally. 'Did you miss me?'

She sent him a scathing look. 'Why did you do it?' she asked. 'Take everything I have. And lie to me about... well, everything else.'

He perched his backside on the arm of the chair across from hers, angling his body so that it blocked the doorway. 'I didn't intend to. Believe it or not, I liked you.'

'Tell that to your wife,' she replied, sniffing.

'But you were too trusting. It was too damned tempting. Our affair had run its course. You were asking too many questions, making demands. It would only have been a matter of time before you forced your friends on me, pretending you didn't know they planned to call round when I was here. You wanted to show me off like a pet dog.' He sighed. 'It happens every time.'

'Don't flatter yourself. I dare say even your most besotted of conquests sees through you eventually. I certainly have.'

Logan shrugged. 'We all have to make a living, darling, and you made it far too easy for me to resist. I would feel a slight pang of remorse about you, perhaps, if you hadn't let Jack park his boots under your bed before you'd had time to bang the imprint of my head from the pillows.'

'You're jealous?' she asked incredulously, shaking her head and blowing air though her lips. 'Talk about arrogant. It might surprise you to hear that he's a decent man who doesn't feel the need to screw anyone over.'

'You know nothing about me, about what drives me,' he replied, his voice hardening.

'I know what Jack's told me, which is that you were born with the proverbial silver spoon and seem to think life owes you a living.'

His expression closed down. 'The silver spoon often comes at a high price,' he said distantly.

Looking at her, her eyes still puffy from sleep, Logan felt a swelling of affection, which jolted him. He also felt a driving need to make her understand what made him tick in the hope that she wouldn't think quite so badly of him. He was as close to being in love with her as he'd been with anyone, he realised, which is why he was prepared to explain something so deeply personal, so humiliating. Something that he'd never spoken about to anyone before in his entire life.

She had got under his skin without his realising it. He wondered if it would have happened if she hadn't taken up with Jack. Possibly, but she was right about one thing, he was insanely jealous.

'Am I supposed to feel sorry for you?' she asked.

He couldn't stand her scorn. 'Being a pretty kid at boarding school is not recommended,' he said. 'Take it from one who knows.'

He said nothing more but studied her face and knew when realisation dawned. 'You were abused?' she asked, unable to completely disguise her sympathy, even though Logan sensed that she didn't want to spare him any. She was so naïve; that was one of the things that endeared her to him, or had. Until she double-crossed him with his partner.

'Not only at school.' He inhaled sharply and looked away from her, feeling the pain almost as acutely now as he had on his fifth birthday; the first occasion upon which his father had visited his bedroom with a special present for him. He'd regularly spent what he referred to as quality time with his special boy after that. And yet, in spite of that, or perhaps because of it, he had desperately wanted to impress the old man.

That was what drove him. *That* was what he had never been able to tell anyone. *That* was what no one else would ever understand.

'I'm sorry,' she said, looking as though she meant it. 'Have you ever sought help? Talked to anyone about it? It wasn't your fault, and you shouldn't bottle these things up.'

'Talk?' He waved a hand. 'You had to be there. Anyway, it's in the past and I'm more concerned with the here and now.'

'Oh, Logan.' She sighed deeply. 'No wonder you're so screwed up. How do you get over something like that without professional help?'

'Your sympathy is touching, darling, but right now I have more pressing concerns. You have Blakely's phone number.'

Her empathy evaporated and she sent him a defiant look. 'What, you're going to ring and make an appointment to murder him?' she asked dispassionately.

He scowled at her. 'What I need it for has nothing to do with you. Nor do I have time to debate the matter. Now, for the last time, I'll ask you nicely.'

He felt the veil descend over his eyes, the one that he tried to fight against.

Sometimes.

The one that had been his constant companion since his fifth birthday. If she didn't do as he asked, and it was a reasonable enough request, then he wouldn't be in control of his actions, and she would only have herself to blame if she got hurt. Isn't that what his daddy had taught him – a lesson that he'd never forgotten?

Everything that had happened to him had been his fault. He wasn't pretty enough, complaint enough, willing enough, which is why Daddy got mad and hurt him. Was it any wonder that he was incapable of loving? Of forming lasting relationships and being *normal*, whatever that was? Relationships were built on foundations of sand. Emotional investment ended in tears.

'The police have been here looking for you,' she said, jolting him back to the here and now.

Logan was furious when he showed a reaction. Callie simply smiled.

'I will be long gone by the time they catch up with me,' he said, with a casual shrug. How the hell had the police got onto him so quickly? Farquhar wouldn't have let Portia report him missing; he'd been depending on that. They must have somehow got wind of his connection to Denning. There was no honour amongst thieves nowadays.

'Not before I get my money back. I'm calling them now,' she said, reaching for the mobile that he'd only just noticed on the table beside her. 'You didn't come here by car so you can only get away on foot. They'll pick you up before you get half a mile.'

Infuriated, Logan reached for her phone, grabbed it from her hand and threw it across the room. It smashed into the fireplace. Her cat, whom Logan had forgotten about, launched an assault on his backside with claws that hurt, but he didn't feel them. He'd learned to deal with worse pain in that area from a much earlier age.

He found himself lying on top of Callie, his hands circling her neck and slowly squeezing. He vaguely wondered how it had come to that and found that he was aroused. He'd have her one more time first.

She fought like a banshee, but he sensed her energy waning. Only the previous day, he'd told Denning that he was incapable of murder. It was true. Logan had never murdered anyone in his entire life.

But Larry, his alter ego, was capable of just about anything. One only had to ask his father, except of course they couldn't. He was now six feet under. Logan still mourned him. Larry had sent him to meet his maker.

He squeezed a little harder.

* * *

Jack drove like a lunatic, worried out of his mind. But as he got caught up in heavy traffic, he used the delay to replay the phone conversation through his head. He'd panicked and hadn't stopped to analyse the weird nature of the muffled call. There had been none of the noises in the background that he'd expect to hear from a busy emergency department.

Stalled at temporary traffic lights, he dialled the hospital. The number was in his phone, it having been necessary to take his mother there several times before at short notice. He eventually got put through to a harried nurse in the emergency department who checked her records and curtly told him that his mother definitely hadn't been admitted that day. He then did what he should have done – would have done – in the first place if he hadn't been in such a blind panic.

He called his mother's number. Her carer answered, and assured him that she was having one of her good days.

'She's looking forward to seeing you,' the chirpy voice told him. 'She's remembered that it's Sunday *and* who you are.'

Assuring her that he would be there later, Jack turned round at the first opportunity and probably triggered every speed camera he passed in his anxiety to return to Callie. Something wasn't right. He'd been lured away under false pretences and left her vulnerable and exposed.

He squealed to a halt outside of Callie's cottage. Odin sprang from the car, hackles raised, with Jack close on his heels. The front door was locked and he didn't have time to knock. He leaned a shoulder against it and pushed. It gave way at the third attempt and slammed back onto its hinges into the wall. He heard sounds coming from the sitting room and dashed in that direction. The sight that greeted him turned his blood to ice in his veins. Logan! How the hell had he got in? He was attempting to strangle Callie, who wasn't moving.

Jack was too late.

Odin wasn't detained by self-doubts. He got there first and, growling, sank his teeth into Logan's backside.

Dear God in heaven, Callie looked so damned pale, and didn't seem to be breathing. This was all his fault. He was such a fool. He'd fallen for a clumsy ruse and was now too late to save the woman he adored.

Odin's efforts caused Logan to slightly relieve his hold on Callie's neck as he cried out in anger and surprise. Despite all the noise that Jack had made breaking in, Logan was so focused that he clearly hadn't heard them. With a spluttered intake of air, Callie lifted a knee and deposited it squarely in the centre of Logan's groin. He cried out and slapped her face, his eyes bulging with insanity in a way that Jack had never seen before.

Jack grabbed the back of his shirt, hauled him off Callie and then punched him with all his considerable strength, right in the middle of his pretty face. Logan crumpled against the fireplace to the accompaniment of shattering bone and a spurt of blood. 'Watch him,' he told Odin, 'and bite him if he comes to and tries to move.'

'God, Jack.' Callie tried to struggle into a sitting position.

'Stay where you are and catch your breath.' He sat beside her, brushed the hair from her face and tenderly took her hand. 'Are you okay? Silly question, of course you're not. Damn it, I never should have rushed off like that. I knew there was something off about that call but it never occurred to me that...'

'It was your mum. Of course you had to go. Is she okay?'

Jack's heart melted when her first thought was for a woman she'd never met. He was in love with her, no question, but now wasn't the time. 'It was Logan calling to get me out of here. He must have been upstairs the entire time. Now, we need to call the police and get you to the hospital.'

'No hospital. I'm fine. I played dead in the hope that he would think he'd killed me. Glad you got here, though. I couldn't have held out for much longer. I think he wanted... wanted to—' She pointed to Logan, whose trousers were unfastened.

Jack ran a hand through his hair. 'Jesus!'

'Thanks for saving my life.'

'Entirely my pleasure, darling. It just so happens that your life is very important to me. Now, if you're sure about the hospital, stay where you are. I'll get you something to drink, then call the cavalry.'

EPILOGUE

A week later, Callie sat beside Jack's mother, listening to her reminiscing about Jack's childhood. She remembered them cooking together, embarrassed him by relating various transgressions during his childhood and then spoke of her other children, mostly remembering their names.

'Thank you for coming,' Jack said when they left together. 'You were good with her.'

Callie told him about her grandmother. 'It's such a cruel disease,' she said wistfully as Jack drove them back to her cottage. 'I often thought that Granny would be better off out of it. There was no dignity in her final years. And then, after weeks of blanking me, I would see a spark of recognition in her eye and figured perhaps the lights might still be on, if dimmed. It's so hard to know. Anyway, euthanasia is illegal in this country, particularly when the patient isn't full cognitive, and rightly so.'

'Could you have done it, if you were able to make that decision?'

Callie shook her head. 'Most likely not. I didn't want to lose what I had left of her.'

They arrived and, as always, Odin was the first out of the car. He and Jinx had reached a sort of impasse. The cat pretended not to notice Odin and Odin kept out of Jinx's way. It was amusing to watch.

Callie went into the kitchen, put the kettle on for coffee, then changed her mind and extracted a bottle of red from the fridge.

'It's a bit early, isn't it?' Jack asked, taking the bottle from her and finding the corkscrew.

'Not if you're going to tell me how your visit to Logan went,' Callie replied. 'Don't think I haven't noticed you making excuses to delay, so it has to be bad.'

'Not so much bad, more sad,' Jack said pensively, pouring wine into two glasses and carrying them into the sitting room. 'Come on, I'll tell you.'

Callie curled her feet beneath her on the settee and leaned the side of her face against Jack's shoulder. 'It was hard for you, wasn't it?' she asked sympathetically. 'Despite what he's done, he was still your friend for all those years.'

'He told you about the abuse, at home and then at school?' Callie bit her lip and then nodded. 'I had absolutely no idea. He never said a word, not one word in all these years. All I knew was that he admired his father and strove to impress him.' Jack's brow creased into a frown. 'How can that be possible when he abused his son in the worst possible way? I just don't get it.'

'Stockholm syndrome. A lot of victims finish up admiring their abusers and wanting to please them. Logan's father told him he was to blame for what happened to him and in the end he believed it. I guess the fact that it carried on at school reinforced that view. He believed he was worthless and deserved everything he got. If he'd only talked to someone about it instead of bottling it up, but then, if he believed that he brought it on himself...'

'He's having mental evaluations on remand,' Jack said. 'They think he has dissociative identity disorder.'

'He turned himself into someone else when he was being abused so that it wasn't happening to him.' Callie made a face. 'That is so sad.'

'It was the other Logan who tried to strangle you. Between you and me, from a few things that Logan let drop, he succeeded insofar as his father was concerned.'

Callie gasped. 'Logan killed his father?'

'Would you blame him if he had? But, as I say, it wasn't Logan but his other personality. He mentioned someone called Larry more than once.'

'He spent his entire adult life trying to please the people he cared about and did it by attempting to over-achieve.'

'I agree.' Jack stroked Callie's hair. 'That's why he married Portia. He was shafted there too because she's always been a few farthings short of a shilling, as my old mum always says, and giving responsibility for her to a mentally disturbed individual was a recipe for disaster.'

'He couldn't impress anyone, it all got on top of him, so he decided to scarper abroad, where no one knows him, and start again.'

'Well, at least you'll be getting your money back,' Jack said. 'As will I. Logan's singing like a canary, aware that he's safer in custody then he would be if Denning gets his hands on him. He's admitted to what he's done. The money is tucked away offshore, but we'll get it back once we can prove what he stole from us.'

'Will Logan get a custodial sentence?' Callie asked.

'It's more likely to be a spell in a mental institution, which is where he belongs. I hope you don't feel short-changed.'

'No, not really. I wanted my money back and I wanted

revenge, but I can see now that what Logan needs is professional help. I hope he gets it. Will Portia have him back?'

'I hope not. He needs to be with someone who can take care of him, rather than the other way around. He's mentally unstable.'

'What will happen to Denning and Blakely?' she asked. 'And won't Logan be in danger in prison? Denning will want his revenge because I dare say he's given the police enough ammunition to finally knock on his door with a search warrant.'

'Ah, of course, I haven't had a chance to tell you. I got a call from our friend DI Renton this morning. Seems Denning was found in a warehouse he owns with a bullet through his forehead and so was someone else. Want to take a guess at his identity?'

'Nope, but you want to tell me.'

Jack laughed and briefly covered her lips with his own. 'Our friendly butler, Davidson.'

'Blimey. Blakely must be responsible. I wouldn't want to get on his wrong side.'

'Renton thinks so but can't prove it. Blakely was at a conference, giving a speech to fifty delegates at about the time the deaths supposedly occurred. He was there for three days and has witnesses who can account for every second of his time. No doubt one of his minions did the honours, but Renton won't bust a gut trying to prove it. As far as the police are concerned, the world's a better place without Denning in it.'

'I guess.'

'By the way, Maisie's husband. I'm thinking of taking on Clydesdale Mews and will need a structural engineer. Logan owns the terrace and has signed it over to the company. I have a feeling that we can redevelop the existing houses rather than knocking them down, but I'll need someone who knows his stuff to...'

Callie flung her arms around his neck and kissed him hard. 'Thank you!' she cried. 'I'm understandably cautious about commitment, but seeing as how you're so compassionate, I think I might keep you around for a bit longer.'

ACKNOWLEDGMENTS

With grateful thanks to my talented and eagle-eyed editor, Emily Ruston, and the rest of the wonderful Boldwood team for making my book the best it can be.

MORE FROM EVIE HUNTER

We hope you enjoyed reading *The Trap*. If you did, please leave a review.

If you'd like to gift a copy, this book is also available as an ebook, digital audio download and audiobook CD.

Sign up to Evie Hunter's mailing list for news, competitions and updates on future books.

https://bit.ly/EvieHunterNewsletter

The Fall, another nail-biting revenge thriller from Evie Hunter, is available to order now.

ABOUT THE AUTHOR

Evie Hunter has written a great many successful regency romances as Wendy Soliman and is now redirecting her talents to produce dark gritty thrillers for Boldwood. For the past twenty years she has lived the life of a nomad, roaming the world on interesting forms of transport, but has now settled back in the UK.

Follow Evie on social media:

twitter.com/wendyswriter
facebook.com/wendy.soliman.author
bookbub.com/authors/wendy-soliman

ABOUT BOLDWOOD BOOKS

Boldwood Books is a fiction publishing company seeking out the best stories from around the world.

Find out more at www.boldwoodbooks.com

Sign up to the Book and Tonic newsletter for news, offers and competitions from Boldwood Books!

http://www.bit.ly/bookandtonic

We'd love to hear from you, follow us on social media:

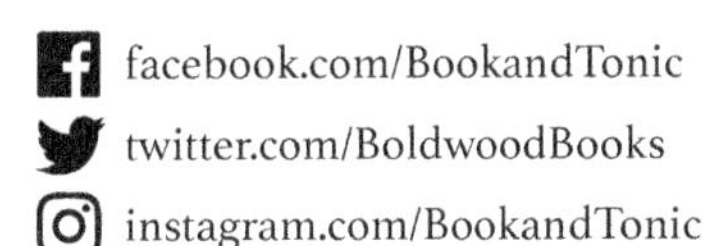

Printed in Great Britain
by Amazon

27208576R00155